"Clara . . . my sweet angel . . . I want to taste of you," he husked, holding her gaze with smoldering need. "Will you allow me?"

She touched the tip of her tongue to her lips, the unwitting motion clenching the muscles of his thighs.

"Taste?"

"I want to kiss you."

"Why?"

"Not everything has a reasonable explanation, Miss Dawson. Indeed, there are some things that should be left a mystery."

"Such as kisses?"

"Such as kisses." He stepped until her soft curves were pressed to his own. Still holding her face in his hands, he lowered his head until he was a breath from her lips. "Give me leave, Clara. I will not steal what should be offered freely."

"Yes," she at last whispered. "Yes."

With a groan he softly touched her lips, fiercely reminding himself she was an innocent. Certainly there was passion enough beneath her proper manner, but she had no experience with the darker desires. He must take care not to startle her with his hunger.

Unfortunately, his silent lecture did nothing to prepare him for the satin sweetness of her mouth. Barely sweeping over her lips, he gasped as a flood of gut-wrenching pleasure surged through his body.

He had expected to enjoy her. A lot.

But this . . . this was magic . . .

Books by Deborah Raleigh

SOME LIKE IT WICKED

SOME LIKE IT SINFUL

Published by Kensington Publishing Corporation

Some Like It Sinful

DEBORAH RALEIGH

ZEBRA BOOKS
Kensington Publishing Corp.
www.kensingtonbooks.com

ZEBRA BOOKS are published by

Kensington Publishing Corp.
850 Third Avenue
New York, NY 10022

All Kensington titles, imprints, and distributed lines are available at special quantity discounts for bulk purchases for sales promotion, premiums, fund-raising, educational, or institutional use.

Special book excerpts or customized printings can also be created to fit specific needs. For details, write or phone the office of the Kensington Special Sales Manager: Attn. Special Sales Department. Kensington Publishing Corp., 850 Third Avenue, New York, NY 10022. Phone: 1-800-221-2647.

Zebra and the Z logo Reg. U.S. Pat. & TM Off.

ISBN 0-8217-7856-0

First Printing: June 2006
10 9 8 7 6 5 4 3 2 1

Printed in the United States of America

Chapter One

It was a typical spring evening in London.

Damp, foggy, and exquisitely miserable. The sort of weather that should have made any reasonable gentleman consider staying nicely tucked by the fire. Or better yet, immigrating to India with all possible speed.

Of course, English gentlemen were a rare breed.

While they might be incapable of tying their own cravat, or removing their boots without a small legion of servants, they would not so much as bat an eye at braving the most formidable weather.

Earthquake, flood, or monsoon, nothing was allowed to interfere with the nightly round of entertainments.

Especially when that entertainment included a few indulgent hours spent at Hellion's Den.

Once a coffee shop that had catered to the various artists spattered about the capital, the narrow, decidedly shabby building had been purchased by Hellion Caulfield and Lord Bidwell to create an exclusive gambling club.

Since its opening last year it had become a favorite gathering for the gentlemen of society.

Dandies, rakes, rogues, and a sprinkling of hardened gamblers were stuffed into the smoky interior.

And then there was Rutherford Hawksley.

No one could claim him a frivolous dandy, nor did rake or rogue entirely suit him.

Oh, he was handsome enough to make any woman forget to say no. Quite often they forgot to say anything at all. Drooling and swooning was by far the more likely response.

Perfectly reasonable.

His features were lean and perfectly carved. He possessed a long, aquiline nose, a broad forehead, and high cheekbones that gave a hint of exotic beauty to his countenance. His eyes were an indigo blue and surrounded by a fringe of black lashes. And if he were not blessed enough, he possessed a set of dimples that could flash with devastating results.

But while women had always and would always lust after him, and more than a few knew the pleasure of his intimate touch, the past months had wrought a change in the once devil-may-care Hawksley.

No longer did he tease and charm his way through society. No longer did he shock London with his madcap dares. No longer was there a ready smile and hint of laughter in the astonishing blue eyes.

Instead there was a hard edge to his features and a hint of ruthless determination about him that kept the women casting longing glances from a safe distance and wise gentlemen stepping out of his path.

On this evening he was attired in his familiar black with his long raven hair pulled into a queue with a satin ribbon. In the muted candlelight a diamond flashed on his ear with cold beauty and the scar that ran the length of his jaw was thrown in sharp relief.

Seated at a private table, he sprawled in his seat with elegant ease. An ease that did nothing to disguise the air of lethal power in his lean form.

He looked precisely what he was.

Coiled danger ready to spring.

Unfortunately, Lord Pendleton, who was currently in the chair across the small table, was far too infuriated to appreciate the risk of baiting the young nobleman. In one short hour he had lost three hundred quid. Not such a terribly large sum, but one he could ill afford to hand over. Especially since his harridan of a wife had threatened to tell her father of his gambling habits.

The clutch-fisted old gudgeon was bound to pull the purse strings even tighter.

God rot his soul.

Tossing his cards onto the table, he glared into Hawksley's unfashionably dark countenance. His annoyance was not lessened by the fact that the . . . the dastard was utterly impassive despite the stack of vowels piled indecently before him.

"You seem to be in the luck yet again, Hawksley," the older man growled.

"So it would seem."

"Some might even say unnatural luck."

Hawksley narrowed his gaze. He had sensed his opponent's frustration early in the game. The fool had been well outmatched, but like most noblemen he had been too proud to admit his incompetence. For such a gentleman it was far preferable to blunder along, somehow hoping that lightning might strike and avert the inevitable disaster.

Rather like clinging to a horse as it tumbled off a cliff.

As a rule Hawksley was content to toy with such prey and move on when they began to twitch. Why bleed a poor bloke dry? It only provoked an ugly scene. And besides which, there was always a ready supply of dupes anxious to hand over their allowance.

On this evening, however, he did not possess the luxury of time.

During the past fortnight he had devoted his nights to shadowing a certain Lord Doulton through the fashionable balls, routes, and assemblies of London. Not to mention the less fashionable brothels that clogged the Dials. It had left precious little opportunity to earn his livelihood.

Now he was without money, without credit, and his rent was due. He needed a bit of the ready if he weren't to be tossed into the streets of the stews. A fate that did not suit his current plans.

And the blustering Pendleton had been the perfect pigeon.

Folding the vowels in his slender fingers, Hawksley tucked them into the pocket of his jacket.

"I prefer to think of it as skill rather than luck," he drawled.

"Skill?" The older man's face was becoming an ugly shade of pink, as if his cravat were choking him. "I could name another word for it."

"Take care, Pendleton. My temper is rarely dependable and I should take great offense if you were to cast aspersion on my honor."

"Arrogant pup, I shall say whatever I damn well please."

Hawksley smiled his cold smile. "Only if you happen to be anxious for a dawn appointment."

There was a moment of shock at the blunt warning. "Are you threatening me?"

Hawksley shrugged. He was in no mood to soothe the twit's wounded pride. He had the man's money. Now he wanted him to leave.

"Merely clarifying your options, Pendleton. You can accept your loss and walk away with a bit of dignity, or we can meet tomorrow on the field of honor."

The pink countenance became puce and then an intriguing shade of purple.

For a crazed moment the older man seemed on the brink of utter stupidity. Thankfully the moment passed and he awkwardly rose to his feet.

"Fah, you aren't worth the cost of a bullet."

Hawksley had devoted a lifetime to disappointing and aggravating others, and the insult slid off without drawing so much as a wince.

"That seems to be a common conclusion among most who know me."

"Bloody sharp," Pendleton muttered even as he backed away with something just short of an all-out run.

Hawksley did not even bother to watch the rather amusing retreat. Instead he silently sipped at his whiskey as he contemplated what to do with the remainder of his evening.

It was too late to pick up on the trail of Doulton. And in truth, he was weary of the fruitless effort. He could always move on to another gambling hell. His luck was in and he could always use the blunt. That, however, held little appeal as well.

He sipped more of the whiskey.

If he was being perfectly honest, nothing seemed to hold appeal. Oh, perhaps a luscious armful of willing woman. That usually managed to lift a man's spirits. Unfortunately he had no current mistress and no desire to go to the effort of locating one.

Bloody hell. He leaned back in the seat. He was weary.

Weary and frustrated and so sick at heart that there were times when he wanted nothing more than to crawl into his bed and never leave.

The bleak thoughts were interrupted as a thin, rat-faced gentleman attired in a shocking pink coat and yellow waistcoat slid into the vacant seat across the table.

A faint smile, genuine on this occasion, tugged at Hawksley's lips.

He had acquired any number of casual acquaintances since being tossed out of his father's home and traveling to make his fortune in London. But there were few he actually considered a friend, and even fewer that he trusted.

Lord Bidwell, better known as Biddles, was one of those few.

Although now a properly married gentleman with the task of ensuring Hellion's Den kept him disgustingly wealthy, Biddles had once been England's most proficient spy. Intelligent, cunning, and possessing the sort of morals that allowed him to climb into the sewers with the best of them, he had done as much as Wellington to save England from defeat.

His retirement from the War Office had been

a decided blow for his country but a blessing for Hawksley.

Never one to allow his talents to fall into waste, Biddles kept himself entertained by turning his attentions to those closer to home. There was nothing that occurred in London, be it in the most elegant ballroom or the seediest backstreets of the stews, that Biddles was not aware of.

Which was why Hawksley had turned to him the moment he realized he needed assistance.

"Ah, Hawk, you are in your usual charming mood, I see," Biddles mocked as he raised a lacy handkerchief to dab at his pointed nose.

Hawksley shrugged. "I find it difficult to be charming when I am being accused of cheating."

"Then you shouldn't win so often, old chap. It makes gentlemen peevish."

"It makes me peevish when I cannot pay my rent."

The pale eyes narrowed as Biddles regarded him with a shrewd thoroughness.

"Difficulties?"

Hawksley choked back a humorless laugh. He could write an epic on difficulties. A father who detested him. Bill collectors yammering at his heels. A title and duties hanging about his neck like a yoke. A murdered brother. Oh, and an investigation that had produced precisely nothing. Well, nothing more than a lingering headache and a bad taste in his mouth.

"No more so than usual," he retorted in wry tones.

"You know I always stand prepared to offer assistance if you find yourself in need," Biddles murmured.

Hawksley gave the faintest nod. He did know. And it offered him a comfort he rarely found these days.

"Not necessary at the moment, although I do appreciate the offer."

Biddles gave a small smile. "I believe I have something you will appreciate even more."

Hawksley lifted his brows. "Is she beautiful?"

"I fear it is not a woman."

"A pity," he drawled. "Now that I have a bit of blunt I could use some companionship."

"A swift means of not having your blunt for long."

He briefly thought of the luscious, dark-haired widow who had been on his scent for the past weeks. And the slender blond actress who had offered all sorts of intriguing possibilities.

Either would do.

"Ah, but what more delightful means of becoming a pauper?"

Biddles gave a soft laugh. "I must refrain from answering such a leading question. I am a married man, after all, and I prefer my head not to be placed upon the platter."

"Where is your charming wife?"

The expression of sardonic amusement faded as a frown of annoyance marred the thin countenance. Hawksley noticed that frown quite often when men spoke of their wives. Only one of a dozen reasons he was not wed.

"She was decidedly pale this morning and I left strict orders that she was to stay home this evening to rest." Biddles grimaced. "Of course, that only ensures that she will be gadding about to every assembly and ball in town. She possesses a remarkable dislike for orders."

Hawksley sipped his whiskey, his lips twitching. "Perhaps you have not been stern enough in teaching her who is master."

"Master?" Biddles tilted back his head to laugh with rich amusement. "I would suggest you not say such a thing in Anna's presence."

"You believe it would be my head upon the proverbial platter?"

"Without a shred of doubt."

"That is the trouble with wedding a spirited woman."

"Ah no, that is the pleasure," Biddles corrected with a wicked glint in his eyes.

Hawklsey briefly thought of the actress again. She was spirited in all the right ways. And without the bother of a wedding ring. Unfortunately, he wasn't entirely certain she was worth the effort or the money.

A thought that entered his mind far too often of late.

Bloody hell. Obviously, the sooner he ended this frustrating search for the truth, the better.

Another few months and he'd be a damn eunuch.

"I should be on my way. Pendleton is no doubt drinking himself into a rage in some corner and I have no desire to have to shoot him."

Biddles glanced about the crowded room. "If you are not in a desperate hurry, I think you should join me in my office."

"Office?" Hawksley grimaced. The word was enough to conjure up his father's large study where he had regularly endured endless lectures, sermons, and an occasional beating. None of which had done the least good. "That sounds tediously dull."

"Actually I think you will find it of great interest."

Interest? Hawksley narrowed his gaze. "I suppose I could spare a few moments."

Together they left the table and climbed the narrow stairs to the upper floor. Out of habit Hawksley glanced about to ensure he was not being watched. He had taken care to hide the fact that he was searching for his brother's murderer, but he was never foolish enough to lower his guard.

Satisfied that the crowd below was suitably entranced by the turn of cards and rattle of dice, he allowed himself to be escorted into a barren room that was only notable for its lack of space.

Giving a lift of his brows, he glanced over at the desk and lone chair that managed to consume the small chamber.

"Not quite what I expected from the notorious Hellion," he murmured, referring to Biddles's partner, who had once been the most successful rake in all of England.

Daintily dusting off the edge of the desk, Biddles perched himself upon the worn wood.

"His wife has ensured that he is not nearly so notorious these days."

Hawksley leaned against the paneling, crossing his arms over his chest. "Poor blighter."

"He wouldn't agree, I assure you."

He offered a dramatic shudder. "Lord save me from happily married gentlemen."

Biddles chuckled. "We are a dull lot, are we not?" Reaching behind him, the slender gentleman produced a bottle to pour Hawksley a measure of the amber spirit. "I think you will find this to your taste."

Accepting the offering, Hawksley took an experimental sip. Ah. A smoky fire slid down his throat. Whiskey, of course. Hawksley always drank whiskey. "Excellent. Your private stock?"

"Of course."

Beyond his skill in spying, Biddles always managed to procure the finest spirits. Another reason to like the man.

"I would ask where you purchased it, but I have a feeling you have no desire to share your source."

Biddles held up his hands in a helpless motion. "I must have something to maintain my intriguing air of mystery."

He gave a bark of laughter. "You become any more mysterious and Parliament will have you locked in the Tower. Prinny already complains you need to have a bell tied about your neck to keep you from lurking about and sticking your nose into places it has no business being."

"My poor nose." Biddles fondly stroked the pointed end. "It is sadly abused."

"It is a lethal weapon."

The pale eyes glittered in the candlelight. "You will not be nearly so condemning when you discover what this nose has managed to sniff out."

"You have information for me?"

"Not precisely the sort you requested, but I think you might find it interesting."

Hawksley did not move, but every muscle in his body tightened in anticipation. Biddles would not have approached him if he didn't think the information was something he could use.

"Tell me."

"There is a rumor floating about the stews that a certain Lord Doulton approached Jimmy Blade with an offer to pay him one hundred quid."

Hawksley abruptly set aside his whiskey. He could not deny a measure of surprise at the information. Although he suspected that the elegant Lord Doulton dabbled in all sorts of nasty business, the man had always been careful to keep his reputation spotless. He preferred to hire others to wallow in the muck.

"He has need of a thief?"

"A highwayman."

Well. This just got more interesting by the moment.

"Why?"

"It seems there is a carriage on its way to London from Kent that Lord Doulton does not wish to arrive."

Hawksley narrowed his gaze even further. "There is something in the carriage he desires?"

Biddles grimaced. "Actually, there is something in the carriage he wants dead."

An icy fury flared through his heart. Damn the ruthless bastard. One day he would overplay his hand and put himself in Hawksley's clutches. And that day would be his last.

"Who?"

"A Miss Clara Dawson."

Shock made him catch his breath.

"A woman?"

"Yes. Is she familiar to you?"

"I have never heard her name before. Bloody hell, why would Doulton want this woman dead?"

Biddles shrugged. "Well, the prig is too much a cold fish to have it be for the usual reasons a gentleman might wish to do away with a woman. Love, hate, jealousy. So it must be that he either owes her money or she has information he does not care to have spread about."

Hawksley shoved away from the wall. Unfortunately, there wasn't the necessary room for a good pacing. He took two steps to the chair and then back to the wall. Still, by the time he turned he had made his conclusion.

He had already discovered that Doulton possessed an astonishing fortune. Too much fortune for a man who had inherited a crumbling estate and a pile of bills. The nobleman could easily afford to pay off any trifling debt.

"Information," he said firmly.

"That would be my guess," Biddles offered.

"You said the carriage was coming from Kent?"

"Yes."

A silence descended as Hawksley debated how best to use his unexpected windfall.

He could lay a trap for Jimmy and force whatever information he might possess out of him. Not a bad plan except for the realization that Doulton sharing his reasons for wanting the woman dead was about as likely as a pig sprouting wings.

No. Jimmy would know nothing.

But the woman . . . ah yes.

She knew something. Something Doulton was willing to kill to keep secret.

"Where is Jimmy to attack?" he abruptly demanded.

"Westerham, just past the King's Arms."

"When?"

"Tomorrow afternoon."

Hawksley gave a slow nod, then with a lethal smile he reached out to lay his hand upon Biddles's shoulder.

"I owe you yet again, old friend."

Biddles grasped his arm before he could move away, his expression somber.

"What do you intend to do?"

A grim determination hardened his already hard features. "Get to the information before Jimmy Blade can make it disappear."

Biddles took a moment before he slowly released his arm. "Take care."

Chapter Two

It was not until she had hired the carriage and was well on her way to London that Miss Clara Dawson discovered she was not at all suited to long journeys.

The swaying carriage made her queasy and the relentless jolting made her head ache. Even worse, her unsettled stomach made it impossible for her to read or work upon her needlework or even count the blasted cows as they passed. She was a prisoner in the cramped confines with nothing to occupy her restless mind.

Who could have known?

Having lived in a small village for all her six-and-twenty years, she had always used her God-given feet to take her about. And the few times she had resorted to accepting a ride by a kindly neighbor, the distance had been short enough to avoid any hint of her weakness.

Besides which, it was not as if she were one of those timid, easily distressed creatures who was overset by every situation that might come her way.

While she might barely stand five foot and weigh little more than a feather, she was a sturdy, sensible woman.

Most would say far too sensible. Or even annoyingly sensible, despite the fact she'd had no choice in the matter. When a woman was left on her own at the tender age of seventeen with a mere pittance and no family to speak of, she either learned to confront life squarely or she found herself begging in the streets.

Still, it was perhaps best that she had not realized just how great her discomfort would be, she acknowledged as another pain shot through her head. As much as she wished to ease the curiosity that had plagued her for the past fortnight, she sensed she would have been far less likely to leap into this carriage and head off so willy-nilly if she had known the nasty surprise awaiting her.

At least she had the comfort of knowing they were less than two hours from London, she told herself. And the small sherry she had enjoyed at the posting inn had helped to ease her heaving stomach. She was bound and determined to survive.

It was, after all, what she did best.

Chancing a brief glance out the window, she noted the sun was slanted toward dusk. It would be dark by the time she arrived at the hotel, but at least the weather was cooperating. After a week of endless rain, the sun had struggled through the clouds to chase away the gloom. She would not be forced to make her first appearance in London wet and bedraggled.

Queasy and weary was bad enough.

Leaning against the worn leather squabs, she resisted the urge to close her eyes. The swaying was horrid enough with her eyes open; with her eyes closed it was unbearable. She barely dared to blink.

They slowed as the plodding team approached a curve, then oddly she felt them being pulled to an abrupt halt.

Clara frowned. There was no toll gate along this road that she was aware of. And certainly there was no traffic to impede their progress.

Had something gone wrong with the carriage? They had hit enough bumps to rattle any number of vital things loose.

Not one to sit about and await problems to be smoothed away, Clara reached up to push open the hatch in the top of the carriage.

"Driver, why have we stopped?" she demanded.

There was a muffled curse from above. "Hold, miss."

Clara's frown deepened. "What is happening?"

"Trouble."

Not at all satisfied with the vague response, Clara reached out to push open the door. If the driver had halted to have another drink from his flask, she would have his hide. Her hand, however, found nothing but empty air as the door was wrenched open without warning.

Nearly tumbling off her seat, Clara was forced to steady herself before she could glance up to regard the large form standing in the opening.

When she did her heart momentarily halted.

Even with his tall form cloaked in a caped driving coat and a hat covering his hair, there was no doubting the stranger was very large, and very, very male.

Precisely the sort of ruffian a woman did not desire to encounter on a lonely stretch of road.

Her mouth went dry and her blood rushed, but she refused to give in to panic. That would surely accomplish nothing. Instead she sternly forced herself to view the man with the logic she had learned from her father.

Breathing deeply, she first studied the coat that was frayed but clearly of good quality. Good enough quality to boast gold buttons and an exquisite tailoring that fit the muscular form to perfection. Not the sort of thing one would expect a highwayman to possess.

Her gaze lifted higher, taking note of the dashing diamond earring and then the hard-edged features of his countenance. He was handsome, she easily decided. By far the most handsome man she had ever encountered. But there was a grimness in his expression that halted him just short of beautiful.

At last she forced herself to meet his glittering gaze.

Her heart once again halted, only on this occasion she could not blame it on fear.

Sweet heavens, she had never seen such astonishing eyes. The blue was as rich as the finest velvet and rimmed in black, while the startling long lashes framed them with artistic perfection.

They were the sort of eyes that women would kill for, but there was nothing effeminate about them. Instead they shimmered with a cold intelligence that sent a small chill down her spine.

Clara gave a vague shake of her head at her ridiculous reaction.

If her inspection had told her nothing else, she

did know for a certainty that this man was no mere highwayman.

From the top of his beaver hat to the tips of his polished Hessians, he spoke of noble breeding.

No doubt a bored aristocrat out on a lark, she told herself with a disgusted sigh. She had heard that many gentlemen who considered themselves Tulips enjoyed daring one another to the most outrageous antics. Including holding up carriages and demanding some sort of token for proof of their foolish courage.

Waiting for him to finish his survey of her slender form, Clara folded her hands neatly in her lap.

"Sir, may I inquire what this is about?"

"Get out of the carriage."

Clara blinked. Not so much at the soft purr of his voice, although it was deliciously compelling, but more at his astonishing demand.

It was one thing to pinch a fan or even a kiss. It was quite another to haul her off to prove his daring.

"Get out of the carriage? Why should I?"

A raven brow flicked upward. "For the simple reason that I told you to do so."

Clara decided his voice was not so nice after all. "I did hear you. Despite my advanced years, I am not deaf."

He paused, as if caught off guard by her response. Not surprising. Clara had learned long ago that she tended to catch others off guard.

Not in a good way.

But in an aggravating, longing to gag her sort of way.

"If you heard me, then why are you still sitting there?" he growled.

"I am not about to be ordered about by a perfect stranger."

His eyes narrowed and he slowly reached into the pocket of his coat to withdraw a pistol. With an ease that was not at all reassuring, he pointed it at her heart.

"Perhaps this will convince you?"

No doubt it should have, but Clara was busy noticing that the pistol was much like the rest of him. Sleek, lethal, and very expensive.

Just the sort of thing a dandy on a childish lark would carry.

"That is a very fine dueling pistol." She leaned forward to inspect the detailed workmanship. "I notice it even possesses ivory inlay. No doubt you had it crafted at Manton's?"

The faux highwayman gave a muffled cough. "Bloody hell, have you been drinking?"

"Of course not . . . Oh, that is not entirely true." She gave an unconscious grimace. "I did have a small sherry at the posting inn. I possess a very sturdy constitution, but I have discovered that it does not care for long journeys. My stomach becomes very queasy."

"I . . . see." The eyes held a growing hint of bemusement. As if the man was not quite certain what to make of her. "You are not about to sick up, are you?"

Clara gave the matter serious contemplation before offering a shake of her head.

"No, I do not believe so. Not at the moment, in any event."

"I cannot express the depth of my relief." He took

a step back. "Now, I am in something of a hurry, so I must insist that you step out of the carriage."

"You still have not explained who you are or why you wish me to leave this carriage."

"And I have no intention of doing so." An edge had entered that honey voice as he gave a wave of the gun. "Get out or I will be forced to use this."

Clara leaned farther back in her seat. She was not opposed to this man having a bit of fun, but she was tired of this dismal journey and not at all in the mood to play. Especially not if he wished to display her to his cronies like some sort of trophy.

"I do not believe you will pull the trigger."

The slender fingers tightened on the pistol.

"What?"

"Well, if you truly wanted me dead you would have shot the moment you opened the door. I cannot imagine a cold-blooded murderer seeking to indulge in conversation. Which leads me to presume that you desire to keep me alive."

"A desire that is waning with every passing moment," he muttered.

A wry smile touched Clara's lips. "Not surprising. I tend to have that effect on most people."

Again there was that startled pause. "You are a most . . . unusual young woman."

She flicked a pointed glance over his elegant attire. "And you are a most unusual highwayman."

"One who does not possess time to wrangle with you. Forgive me, but you leave me no choice."

"What do—" Clara's words ended in a startled shriek as the stranger reached into the carriage and wrapped an arm about her waist. With surprising ease she discovered herself being hauled from the carriage and slung over the man's shoulder. "Sir."

He paid no heed to her protest, not even when she beat her fists upon the broad width of his back. Instead he calmly moved to a massive black stallion and smoothly vaulted into the saddle.

Real panic flared through Clara. Not so much at being kidnapped, since she still did not believe this man intended to harm her, but at the thought of riding over the man's shoulder. Sweet heavens, she was guaranteed to be violently ill.

As if sensing her distress the stranger tugged her downward, settling her across the hardness of his thighs and clamping a firm arm about her waist.

Clara discovered her new position somewhat of an improvement. At least her head was not dangling downward and her stomach threatening a revolt. But she had to admit she was not entirely pleased with her awareness of the hard muscles that pressed into her legs.

It did not seem entirely respectable to be so conscious of the warm sensations that flushed through her body.

Barely given time to catch a glimpse of the two gentlemen who were seated on horses and pointing guns at her poor driver, she felt the horse taking off with a sharp leap. Clara bit her lip, ridiculously glad of the strong arm that kept her from tumbling onto the ground. She might be furious at being hauled off in such a manner, but falling from the huge beast seemed a somewhat worse fate just at the moment.

In silence they thundered down the narrow lane, and then without warning the man tugged on the reins and they were angling toward the shallow ditch before plunging straight into the trees.

Out of necessity the galloping nightmare was forced to slow its pace, and Clara took her first breath since being hoisted onto the horse.

She had not fallen and been trampled to death.

That had to be a good thing.

As her heart slowed to something approaching bearable, her simmering anger was allowed to resurface. Blast it all, what was this man doing? She was never going to get to London.

"I really must demand that you halt, sir," she said in the sort of stern tones that frightened even the old squire in her village.

Casually reaching out, her captor knocked aside a twig that threatened to hit her legs.

"Eventually."

"This is no longer a jest. You will find the law takes a very dim view of kidnapping young ladies."

He bent his head so that his lips brushed her ear. "Then I must make certain that I am not caught."

Clara suddenly realized that it was not only the hard muscles beneath her that could cause that peculiar heat to stir within her. The wide chest pressed against her back and the tickle of his soft breath seemed equally capable of accomplishing the same feat.

Perhaps sensing her distraction, he tightened his arm about her waist.

"You have not fainted, have you?"

Clara frowned at the insulting question. "I never faint."

"You are being remarkably quiet."

"I am thinking."

"Gads. A most worrisome notion."

"I could be screaming," she reminded him in tart tones.

"True enough," he agreed, his lips still touching her ear. "Why are you not?"

She turned her head to regard the thicket that surrounded them. In the gathering gloom little could be seen. Nothing beyond trees, brush, and emptiness.

Maybe an inquisitive grouse.

"There is no one about to hear me, and it would only annoy you. I do not believe you are a violent man, but it seems best not to overly provoke you."

She felt his chest expand, as if he had abruptly caught his breath. Then the faintest hint of laughter whispered through the silent air.

"Do you know, I begin to suspect you are an utter lunatic."

Clara stiffened as he unwittingly hit a sensitive nerve. Having been called odd, peculiar, and outright daft most of her life, she should perhaps be accustomed to such accusations.

She was not.

"I am an eccentric, not a lunatic."

"Is there a difference?"

She grimly turned her head to stab him with a condemning glare.

"It is bad enough you have kidnapped me for God knows what nefarious purpose. Is it also necessary to insult me?"

His eyes narrowed, as if he was belatedly realizing just how deeply he had offended her.

"Forgive me," he said, his voice soft. "This is my first kidnapping, I fear. And you are not at all what I expected you to be."

"What did you expect?"

"An older woman." His gaze drifted slowly over her upturned countenance. "And one not near so lovely."

A portion of her annoyance faded. Mostly out of shock.

Gentlemen, whether they were ruffians or not, never found her lovely.

Annoying, strange, and sometimes frightening, but never lovely.

"You think me lovely?"

"Shall I tell you how lovely?" His arm tightened about her waist as his head lowered until she could feel his lips lightly touch her neck. "Your hair shimmers like moonlight on water. Your eyes are the purest green I have ever seen. And your skin is so soft it makes me wish to explore you from head to toe."

Clara decided she quite liked the small shivers that were racing down her spine. What was not to like? There was heat and tiny flutters of excitement and an undeniable urge to tilt her head so he could have better access to the curve of her throat.

She also decided that such sensations were no doubt quite dangerous.

She could almost feel her well-honed intelligence melting to mush.

A deliberate strategy on his part, no doubt.

"You are attempting to distract me," she accused.

"I was," he agreed without apology. His tongue reached out to touch the pulse beating at the base of her neck. His tongue! Clara barely resisted the urge to squirm, feeling his lips continue up her throat to stroke the curve of her cheek. "Now that

I have begun, however, I am quite willing to continue if you feel so inclined."

Clara swallowed. If she was perfectly honest with herself, she would have to admit she was not nearly as opposed to the thought of him continuing as she should be.

She had never before experienced such a sharp physical attraction. It clutched at the pit of her stomach and raced through her blood. A heady mixture.

Unfortunately, the gentleman creating the delicious sensations was not all suitable for a proper lady. Not even one who had been on the shelf for so long that she had grown more than a tad moldy.

"Certainly not," she forced herself to say.

She felt his lips curve in a smile against her skin. "Why? It could be pleasurable for the both of us."

"No doubt, but I will not have my first kiss given to me by a ruffian."

"Your first . . . Bloody hell." The gentleman gave a sudden cough as he abruptly straightened. Almost as if she had just told him she had the pox. "You must be jesting?"

"Why should I jest about such a thing?"

"Good God," he muttered, "what sort of female are you?"

Turning her head, Clara offered a dark frown. Despite his undoubted skill to make her heart flutter, she found him more than a bit annoying.

"I happen to be a proper woman who does not allow—"

"Never mind," he rudely interrupted, his attention focused over her head. "We have arrived."

* * *

Hawksley had not given a lot of thought to his role as kidnapper.

After all, how difficult could it be?

He would send out his accomplices to locate Miss Dawson's carriage while he waited in the trees to ambush it. Once he had captured the woman, he would carry her off to an isolated cottage. After that it would be a simple matter to learn her secrets.

A nice, straightforward plan that left little room for mistakes.

Unfortunately his nice, straightforward plan had not included Miss Dawson.

Angling his horse toward the crumbling stables, Hawksley shifted to study the pure line of his captive's profile.

My God, she looked like an angel, he acknowledged with that shocking flare of awareness that had plagued him since first clapping eyes upon her.

This was not the hardened tart he had been expecting.

Far from it.

In the gathering dusk, her hair shimmered with a silver beauty. The sort of hair that made a man long to rip out the offending pins and allow it to flow over her shoulders.

And her eyes . . . so pure a green they reminded him of a mischievous kitten. One he suspected he would take great pleasure in making purr.

Strange, considering some of the most beautiful, most experienced women in all of London had not been capable of stirring even a vague interest lately.

Perhaps it was her body, he decided, allowing his gaze to slide down the slender form currently pressed against him.

For the most part his mistresses had been well curved in all the right places. The sort of women that made a man think of lust.

But for the first time in his thirty years, he realized that there was something rather enchanting in having such a slender female snuggled close to him. She felt fragile and as delicate as the finest crystal.

Or at least she did until she opened her mouth.

A rueful smile tugged at his lips as he rode into the dusty shadows of the stables and pulled his mount to a halt.

By the fires of hell, she was the most peculiar of females.

Not once had she revealed the fear or fury he had prepared himself to endure. Indeed, she had appeared little more than annoyed at being carted off by a stranger. Rather as if he was no more than a tedious interruption to her journey.

It was difficult to imagine that this practical, frighteningly sensible woman could have any nefarious dealings with Lord Doulton. Actually, it was damn well impossible.

But Biddles was never mistaken.

There had to be some reason for the nobleman to wish this woman dead.

And he intended to discover precisely what that reason was.

With a smooth motion he vaulted out of the saddle and reached up to tug Miss Dawson onto the ground next to him. Leading his restless horse into a nearby stall, he set about settling him for the night.

Out of the corner of his eye he kept a close watch on his captive. Not that she appeared ready to bolt.

Instead she was taking a careful survey of her surroundings.

Sensible and practical.

And oddly kissable.

Strange.

"What is this place?" she at last demanded.

"Just a small cottage. It is barren and lacking in many amenities, but it is isolated enough so we can speak in private."

The green gaze shifted to regard him with a frank speculation. "And that is all you desire from me? To speak in private?"

All he desired? Not bloody likely.

"Unless you change your mind about that first kiss."

"I do not think so," she retorted primly. He merely smiled, reaching for a brush. After a time she took a step closer. "That is a beautiful animal. What do you call him?"

"Brutus."

"Brutus?"

"He attacks anyone foolish enough to turn their back on him."

"Oh."

Straightening, Hawksley shot his companion a warning glance. "If you attempt an escape, I would suggest you not try it upon this beast. He is ill-tempered and more likely to break your neck than take you to safety."

With her odd habit she silently considered his words. "You intend to keep me here?"

"Only for a short time."

"And then what?"

"That depends upon what you have to tell me."

She once again fell silent as he spread out fresh hay. He did not even attempt to guess what might be passing through her mind.

Nothing that would be passing through an ordinary woman's mind, he was certain.

"Do you know, when you first halted my carriage I assumed you were just a ridiculous dandy having a lark," she murmured.

Hawksley gave a lift of his brows. "You did not consider the possibility that I might actually be a highwayman?"

The faintest hint of humor entered her beautiful eyes. "You do not have one possession, from that horse to your boots, which a highwayman could possibly afford. Indeed, the buttons on your coat alone could feed a family for a month."

"They could all have been stolen," he pointed out, just a tad annoyed by her sharp perception.

She should be shrinking in terror, not calmly assessing the worth of his property.

"Perhaps the clothing and even Brutus could have been stolen, although it is more likely they would have been hocked than kept." She gave a shrug. "But not the ring."

He glanced down at his hand. "Why not the ring?"

"From Oxford, is it not? Not the sort of jewelry to catch the eye of a thief. Not unless he happened to be one of the rare highwaymen who attended the school and possessed a sentimental nature."

Hawksley's lips twitched. Damn. The woman was downright freakish.

"I see. You have determined that I am no highwayman and no dandy on a lark, so what conclusion has that clever mind devised?"

She faced him with that calm poise he found so intriguing.

"There seem to be only two possibilities. Either you are a dangerous lunatic, or this has all been some horrid mistake."

Chapter Three

He resisted the urge to laugh. In truth, her conclusions were not far from his own, Hawksley had to concede.

Oh, not so much that bit about the dangerous lunatic, although he had been accused more than once since his brother's murder of becoming a ruthless bastard.

But maybe there had been a mistake made.

Or perhaps you simply hope there has been a mistake made, a voice whispered in the back of his mind. *Perhaps you do not want this strange and fascinating angel to be involved in Fredrick's death.*

Startled by the ridiculous fancy, Hawksley sternly squashed the traitorous thought. Dammit all. This woman was here for one purpose and one purpose only.

And that was to discover what connection she had to Lord Doulton.

He folded his arms over his chest. "You are Miss Clara Dawson?"

She gave a startled blink. "I . . . Yes."

"From Kent?"

"Yes."

So. No mistake.

"Then you are indeed the woman I want." He reached out a commanding hand. "Come along."

Her lips thinned as she took a step back.

"No."

"Oh, for God's sake, now what?"

"I refuse to go anywhere with you until you tell me who you are and why I am here."

Hawksley did not hesitate. With one motion he was moving forward and scooping her over his shoulder. Not a difficult task considering she was nearly tiny enough to slip into his pocket.

"Do you know, kitten, I begin to suspect you simply enjoy being in my arms," he mocked as he carried her out of the stables and toward the cottage. "Why else would you continue to challenge me?"

A small hand smacked him in the center of his back. "Brute."

"You have left me little choice."

"Of course you have a choice," she gritted. "You could do the honorable thing and return me to my carriage."

Reaching the cottage, Hawksley pressed open the door and stepped inside. He cast a swift glance about the darkened interior, resisting the urge to grimace. While a poet might claim the aged timbers and uneven flagstones picturesque, he was quite certain the woman squirming in his arms would claim it shabby, damp, and not at all fit for a proper lady.

And she would not be wrong.

Although it was relatively clean, the only furniture was a rough table and chairs set by a large fireplace and a battered bench below the single window. There were no curtains, no pretty pottery or pictures hung upon the walls.

It looked precisely what it was. A convenient hideout for a notorious smuggler.

With an inward shrug, Hawksley slowly lowered his captive to her feet. He wasn't here to entertain the lady or see to her comfort.

"There would be nothing honorable in allowing you to continue on to London," he assured her, thinking of the murderous Jimmy still awaiting his prey.

She planted her hands on her hips to glare at him. It might have been more effective if the cloud of silver hair had not slipped from the tidy knot to float about her shoulders.

Holy hell.

"What on earth do you mean?"

Against his will his hand reached out to catch a strand of the silken silver in his fingers.

"It would be a sin against nature to have you harmed," he murmured. "And I have need of you."

"What need?"

He smiled wryly at her suspicious tone. "All in time." Turning, he walked to peer out the small window. "First I must ensure we were not followed."

"Who do you believe would follow us?" she demanded.

A swift glance revealed no angry cutthroats in the yard, but Hawksley kept his back turned as he carefully watched his prey in the reflection of the window. He had discovered that he could learn a great deal about others when they were unaware they were being observed.

"There are all sorts of nasty creatures roaming about," he assured her.

Edging sideways, Miss Dawson kept a wary gaze on his back. "No, I believe you have someone specific in mind."

"Why do you say that?"

A few more steps to the side. "People as a rule do not fear they are being followed unless they have reason to believe it might be so."

Hawksley gave a short laugh. "Obviously you have never been to the stews."

Her hand reached out to grasp the heavy candlestick from the mantle. "But you have?"

His lips twitched even as he took careful note of her courage. She was obviously not the sort of woman to hide in the corner and hope to be rescued.

Something he would do well to remember.

"Put it down, kitten, unless you desire to be tied to the bed," he murmured, presuming there must be a bed somewhere in the loft. "Something I assure you would give me a great deal of pleasure."

He saw her eyes widen as the candlestick was abruptly thumped back onto the mantle.

"How did you . . . Oh, of course. My reflection in the window. Blast. I should have taken that into consideration."

Slowly turning, Hawksley flicked a glance over her tiny form. "Would you truly have hit me with that?"

"Would you truly have tied me to the bed?"

He smiled. "Touché."

There was silence as they both measured one

another, then the faint sound of hoofbeats had Hawksley spinning back toward the window. His hand instinctively reached into his pocket to grasp the pistol until the rider came into view. Only when he recognized the dark, swarthy gentleman with a long mane of pitch-black hair and hawkish nose did he relax.

Leaving the lethal weapon tucked in his pocket, Hawksley moved toward the door. Pulling it open, he paused to stab his captive with a warning glare.

"I will return in a moment. In the meantime do not even think of attempting to flee. If I have to chase after you, I shall be very displeased."

She folded her arms over her chest. "You have already kidnapped me, hauled me about as if I were no more than a sack of flour, and are now holding me against my will in this filthy cottage. I do not give a fig if you are displeased."

Hawksley was crossing the floor and wrapping his hands about her waist before he could halt his progress. Not that he particularly wanted to halt his progress, he realized as he easily hoisted her off the floor until they were nose to nose. He might as well accept that he would use any excuse, no matter how pathetic, to touch this woman.

"Let me put it this way, kitten. If I have to chase you, I will expect some sort of compensation for my efforts." He gaze deliberately drifted to the soft lips.

Her eyes widened. "No. No kisses."

"There are many pleasures beyond kisses," he murmured, angling his head to gently nip at the lobe of her ear. Then for good measure he stroked his tongue down to the pulse fluttering at the base of her throat. It was pleasant to know when his efforts were being properly appreciated.

Her head turned to allow him greater access before she abruptly decided she should be protesting his touch rather than encouraging it.

"What is that if not a kiss?" she breathed.

Slowly he angled her down his body until her feet touched the ground. He smiled deep into her eyes.

"A prelude." Hawksley gave a tug on a silver curl. "Now behave yourself."

He left the cottage before he could conjure yet another reason to snatch Miss Dawson off her feet and firmly closed the door behind him. Only then did he cross the yard to where Santos was leaping from a pure white stallion.

Hawksley knew little of this dark recluse known only as Santos. No one knew much. He was a pirate, a smuggler, and lethal when crossed. He moved through the underworld of London with smooth ease and was reputedly the son of an English duke and a Portuguese actress. No one was foolish enough to actually inquire if it was true. Certainly not Hawksley.

What he did know was that the man had proven to be an invaluable asset in his quest for revenge. And that he would trust him with his life, if not his valuables.

Santos flicked a black gaze toward the cottage. It belonged to him. Just one of a dozen hideaways he possessed outside of London.

"Any trouble?" he demanded.

Hawksley grimaced. "That depends on what you consider trouble."

A dark brow arched in amusement. "Miss Dawson?"

"She is not precisely what I expected."

"Does that please or disappoint you?"

A wry smile twisted his lips. "She makes my head ache."

"Ah . . . She pleases you, then."

Hawksley gave a short laugh. Only Santos could consider a woman who made his head ache as pleasing. No doubt he thought being shot at by Excise men a nice means to round out the evening.

"Did you discover Jimmy?"

There was a brief nod of the dark head. "Yes, he is still hidden just beyond Westerham."

"It will not take him long to realize the carriage is never going to arrive," Hawksley murmured. "Did you cover our tracks?" He glanced up to meet a steady black gaze. "Ah, of course you did, forgive me. Where is Dillon?"

"He will keep watch on the cottage. You need not fear any unexpected visitors."

"And what of you?"

A faint smile touched the dark eyes. "I have some business in the area. I will not be far away."

Hawksley did not inquire into the nature of the man's business. He was fairly certain he did not want to know. Instead he turned back toward the cottage, not surprised to discover Miss Dawson standing with her nose pressed to the window.

At least she had not attempted to escape up the chimney.

"I do not know how long this might take. I sense Miss Dawson will not make this simple."

"Women rarely do," Santos murmured, stepping to his side. He seemed to still as a lingering slant of sunlight suddenly fell across the woman's silver cloud of hair and delicate features. "*Mãe de Deus*, is that her?"

Hawksley discovered a frown forming on his forehead.

"Yes."

"Ah . . . *anjo magnifico*. Perhaps my business is not so pressing after all."

The frown deepened. "Do not even consider it, old friend. For the moment she is mine."

A knowing gaze slashed in his direction. "And when you have your information?"

"That remains to be seen."

An expression that Hawksley did not care for settled on the too-handsome features.

"Yes . . . it does."

With one last glance toward the window, Santos moved to swing himself atop his horse, barely hitting the saddle before he was reeling his mount around and charging toward the trees.

Hawksley watched his departure before striding back toward the cottage and the woman waiting within.

No, not *the* woman.

His woman.

At least for the moment.

Clara was in a decided quandary.

As a rule, she had discovered that her logical approach to life kept most troubles at bay. She did not impulsively leap into decisions or allow her heart to lead her into foolishness. Indeed, her days were carefully planned, with few opportunities for surprises to occur.

Most maidens would no doubt find her existence tedious.

There might even be a few occasions when *she* found her existence tedious.

But her current situation did not lend itself to her usual sensible approach. Kidnappings rarely did.

And certainly her kidnapper defied any sort of logic.

How was she to reason with a man who utterly aggravated her one moment and the next made her heart leap with shivering excitement?

No closer to an answer, Clara turned from the window. Her captor was returning, and his expression was once again set in those grim lines.

More aggravation and less heart leaping, she acknowledged with a faint sigh.

As if to prove her point, the gentleman entered the cottage and shut the door with far more force than necessary. Walking across the floor, he stood before her with his arms crossed and his gaze narrowed.

She crossed her own arms and met his gaze squarely. "Who was that?" she demanded, referring to the dark, rather frighteningly beautiful stranger. "Is he an accomplice of yours? Does he know I am being kept here against my will?"

"You ask a great number of questions," he retorted.

Clara shrugged. "So I have been told."

"Well, from now on I shall be the one asking the questions."

"That does not seem entirely fair," she protested.

"I rarely play fair." He took another step closer. "You might as well have a seat and make yourself comfortable."

Clara glanced over her shoulder at the small bench directly behind her. Then her head swiveled back to discover the impossibly blue eyes watching her closely.

"You want me to sit there?"

His brows drew together. "Is there a problem?"

"I am not convinced the bench is entirely clean."

He regarded her for a long moment, as if not certain he had truly heard her correctly. Then, glancing toward the heavens, he reached into his pocket to remove a handkerchief.

"Bloody hell," he muttered, moving to dust the bench with a bristling impatience. "Now are you satisfied?"

"Actually I believe you missed a place just—"

Strong arms grasped her shoulders and pressed her downward. "Sit."

Clara pursed her lips. There had been dust. And now it was no doubt staining her best carriage gown.

"You need not growl at me," she said.

Again his eyes lifted to the heavens. "How old are you?"

"Six-and-twenty. Why?"

"I was just curious as to how you lived to such a great age without being throttled."

"More luck than skill, I expect."

His gaze shot back to her countenance, then without warning he gave a short, reluctant laugh. Clearly he found her brilliant ability to annoy others a source of amusement.

Ah well, at least the grim features had softened and the air of danger crackling about him lessened to a muted tingle.

He was once again the handsome ruffian who made odd things flutter within her.

"Enough," he murmured. "You possess information I need."

Clara sighed. He was certainly persistent. Like a fly that refused to be shooed away.

"I cannot imagine what it might be. Not unless you possess an interest in mathematics or riddles."

He shifted back on his heels and peered down the long length of his nose.

"What is your relationship to Lord Doulton?"

This was the information he desired? "Lord Doulton?"

"Do not pretend you do not know of him."

She stiffened. She did not care for his tone. It sounded decidedly accusing.

"Of course I *know* of him," she said tartly. "My governess insisted I learn all the names of the titled families as well as their tedious heirs, although I could never comprehend why. It is not as if I shall ever have need to move among society."

"What is his connection to you?"

"There is none. He is not related to me, nor have we ever met."

The thin nose flared. "You are lying."

Clara surged to her feet, an angry heat flushing her cheeks. Why . . . the . . . the . . . She was too angry to conjure an appropriate insult. He had just branded her a liar. Her. Miss Clara Dawson, who never lied.

If her father had not insisted that good manners were essential no matter what the situation, she would have stomped on his toes.

"I do not lie, sir," she gritted. "Why should I?"

His eyes narrowed. "That is what I intend to discover."

"There is nothing for you to discover."

"There has to be something."

Clara forced herself to suck in a deep breath. His tenacity was becoming less a source of annoyance and more a source of downright harassment.

"Why? Why do you presume I have something to do with this Lord Doulton?"

There was a silent beat before he stabbed her with a glittering gaze.

"Because he wants you dead."

Clara's heart stopped beating and then an odd buzzing entered her ears.

"What did you say?"

"He has hired a gang of ruffians led by a very nasty bloke named Jimmy Blade to ambush your carriage and murder you. There must be some reason why."

Clara swayed in shock.

Dead? Someone wanted her dead?

No. It was not possible. She opened her mouth to protest but no sound came out. Instead a wave of darkness slammed into her. She thought her knees might have buckled, but it was impossible to determine. The darkness had taken hold and she thankfully knew no more.

Hawksley muttered his way through his favorite list of curses as he snatched up the unconscious Miss Dawson and carried her to the loft. It was a long list, but he went through it twice more as he carefully tucked his captive on the mattress tossed on the floor and covered her with his caped coat.

He did not want to miss one.

Returning down the narrow flight of stairs, he tore his way through the cupboards, shifting aside the inevitable bottles of brandy until he at last discovered the small flask of whiskey. Taking several long pulls, he waited for the fiery spirit to settle his rattled composure before collecting a glass of water and returning to the loft.

Damn and blast.

The woman had scared the hell out of him when she had so abruptly fainted. It had occurred so quickly he had barely managed to take a step forward before she had toppled backward, banging her head on the bench before crumpling onto the floor.

Just for a moment he had been terrified the blow to her head had killed her. Although there was no blood, she had been shockingly pale as she lay in a motionless heap. Dropping onto the floor beside her, he had nearly swooned himself when he felt the steady pulse.

It was then he had gathered her in his arms and taken her to the loft.

And began swearing at his stupidity.

Setting aside the water, Hawksley settled himself on the edge of the mattress and studied the woman lying beneath the blanket.

Darkness had nearly enveloped the cottage, but there was still enough light to make out the delicate features and the dark fringe of lashes that rested against her pale cheeks. Instinctively he reached out to brush a silver curl behind her ear.

Damn, but she looked so fragile. And far too

innocent to be involved with a scurrilous creature like Lord Doulton.

Whatever the reason the blackguard desired this woman dead, Hawksley was finding it increasingly difficult to believe she had been intimately involved in his brother's death.

She might be aggravating to a near-historic degree and far too outspoken for a proper lady, but she was incapable of deception. He was certain of that.

How he could be so certain was a matter he did not bother to ponder.

Keeping his vigil at her side, Hawksley was at last forced to go in search of a candle as the darkness filled the loft. He had just set it on a low stool when Miss Dawson gave a moan and her lashes slowly fluttered open.

Returning to the mattress he hovered over her, his hand pressing against her shoulder when she attempted to lever herself upright.

"No, do not move," he commanded softly.

Baffled green eyes clung to his countenance, as if attempting to determine why she might be lying on her back in a darkened loft.

"What happened?" she at last demanded.

"You fainted."

Her brows snapped together. "I told you, I never faint."

"Then you must be an extraordinary actress," he retorted in wry tones. "I have seen any number of women swoon on cue, but you are the first to roll your eyes back and thump your head upon a bench."

Her hand lifted to gingerly touch the lump that no doubt was still aching.

"Ah. That would explain the pain in my head."

Hawksley resisted the urge to smile. He was beginning to expect the unexpected with this woman.

"You collapsed too quickly for me to prevent your plunge to the floor. On the next occasion you might at least offer some small signal. That way I can be properly prepared to avert disaster."

"I have no intention of fainting again." Her lips thinned in disapproval. "I would not have done so in the first place had you not made that absurd claim."

His amusement died a swift death. "Kitten, there is nothing absurd about it."

"It must be," she insisted. "Why would anyone desire to kill me? I live alone in a small village with no relatives, little money, and few friends. The only things I possess of value are my father's books, and they are not worth more than a few pounds."

"Lord Doulton must possess some reason."

"There can be no reason. He does not even know me."

"Then how do you explain the fact that Lord Doulton not only knew your name as well as where you live, but he also knew the precise day you would be traveling to London?"

She bit her bottom lip, her brow creased. "I cannot say, although my trip was no secret. I would suppose most of my neighbors knew of my travel plans."

He considered the possibilities for a moment. Could Lord Doulton have some association to the village? Some nefarious dealings there that this woman might be jeopardizing?

Possible, but he was not going to leap to conclusions.

"Did you write to tell anyone in London of your arrival?"

"I . . ." Surprisingly, her words trailed away as a hint of a blush touched her cheeks.

Hawksley discovered his curiosity fully roused. "What?"

"I did send a message to Mr. Chesterfield, but I cannot be certain he received my note."

"Chesterfield? He is a relative?"

"No . . . he is . . . an acquaintance."

Hawksley shifted on the mattress, planting a hand on each side of her shoulders. He did not care for the notion that this woman was traveling to London to visit some male acquaintance. And he certainly did not care for the notion that this male acquaintance might be the reason Miss Dawson was hoarding her first kiss.

"You were slipping off to London to meet a gentleman? Really, Miss Dawson. That is hardly the behavior of a proper lady."

She tightened her lips, although he could sense a lingering embarrassment she attempted to keep hidden.

"I was concerned for him."

"Why?"

"I really do not feel it is any of your business."

Hawksley smiled. Ah, she had no notion.

"At the moment, everything about you is my business."

"You cannot force me to tell you."

Her words echoed through the empty cottage. Rather audacious for a woman being held captive by a strange gentleman far from any hope of rescue.

Of course, he was beginning to suspect that Miss Dawson made a habit of audacity.

He lowered his head until their noses were nearly touching. "I may not be capable of forcing you, but I can certainly keep you in this bed until you do so."

She unwittingly licked her lips, although he did not believe it was from fear. Or even from intimidation.

Not when her eyes had darkened to that intriguing shade of emerald.

"You cannot keep me here," she breathed. "My reputation will be ruined."

Her reputation was not precisely what was on his mind at the moment.

"Then tell me what I wish to know."

"I have nothing to tell."

Turning his head, he allowed his lips to softly stroke the tender skin just below her ear. She sucked in a rasping breath, but she made no move to push him away.

"Why were you going to visit Mr. Chesterfield?" he demanded. "Did you hope for him to become your lover?"

He felt her stiffen beneath him. "Certainly not. Our relationship was not of that sort."

A hot rush of satisfaction flared through him. Ridiculous, but what was a gentleman caught in throes of lust to do?

"What sort of relationship was it, then?"

"We knew each other on an . . . an intellectual level."

Hawksley pulled back to regard her with a lift of his brows. "On a what?"

"An intellectual level."

"And what precisely would that be?"

Perhaps sensing his stirring amusement, she gave a small sniff. "We have corresponded with one another but we have never actually met in person."

"Never so much as exchanged a glance? Hellfire. I must say that this Mr. Chesterfield must possess a golden quill to lure a proper young lady from her home to join him in London," he murmured. "Did he bewitch you with love poems and promises of happily ever after?"

Her expression became decidedly huffy.

"If you must know, he sent me mathematical equations."

"Math . . ."

Hawksley could not help himself. Tilting back his head, he laughed with startled enjoyment.

Chapter Four

Clara was not surprised by her kidnapper's amusement. Although naïve, she was not a fool. She knew that most gentlemen did not seek out ladies for their intelligence, or for their sensible nature. How could she not know?

They wanted women they desired. Women who charmed them and played those mysterious games she had never been capable of learning.

Still, she did not entirely appreciate his boorish reaction. So, she was not the sort of female to attract gentlemen. So, night after night she found herself sitting at home rather than being invited to the numerous entertainments held about the village. At least Mr. Chesterfield appreciated her unique qualities.

There was no need to mock.

Glaring into the beautiful features that could make a woman's heart forget to beat, Clara waited for him to gain control of his mirth.

"Are you quite finished?" she at last demanded.

The blue eyes continued to smolder in the flickering candlelight. "I must admit that I have never con-sidered using mathematical equations to seduce a woman."

Clara was not about to reveal that the equations were only the beginning. That they formed the basis of a secret code that when properly calculated spelled out a poem. The beast might choke himself laughing at her.

Perhaps not entirely a bad thing.

"Mr. Chesterfield was not attempting to seduce me," she bit out, shifting on the mattress. She was not at all certain how clean it might be. A worri-some thought. Perhaps even more worrisome than the large gentleman who was hovering over her like a hawk circling for a kill. "We simply possess a shared interest."

"Kitten, you are either astonishingly gullible or the best liar I have ever encountered," he taunted softly.

"Whatever do you mean?"

"You might consider an intellectual relationship the stuff of dreams, but I assure you any red-blooded male is interested in something a bit more . . ." His gaze deliberately lowered to her lips. "Tangible."

Oh my.

A hot flash seared through her before Clara was sternly squelching it.

"I will not discuss this with you, sir."

The blue gaze reluctantly returned to her flash-ing eyes. "You would prefer we do sums?"

"I would prefer you tell me what is occurring. First you kidnap me, and then you announce that some gentleman I have never encountered desires me dead. I believe I am due some explanation."

He considered her demands for a brief moment. "Perhaps, but I have yet to decide if I trust you."

Trust her? Trust *her*? Well, that took some bloody nerve.

"If anyone is untrustworthy it is you, sir."

He lifted a brow at her tart tone. "Now, my dear, is that any way to speak to the gentleman who saved you from a nasty ambush?"

"I have only your word to prove I was in any danger in the first place. And since you are a kidnapper and a ruffian, it is only logical to assume that I am the more honest person."

He shrugged. "But I am larger."

"Larger? What does that have to do with anything?"

"It ensures that I am the one who gets to decide who is to be trusted and who is not."

"That makes no sense."

"It does not have to."

Her lips thinned. "Barbarian."

"Not entirely." Shifting back, her captor slid his arms beneath her and gently lifted her to a sitting position. Then, reaching to one side, he produced a glass of water and held it to her lips. Clara's throat was too parched for her to dwell overmuch on whether the glass had been recently washed or if the water was fresh from the well, and taking a large gulp, she closed her eyes in relief. "Better?" he murmured.

"Yes."

He pressed the half-empty glass into her hand and reached up to tuck a curl behind her ear.

"Let us start from the beginning," he said, ignoring her heavy sigh. "You claim you have no knowledge of Lord Doulton."

"None whatsoever."

"And you were traveling to London to meet with a Mr. Chesterfield, whom you only know through correspondence."

"Yes."

"Alone?"

"Yes."

His gaze skimmed her pale features. "Your family did not object to such a scandalous journey?"

Drinking down the last of the water, Clara set aside the glass with a small click.

"There is nothing scandalous in my traveling to London. Besides which, I have no family. I am a lady of independence who is perfectly capable of making decisions for myself."

He seemed oddly displeased with her confession. Obviously he did not consider the notion that if she did possess a mythical relative, he might very well discover himself gazing down the barrel of a loaded pistol.

"You have no guardian? No one to protect you?"

"I have no need for protection." Her brows drew together as he gave a short, humorless laugh. "What?"

"For God's sake, if any woman is in need of protection, it is you," he growled. "Not only is a gang of thugs currently attempting to do away with you, but you are being held hostage in a bed with a dangerous ruffian."

She blinked at his fierce tone. "Are you dangerous?"

With an exasperated shake of his head, he allowed his features to soften. "That depends on what sort of danger you mean. I do not intend to slit your throat or dump you in the nearest well."

"What do you intend to do?"

The blue eyes darkened in what was becoming a familiar manner. "Now that is a most intriguing question."

Distracted by a pair of green eyes and kissable lips, Hawksley nearly missed the faint sound from below. Tensing, he reached behind his back to withdraw the pistol he had shoved in the waistband of his breeches.

Beside him Miss Dawson abruptly scooted away, clearly not having heard the soft scrape of the door opening.

"What are you doing?"

Leaning close, he whispered directly in her ear. "Remain here and do not make a sound."

He waited for her slow nod before lifting himself off the mattress and inching his way down the narrow stairs. Careful to keep low and to remain in the thicker shadows, Hawksley reached the lower floor and leaned against the wall. He had no intention of moving until his eyes managed to adjust to the darkness.

Several moments passed before a figure slid through a slanting ray of moonlight, and his tension eased. Straightening, he stepped away from the wall.

"Dillon."

Little was visible beyond a squat, blocky body. Had there been light, however, he would have seen a pug face crisscrossed with knife scars and a squashed nose that had been broken more than once. He had hired Dillon as his manservant shortly after arriving in London, more for his ability to watch his back than for any talent as valet.

Thank God, since no sane gentleman would allow the brute near his throat with a razor.

"What is it?" he demanded.

"Jimmy just left the road," the servant warned in a raspy voice.

Hawksley gave a slow nod. He had expected as much. Jimmy Blade would not easily allow a small fortune to slip through his fingers. Especially not when it would mean returning to Lord Doulton and confessing he had failed.

"Is he coming in this direction?"

"I'd say there is the likelihood that he'll eventually stumble across this place."

Hawksley shoved the pistol back into his pants. "Take Brutus and hide him in the woods."

"What of you?"

"We will wait in the tunnels. Signal when it is safe to come out."

"The wench may not be so pleased with your plans."

Hawksley gave a dismissive shrug. "The wench would not be pleased if I got down and kissed her feet, but she will do as she is told."

There was a moment of silence, warning Hawksley that his friend was battling a surge of amusement.

"Or?"

Hawksley's lips twitched as the image of seducing Miss Dawson to his will rose to mind.

"There are any number of possibilities I am considering," he at last murmured.

Dillon gave a short laugh. "Just make sure those possibilities are done quietly."

"I will be as silent as a mouse."

"And her?"

Hawksley smiled. "Now that I cannot promise."

Turning on his heel, he made his way back up the stairs. He was careful to ensure that Miss Dawson was not poised to knock him upside the head or tumble him backward before stepping into the loft. He would never be fool enough to underestimate his competent angel.

Finding her waiting upon the mattress, Hawksley moved forward. With one smooth motion he had scooped her into his arms. He paused only long enough to wrap his caped coat about her and pinch out the candle before returning to the stairs.

"Sir, what are you about?" Miss Dawson squeaked, obviously not quite as pleased as she should be at finding herself in his arms. "Put me down at once."

He pressed her closer, not at all prepared to risk allowing her to walk down the steps on her own. She had taken a sharp blow to her head. He had no intention of having her take another tumble. Not while she was in his care.

"Halt your squirming, kitten," he commanded.

"Or?" she tartly demanded.

"Or I shall toss you out the door for Jimmy Blade to find," he chided, carefully negotiating the stairs. Thankfully, without breaking either of their necks.

"He is here?"

"He soon will be."

"For goodness' sake, why did you not simply say so? I have no desire to have my throat slit. There was no need to manhandle me."

Crossing the short hall into the kitchen, he smiled at her exasperated tone.

"Perhaps I simply desired to manhandle you," he murmured.

His blunt honesty momentarily stilled her tongue. A rare occurrence, and one he was certain would not last for long.

It didn't.

As he located the hidden latch that swung the china cupboard forward and stepped onto the narrow stairs that led downward, her lips were already parting.

"Where are we going?" she demanded.

"The cellar."

Hawksley made certain the cupboard was firmly back in place before continuing down to the narrow tunnel below. Only then did he slide Miss Dawson to her feet.

"This does not feel to be a cellar," she whispered in the thick darkness. "I believe it is a tunnel."

"Perhaps."

She pondered the knowledge a moment before drawing in a sharp breath. "Good heavens, you are a smuggler."

His lips twitched at her shocked tones. "Not guilty."

"Then why do you have a hidden door and tunnel in your cottage?"

"It is not my cottage."

"Oh."

He smothered a chuckle. "Disappointed, kitten?"

"Well, at the very least you are in collaboration with a smuggler."

Hawksley could hardly argue with her accusation.

His friends included smugglers, spies, thieves, and gamblers. Most of whom possessed greater honor and higher morals than so-called noblemen.

"Actually, Santos prefers to think of himself as a purveyor of rare objects."

"Rare objects such as brandy and French silk?"

"Those might be included."

"Good heavens, do you possess no appreciation for the law?"

Hawksley felt his muscles tighten. An instinctive reaction to his still-raw anger.

After the death of his brother he had naively turned to the authorities. He had presumed they would be anxious to hang those responsible for the death of a viscount.

What greater crime was there in all of England?

And, indeed, they had been anxious to arrest the culprits. Only they had possessed little concern whether the culprits they arrested were actually guilty or not.

He discovered that guilt and poverty were irrevocably linked in the minds of most gentlemen of power. The less money in your pocket, the more guilty you became. And if you happened to be foolish enough to be a foreigner in the bargain, you might as well place the noose about your own neck.

It had taken Hawksley less than a fortnight to wash his hands of the lot of them.

"I make my own laws, kitten," he said in harsh tones. "A fact you would do well to recall."

Miss Dawson abruptly stiffened, no doubt sensing she had touched a raw nerve.

Hawksley discovered himself regretting his sharp retort and instinctively began to offer an apology, only to hastily snap his lips shut when he realized he was being ridiculous.

Dammit. This woman was his captive, was she not? A mere piece in the puzzle of his brother's murder. Beyond that, she was annoying as the devil.

But that protective urge that she seemed to stir in him refused to be denied.

Almost as if to prove the point, she shivered, and Hawksley instinctively reached out to ensure the coat was tucked about her.

"Are you cold?" he demanded.

"No, I am quite warm."

"I felt you tremble."

"I was just thinking of some stranger wishing me dead. It is not a pleasant thing to consider."

His hands lingered, pulling her close to him. "No one is going to harm you, that I promise."

She shifted in his arms, as if attempting to peer at him through the thick blackness.

"That is rather an odd promise considering that you are the gentleman currently holding me hostage," she said dryly.

He chuckled softly. "If you will recall, I am also the gentleman who saved your life."

"There is that, I suppose." There was a moment of silence. "Why?"

"Why what?"

"Why did you rescue me?"

Hawksley took a moment to consider his response. It would be easy to blithely assure her that he would never allow a young maiden to fall into the hands of a ruffian such as Jimmy Blade. It was, after all, no less than the truth. No gentleman with the least conscience would turn his back on a cold-blooded murder.

But Miss Dawson was not stupid. Far from it. She would not believe for a moment his motives were completely altruistic.

Not when he had promptly carried her off to this isolated cottage.

"Because I thought you had some connection to Lord Doulton and I desired information from you."

As was her way, she accepted his less than chivalrous admission with remarkable calm.

"You have yet to tell me what information it is you desire."

His fingers absently toyed with a silky curl. "Yes, I know."

"Perhaps I could be of some assistance if you would confide in me. I do not mean to boast, but I am rather renowned for solving problems."

Hawksley hastily choked back a startled laugh. "Is that so? And what sorts of problems would you be renowned for solving?"

He felt her give a small shrug. "Oh, all sorts. Just last week the squire's wife requested that I discover the location of the brooch she had misplaced."

Caught somewhere between amusement and astonishment, Hawksly cleared his throat. What other woman in all of England would be offering to assist the man who had callously kidnapped her?

"Ah, a dire problem, indeed," he murmured.

"Do not sneer," she retorted, bristling in swift offense. "It was a rather tangled investigation."

"Allow me to guess. The upstairs maid slipped it into her pocket?"

"Not at all."

"Then it fell behind cushions of the sofa?"

"No, indeed. All of the family rooms had been searched quite thoroughly, as well as the grounds."

"Then where was it?"

"In the pantry, just as I had suspected."

Hawksley discovered himself reluctantly intrigued. "The pantry? Why the devil would you suspect it would be there?"

"Because it is well known that the doctor has put Millicent on a diet to help cure her gout."

Hawksley had always considered himself a rather shrewd gentleman. Perhaps more than merely shrewd. But not even he was capable of following her obscure reasoning.

"What does that have to do with a brooch?"

"Well, I could not help but notice that while Millicent was quite contentious in avoiding sweets and richer foods when in company, she still had not lost the weight that must have been expected by such a rigid diet. Indeed, she was quite obviously gaining."

"And?"

"And it occurred to me that she must be sneaking into the pantry to enjoy those treats being denied her," she concluded, not quite able to hide the note of pride in her voice. "It was, of course, a place no one would think to search for a missing brooch."

Hawksley smiled at her undoubted skill. Gads, if Bow Street possessed such intelligence, then his brother's murder would have been solved months ago.

"No one except you."

"I merely used logic," she murmured, although it was obvious that she was pleased with his admiration. "It is an approach I have found quite effective in solving most problems."

"Clever, indeed, but—" Hawksley abruptly cut short his words as he heard a faint sound from above. Someone had entered the cottage. Pulling Miss Dawson close, he whispered directly in her ear. "We are no longer alone."

She gave a nod of her head, her hand reaching up to clutch at his lapel. Hawksley covered her fingers with his own, rather surprised to discover how cold they felt.

Damnation. She maintained such an air of implacable calm that he continually underestimated just how frightened she must be.

He tugged her even closer, laying his cheek upon the top of her head. He would get her away from this cottage, he abruptly swore. He would not allow Lord Doulton to harm a silken hair upon her head.

Hearing sounds from behind the cupboard, Hawksley placed a finger upon Miss Dawson's lips in silent warning before removing his pistol and cautiously creeping up the stairs. He had no true fear that the villains would manage to discover the hidden door, but he desired to know what their plans might be.

If they sought to lay another trap he needed to know the details.

Pressing his ear to the wall, Hawksley closed his thoughts to all but the muffled voices that echoed through the heavy wood. At first he heard nothing more than the usual curses and barks of command as Jimmy ordered his men to make a thorough search of the cottage. Then, as it became obvious nothing was to be found, there came a growing rumble of complaints from the gang of cutthroats.

It was obvious the men were beginning to suspect

that Jimmy had led them upon a fool's errand and were none too pleased with the notion of continuing the search in the damp night air.

Especially not when the cottage offered a roof over their head and a nice stash of brandy.

Hawksley gritted his teeth, sensing the inevitable even before Jimmy disgustedly agreed that there was little hope of finding Miss Dawson at such an hour.

Replacing his pistol, he silently moved back down the stairs and placed his arm about his companion's stiffly held shoulders. Keeping his other hand upon the wall to guide himself, he cautiously led her farther down the tunnel before coming to a halt.

"I fear that this shall not be so simple as I had hoped," he whispered softly.

"What is it?"

"They have determined to remain at the cottage for the night."

She caught her breath at his unwelcome confession. "We surely are not to remain in this tunnel?"

"It is certainly preferable to joining Jimmy Blade and his merry band," he pointed out dryly.

"I . . ."

"What is it?"

There was a long pause before she at last heaved a sigh. "I do not like enclosed places. They make me . . . uneasy."

Hawksley pondered their options. He had to admit he was not particularly fond of the notion of remaining in the damp tunnels either. Not when they offered the opportunity to become trapped in the enclosed space.

But fleeing would leave them vulnerable until he could locate Dillion and his men.

Silently considering the best course of action, Hawksley felt Miss Dawson wrap her arms about herself. It made his decision simple.

Fredrick had possessed precisely the same sort of irrational fear of enclosed places. Hawksley would make no one suffer an entire night of such discomfort.

Keeping her close, he began steering her firmly down the tunnel. "Come."

"Where are we going?" she demanded.

"These tunnels lead to the woods. We will be safe enough there."

She said nothing, but Hawksley did not miss her small sigh of relief. The faintest smile curved his lips. For all her staunch courage and undeniable cleverness, Miss Dawson was not invulnerable.

It was a knowledge that somehow made her all the more intriguing.

Chapter Five

They traversed the tunnels in silence, Hawksley on alert and Miss Dawson lost in the Lord only knew what peculiar thoughts.

As they walked, Hawksley kept himself sharply aware of his surroundings.

The faint moisture in the air, the rustle of muslin skirts, the distant croak of a frog, and overall, the sweet hint of vanilla that clung to his companion's skin.

It was a scent, he absently decided, that he preferred to the usual perfumes that women drenched upon themselves. It was not exotic or deliberately sensual. Instead it was enticingly fresh and without the artifice he disliked.

Perfectly suited to his angel.

Nearly a quarter of an hour later there was a subtle incline and Hawksley slowed their hesitant pace even further. He sensed they were nearing the end of the tunnel and he had no desire to abruptly charge out into the open.

Another five minutes and he came to a complete

halt as he heard the unmistakable sound of rock striking against rock.

"What was that?" Miss Dawson demanded.

There were two more strikes, followed by silence. One strike then another.

Hawksley smiled. "Santos."

"Why is he tapping on the wall?"

"So I do not lodge a bullet in his heart."

"Oh."

With a slight tug he had her moving forward again, and in next to no time they were pressing their way through the branches that hid the entrance to the tunnel.

As he had surmised, Santos was standing in the moonlight, his magnificent white stallion tied a short distance away.

"It seems your cottage has been invaded by a horde of unwelcome pests," Hawksley murmured as he plucked a stray leaf from Miss Dawson's tangled curls.

Santos noted the unwittingly possessive gesture with a mysterious smile, but keeping his thoughts to himself, he turned his head toward the distant cottage.

"Yes, and in the process have inconvenienced a most lovely lady." His voice was smooth but edged with a lethal intent. "Clearly they need a lesson in manners. One I intend to deliver quite forcibly."

Hawksley was in full approval of wiping out the scourge currently drinking themselves insensible, but first he had a more pressing concern.

"A word, Santos," he murmured with a pointed glance toward the woman at his side who had pulled out a handkerchief to futilely brush at the dust on her gown.

Following his glance, Santos allowed his gaze to rest upon the curls shimmering like a silver halo in the moonlight.

"If you insist."

Hawksley's lips tightened. He discovered that he did not care for a gentleman regarding Miss Dawson with such open male speculation.

Especially not a man who had only to cast a lady one of his smoldering smiles to have her doing whatever he might bid.

"I do."

A hint of amusement entered the dark eyes, but with a sweep of his hand he led Hawksley toward the nearby trees.

"What is is it?"

"There is nothing more to be gained here." Hawksley shoved his fingers through the long strands of his hair. He had not slept in nearly two days and he abruptly realized he was weary to the very bone. "I need to return to London."

Santos considered his words a moment. "What of the woman?"

Well, that was the question, was it not, he ruefully conceded.

When he had first planned his brilliant kidnapping scheme, it had been with the certainty that the woman in the carriage was either a conspirator to murder or at the very least a hardened tart who made a living in blackmailing others.

Why else would she be involved with a gentleman such as Lord Doulton?

Now he discovered himself at a distinct loss.

"I am not yet entirely certain." He sucked in a deep breath. "After the past few hours, she is no doubt anxious to be returned to the comfort of her home."

"That notion does not appeal to you?"

Appeal to him? Hawksley swallowed a self-derisive laugh. If he were perfectly honest, he would admit that it was a notion he refused to even contemplate.

Why? Well, he was intelligent enough to come up with a dozen different reasons without examining any of them too closely.

"Not when I still do not know why Lord Doulton wishes her dead." He furrowed his brow. "It may be he would be content to simply keep her out of London. On the other hand, there is nothing to keep him from sending Jimmy or another ruffian to her village to do away with her."

"There is that," Santos murmured.

"Beside which, she must have something that threatens Lord Doulton even if she does not know what it is. I mean to find what that something is."

The dark eyes slowly narrowed. "You intend to take her to London?"

Hawksley shrugged. "I do not think I have a choice."

The smuggler regarded him with an enigmatic expression for a long moment. "You could place her in my hands. I have many places to keep her hidden while you conduct your investigation."

"No." The refusal came swift and fierce.

Not surprisingly, Santos lifted his brows at the vehement refusal. "Why?"

"I desire to keep her with me."

"You do not trust me?" Santos demanded with a hint of amusement.

"With a beautiful woman?" Hawksley gave a humorless laugh. "Only a fool would trust you. But it is more than that." Shifting, Hawksley glanced toward the woman still dabbing at her skirts. In the moonlight she appeared even more ethereal. So tiny and fragile it was difficult to believe she was more than a creature of moon and mist. Thankfully, he was well aware her appearance was deceiving. Beyond her staunch courage, she possessed a near-brilliant ability to view the world about her with perfect logic. A talent that he could not deny was precisely what he was in need of at the moment. "As much as I hate to admit it, I am at a standstill in searching for Fredrick's killer, and Miss Dawson possesses a most remarkable intelligence. I sense she might be of more assistance than I first hoped."

Santos laughed softly at his words. "And you desire to bed her?"

Hawksley stiffened in annoyance before a rueful smile curved his lips. Only an utter idiot would mistake the manner with which he watched Miss Dawson. And Santos could never be taken for an idiot.

"Of course I desire to bed her. She is extraordinarily beautiful." He offered a grimace. "Unfortunately, she is also a proper lady. I do not trifle with virgins."

Their gazes met, each man judging the other, before Santos gave a slow nod of his head.

"She will be in danger in London."

"I will protect her. Indeed, she will be safer with me than she would be if I simply cast her to her own devices. I am not quite certain how she has managed to survive for so long."

"Your mind is set?"

"Yes."

Santos gave a slow nod. "What do you desire from me?"

Hawksley considered for a moment. He knew without doubt he had only to say the word for this man to rid the cottage of every ruffian within. Santos was even more a ruthless bastard than Hawksley himself.

But common sense warned that the sudden death of the highwaymen, along with the disappearance of Miss Dawson, would alert Lord Doulton that his devious plot had been uncovered. He would become more vigilant than ever, and any hope of luring him into revealing his sins would be lost.

Far better for him to presume that Miss Dawson had innocently slipped through the ambush and leave it at that.

"If it is possible I would like to you to distract Jimmy," he at last requested.

"Lay a false trail?"

"Precisely."

Santos slowly smiled. "Actually, I can do better than that."

Hawksley fully approved of that devious smile. It meant that his friend was considering something wickedly brilliant.

"What do you intend to do?"

Santos turned back toward the cottage. "I think I can convince the fools that Miss Dawson has met an untimely accident. Hired carriages are forever overturning; in truth, they are little better than a death trap. It will keep Lord Doulton from continuing his search for her and perhaps lull him into a false sense of comfort. In my experience, gentlemen who are overconfident tend to make mistakes."

Hawksley gave a short laugh as he reached out to clap his companion on the back. "I am in your debt, my friend."

Santos gave a lift of his brows as he swiveled to deliberately study the lovely angel now regarding them with a hint of impatience.

"Hmm. I shall think of some means of payment," he murmured.

Hawksley shifted until he was nose to nose with his companion. "Not for all the gold in England."

Santos gave a quick laugh before stepping back and offering a fluid bow. "Take care."

He moved toward his waiting mount, but Hawksley had already turned to study the thick shadows about him. He had heard his servants approach several moments ago. They would be silently awaiting him to signal his intent.

"Dillon, bring Brutus," he commanded as his gaze caught the square form standing beside a large bush.

"Aye."

With a renewed burst of energy, Hawksley crossed back to join Miss Dawson. Allowing his gaze to sweep over her countenance, he noticed her expression was set in determinedly calm lines, but not even this formidable female was capable of disguising the weariness that darkened her eyes or the brittle tension that shimmered about her slender form.

Hawksley was forced to stifle a pang of regret. She should be nicely tucked in her cottage, far away from ruthless men such as Lord Doulton.

And himself.

The Miss Dawsons of the world were meant to

be protected from evil, not hoisted into a cesspit of murder and treachery.

Unfortunately, he could think of no means to return her to her innocent country existence. Not until he managed to rid London of Lord Doulton.

With her determined insistence to appear unshakable, she briskly tucked her handkerchief back into the sleeve of her gown.

"What are we to do now?" she demanded.

Hawksley carefully hid his smile. If nothing else, he had discovered her temper could be remarkably prickly when she felt she was being patronized.

"We are off to London."

"Oh." She caught her bottom lip between her teeth. "We are not taking a carriage, are we?"

"Certainly not," he assured her, not having forgotten her distaste for the sickening sway of a carriage.

Just for a moment she appeared relieved. Then, as she glanced over his shoulder at the sound of approaching footsteps, her gaze widened.

"No. Absolutely not."

Hawksley gave a low chuckle. Turning, he vaulted in the saddle of the waiting Brutus. With the same ease he urged the large stallion forward, reaching down to sweep the reluctant Miss Dawson off her feet and across his legs. "Do not be frightened, kitten. Nothing will happen to you while you are in my arms."

His assurances were met with a glare, but thankfully Miss Dawson preferred to keep her sharp words to herself. At least for the moment, he acknowledged wryly. He was not foolish enough to hope he wouldn't be due for a nice trimming as soon as they reached London. For now, however, she tightly wrapped her arms about his waist and clung to him for dear life.

With a surge of satisfaction Hawksley gave a shift of the reins and charged into the darkness.

Astonishingly having fallen asleep as they had galloped down the narrow lanes, Clara awoke to discover herself lying upon a strange bed in a strange bedchamber.

She should no doubt have been terrified, she ruefully acknowledged. Proper ladies did not find themselves awakening in strange bedchambers. Indeed, they did not awaken in any bedchamber but their own.

Not even if they had been kidnapped by a handsome ruffian.

As it was, however, it was rather a predictable end to the peculiar day.

Scooting to a sitting position, Clara ran a hand through her tumbled curls. A brief glance about the chamber revealed a stark simplicity to the narrow bed and square armoire in the corner. The washstand did possess a lovely pitcher and matching bowl, and the curtains were freshly laundered, but there was no mistaking the lack of feminine influence.

The chamber was functional, nothing more. But it was clean, thank the Lord, and not nearly as shabby as the previous cottage.

A suitable setting for her captor.

Her captor.

Clara leaned against the pillows with a faint sigh.

She knew she should not be here. Despite her reputation of being an eccentric, she had always been careful to avoid the least hint of scandal. Indeed, anyone acquainted with her would be deeply shocked by the mere notion that she might do anything that was not rigidly proper.

How else could a young lady live on her own without causing social censure?

Unfortunately, at the moment she knew that she was not particularly interested in her reputation. Oh, she could perhaps convince herself that it was not as if she had much choice in the matter. Her captor had not politely consulted with her on his decision to halt her carriage, or carry her off to the cottage, or even to take her to his home in London.

She had been utterly at his mercy and in no way responsible for her current position.

Clara was too honest, however, to simply blame fate and a wicked pirate.

Throughout the ordeal she had made few genuine attempts to flee her captor. Or even to plead for her release.

And if she were to closely examine her heart, she would admit that when she had briefly assumed her kidnapper might put her in a carriage and send her on her way, she had not felt relief.

Instead she had been struck with the most amazing sense of regret.

Admit it, Clara Dawson, she chided herself. *For years you have harbored a renegade dream of being shaken out of your dull existence. And now that you have, you are not at all eager to return to your cottage and the tedious future awaiting you.* Especially when that future did not include a certain fascinating, sinfully bewitching gentleman.

Besides which, she acknowledged, there was the small matter of some lunatic desiring her dead.

How could she possibly settle back into her usual routine when she was plagued with the constant fear of Jimmy Blade arriving upon her doorstep?

The distant sound of approaching footsteps had Clara hastily tugging the covers to her chin. She had not seen her captor since she had fallen asleep in his arms. Now she discovered her heart beating at an oddly swift pace.

A wasted effort on the part of her heart, she discovered, as the door was pushed open to reveal the short, square servant who had ridden to London with them the evening before.

Glancing toward the bed, the man set down the modest cases that Clara had last seen strapped to the back of her hired carriage.

"Awake, are you?" he said in abrupt, but not unkind tones.

Clara gave a slow nod. The man looked as if he was well acquainted with violence, but she sensed no danger. If anything, she was forced to concede that he was the sort of man one might desire to have about in times of trouble.

"Where am I?"

"Most call it the Hawk's Nest. And I am Dillon."

Hawk's Nest? Unusual, but somehow perfectly suited to the raven-haired gentleman.

"We are in London?"

"Aye. I suppose you must be hungry?"

Clara offered a rueful smile. It had been hours since her last meal. She had been far too queasy during her journey to even contemplate food. And in truth, she found it difficult to eat anything that came from an unfamiliar kitchen.

Just another one of her many and varied eccentricities.

"Starving," she admitted.

"Then have a wash and I will fix you a bite."

Clara delicately cleared her throat. Hostage or not, she possessed the habit of situating her surroundings to suit herself. She had no intention of altering her routine.

"Actually, if you will wait for me to change my clothes I will cook my own breakfast, or luncheon, I suppose I should say," she stated in firm tones.

A sudden frown marred the battered countenance. "I may not be a bloody French chef, but I shan't poison you."

Belatedly realizing she had managed to insult the poor man, Clara offered an apologetic smile.

"Oh, forgive me. I never meant to question your skills in the kitchen, Dillon," she said in genuine regret. "It is just that I enjoy cooking, especially when I have need to consider a thorny problem. I find it soothes my nerves."

Dillon continued to frown, but it was obvious he was pleased by her proper apology. Indeed, the pale eyes held a hint of amusement.

"Well, I would say you have your share of thorny problems."

Clara gave a sudden laugh. "Indeed, I do."

"The kitchen is downstairs at the back. Just give a call if you have need of anything."

"Thank you, Dillon."

With a brusque nod of his head the servant

turned to leave the room, closing the door firmly behind him.

Once alone Clara lost no time in scurrying from beneath the covers and giving herself a thorough wash. Later she would demand that a bathtub be carried to her room, she promised herself with a grimace. Until then she could only do her best to appear reasonably tidy.

In the minimum of time she had scrubbed herself rosy from head to toe and brushed her hair into a long braid that she tucked into a knot at the base of her neck. It did take a bit longer to open her cases and arrange her handful of belongings in the armoire before pulling on a sensible green gown. She did not know how Dillon had managed to retrieve her property, and she had no intention of inquiring. She was far too relieved to have on a clean gown to care.

At last prepared, she left the chamber and made her way down the narrow flight of stairs.

She paused for a moment upon the landing, considering a swift tour of her temporary abode only to give an unconscious shake of her head. Although the lack of prickling awareness assured her that her kidnapper was nowhere near, she was too hungry to indulge in any immediate prying.

First things first, she told herself briskly. First luncheon and then a spot of snooping.

Like the rest of the house, the kitchen was narrow and without more than the basic necessities. There was, however, a nicely stocked pantry, and rolling up her sleeves, Clara soon found herself happily distracted in the pleasure of kneading dough and slicing vegetables.

Two hours swiftly passed, and removing the apple tarts from the oven, Clara was in the process of determining whether her shepherd's pie was in need of another few moments when a harsh voice suddenly rasped behind her.

"What the devil are you doing?"

With a startled squeak Clara spun about to glare into the dark, impossibly handsome countenance.

"Sir, you nearly made my heart fail," she chastised, attempting to keep her gaze focused upon the glittering blue gaze. Not an easy task when she longed to fully appreciate the exotic beauty of his male features and the long raven hair that was pulled to a tail at the nape of his neck. Attired entirely in black with the diamond flashing with cold brilliance upon his ear, he appeared a dangerous, elegant predator. Even more unnerving was the smoldering power that seemed to overwhelm the cramped space. It was rather like being caged with a stalking panther, she inanely concluded. "Do not sneak up on me in such a fashion."

Not at all put off by her scolding, her captor folded his arms over his chest.

"I asked you a question."

She gave a pointed glance about the kitchen. "One I assumed needed no reply considering it is perfectly obvious what I am doing."

"I did not bring you here to play servant. Where the hell . . . blazes is Dillon?"

Clara frowned, not quite certain why he appeared so irate. Of course, she often wondered why those about her seemed irate, she acknowledged with a faint sigh. She possessed a rare talent to annoy without even trying.

"I am not playing servant and I have no notion where Dillon is," she retorted tartly. "Hopefully he is out purchasing proper beeswax so that he may polish the furniture, which does not seem to have had a good waxing for some time."

He ignored her pointed comment with his usual arrogance. "If you were hungry, he would have made you something. In fact, I commanded him to do so."

"He did offer, but I prefer to make my own meals. Cooking is a particular hobby of mine."

"Hobby? Proper ladies do not consider cooking as a hobby."

"This proper lady does."

He continued to glare at her for a long moment until at last his lips began to twitch with that humor she found so disarming.

"Very well, Miss Dawson. I will have to admit I have never smelled anything so delicious coming from the hands of Dillon, although I will throttle you if you dare tell him I said so. He is rather proud of his dubious skills," he murmured, stepping around her to pull open the oven door. "Ah, shepherd's pie, my favorite. I hope you intend to share your efforts?"

Clara refused to acknowledge she might be pleased by his obvious flattery. Or to even consider the notion that she might have gone to such effort to impress this wicked pirate.

That would make her . . . well, nothing short of pathetic.

Instead she forced herself to meet the teasing gaze with a stern expression.

"I might be convinced."

"Ah . . ." A worrisome smile curved his mouth as he straightened and moved toward her. Too late Clara recognized the dangerous glow in his eyes and hastily backed away. She did not halt until she had bumped into the wooden counter, but even then he continued forward until he was nearly pressed against her. Without warning his hands landed on the counter on either side of her hips, effectively trapping her. "What will it take, my kitten?" he husked softly, his gaze slowly sliding over her pale features. "I have several skills of my own. Many of which I would be quite happy to share with you."

She clenched her hands together, staunchly battling the urge to reach up and test the hardness of his broad chest.

Oh, Clara, you are treading in waters that are far beyond your depth, she warned herself.

However innocent she might be, she could not pretend that the dark, fluttering excitement lodged in the pit of her stomach was anything but sensual awareness.

Unfortunately, she could not seem to stir up the proper sort of dismay for her traitorous reaction.

Wetting her lips, she did her best to ignore the tingling sensations and instead forced herself to concentrate upon more pressing matters.

"I desire to know your name," she at last demanded.

A raven brow arched. "My name?"

"It is awkward enough to be trapped with a stranger without at least knowing his identity."

There was a short pause, almost as if he was somehow reluctant to confess his name. Then with a twist of his lips, he gave a resigned shrug.

"Hawksley."

She frowned, sensing that he was deliberately hiding something from her.

"Is that your true name?"

"Yes." He shifted until his thighs brushed her own. A magical fire flickered through her blood. "Anything else?"

She swallowed heavily, astonished her skirts did not burst into flames.

"I wish to know why you are interested in Lord Doulton and why you have brought me to London."

He narrowed his gaze as he blatantly shifted his attention to the uncertain line of her mouth.

"I will agree to reveal a portion of my interest in Lord Doulton," he conceded slowly, "but only over a very large slice of shepherd's pie."

"I will not be fobbed off," she warned, her voice strangely breathless.

"Or?"

"Or you shall not have one bite of the apple tarts."

He gave a husky laugh as his dark head swooped down to gently nip at the lobe of her ear. "You do not play entirely fair, Miss Dawson, but I am too hungry to quibble. Allow me to change my coat and I will return."

His lips stroked the line of her jaw before he was abruptly pulling away and striding from the kitchen.

Still leaning against the cabinet, Clara gasped for air.

Oh . . . my.

Until Hawksley had stormed into her life, she had always presumed that passion was one of those fussy emotions that she could never quite feel as she ought. After all, she had known gentlemen throughout the years. Perhaps not suitors, but friends and acquaintances.

Certainly none of them had managed to make her face flush and her body tremble.

But Hawksley . . .

Well, at least she now knew beyond a shred of doubt that she was more than capable of experiencing desire.

Whether that was a good or bad thing had yet to be decided.

Chapter Six

"Good God. This is ambrosia."

Leaning back in his seat, Hawksley regarded his slender angel with astonishment. He supposed he should not be surprised that he had just enjoyed one of the finest meals ever set before him. Miss Dawson was clearly a woman who demanded the highest standards in whatever she did. Whether it was baking a tart that would melt in the mouth, or driving a man to Bedlam.

Still, he found himself continually caught off guard whenever in the presence of this woman.

Perhaps it was the fact that she appeared so fragile, he inanely acknowledged. She looked as if she should be lying upon satin pillows with a gown of gossamer lace. Not marching through life with the skill and determination of a seasoned general.

As if sensing his ridiculous imaginings, his companion set aside her napkin and tidily folded her hands in her lap. She regarded him with the same expression his governess used to conjure when about to wring an unwilling confession of his latest sin.

His lips twitched. It was an expression that was doomed to failure. How could he possibly think of her as a forbidding governess when the entire meal he had been plagued with the image of sweeping aside the plates and spreading her across the worn wood of the table?

An erotic fantasy easily trumped even the most prudish expression.

"I believe you know that it is not your compliments I desire to hear, sir," she prompted.

Hawksley remained silent a long moment. He had known from the moment he made his decision to bring Miss Dawson to London he would have to reveal at least a portion of his troubles.

The only question was how much.

"Very well." Meeting her gaze squarely, he offered the blunt truth. "I believe that Lord Doulton is responsible for my brother's death."

The emerald eyes darkened with swift sympathy. "Oh. I am sorry," she breathed. "Was it a duel?"

Hawksley's expression hardened with the bitter frustration that had haunted him for the past three months.

"No. My brother was found floating in the river with his throat slit."

There was a stunned silence as his companion absorbed his stark words. Hardly surprising. Such violence was rare even by London standards.

"Dear heavens," she at last managed to choke out. "And you think Lord Doulton did such an evil deed?"

"I do not think he actually put the blade to Fredrick's throat, but I am certain he hired the villain who did so."

"I see." Sucking in a slow breath, Miss Dawson slowly gathered her thoughts. Hawksley could almost feel her odd mind beginning to grind over his startling confession. "Why would he do such a thing?"

A good question, he ruefully acknowledged. Unfortunately, he possessed little more than conjecture and gut instinct.

And, of course, a healthy dose of intense dislike for the weasly bastard.

"It is my belief that my brother foolishly stumbled across information that would be harmful to Lord Doulton."

"Do you have any proof?"

"Nothing tangible," he reluctantly conceded. He was certain Miss Logic would not consider vague instinct and prickly dislike quite the irrefutable proof that he did. "I do know my brother was very distracted just before his murder. I quizzed him upon his odd manner, but to be honest, I assumed it was a woman preying upon his mind." His lips twisted as he recalled his brother's habit of tumbling in love with every pretty chit who crossed his path. "He tended to be a hopeless romantic, always tossing his heart at the feet of some female or another."

She leaned forward, folding her arms upon the table. "Now you think his distraction was due to something else?"

"Just before his death his townhouse was broken into. The thieves managed to make a mess, but there was nothing missing."

"That is odd. Could they have been interrupted?"

Hawksley shrugged. "That was what Fredrick claimed, although after his death I am no longer so certain."

"Why?"

"His home was broken into again a fortnight after his funeral, only on this occasion the thief took far greater care to hide his search. It was only because I noticed that the papers in the desk had been disturbed and several books my brother kept in precise order moved on the shelf that I knew anyone had been there at all."

"What was the thief searching for?"

"I cannot say for certain, but I believe it had something to do with this."

Reaching into his pocket, Hawksley withdrew the small journal that he had not revealed to anyone.

Strange that he would share it with this woman he barely knew. Perhaps it was because she was regarding him with intense concentration rather than that pitying expression that implied she thought his grief had driven him mad. Or perhaps it was because he had grown so desperate that he was willing to clutch at any straw, no matter if it was an innocent wench fresh from the country, he wryly acknowledged.

Whatever the reason, he found himself wanting to discover her unique opinion on the mystery surrounding his brother's murder.

"Your brother's diary?" she murmured, taking the journal and glancing over Fredrick's meticulous notes.

"It was hidden beneath the floorboards of my brother's study. It was only by accident the butler stumbled across it and brought it to me."

"Does it reveal who your brother might have feared?"

"No, but it did include these."

Once again reaching into his pocket, Hawksley revealed the folded scraps of paper that had been tucked within the diary. Taking them, Miss Dawson smoothed out the wrinkled notes with a frown.

"What are they?"

Hawksley was not surprised by her puzzlement. Proper young ladies were not supposed to be familiar with such things. Of course, when it came to his angel he was learning to be prepared for anything.

"Gambling vowels."

"Ah." She peered at them more closely. "From Lord Doulton?"

"Yes."

She pondered a moment before lifting her head to regard him with obvious curiosity. "You think Lord Doulton killed your brother because he could not pay his debts?"

Hawksley grimaced. "That was my first thought, but no longer. Those vowels add up to a little over two hundred pounds. A paltry sum that is not worth the risk of murder."

She nodded her head, no doubt having come to the same conclusion. Only at a much quicker pace.

"But . . . you still believe Lord Doulton was involved?"

His features hardened. "Yes."

"Why?"

His hand reached out to point to the open journal. "In his diary my brother was painstaking in listing his appointments. A fortnight before his death he had dinner at Lord Doulton's home and stayed to play cards."

She glanced toward the paper in her hands. "The vowels?"

"Precisely. After that night his usual schedule has obviously been rearranged. He scratches out appointments with both the prime minster and the prince and inserts a meeting with a mysterious MC." Hawksley caught and held her gaze. "He would never have cancelled an appointment with the prince unless it was a matter of vital urgency."

Her expression became distracted, her brows furrowed together. Hawksley settled back in his chair, sensing that she was busily shifting and sorting in her usual method. He presumed such deep pondering could not be rushed.

Oblivious to his presence, Miss Dawson absently shifted the vowels she still held in her fingers, turning them this way and that in silence. He watched her in a rather bemused fascination.

He had never before allowed a female in his home. Partially because the cramped, barren chambers were hardly suited to entertain the fairer sex, but more importantly because he had no desire to encourage any woman to believe she might domesticate him.

Allow a woman into your home and before you knew it, she was fussing and clucking over a gentleman as if he were a mere child.

Somehow, however, he did not resent the sight of the silver-haired beauty seated so comfortably at his table.

He tried to tell himself it was because she was not the sort to bother a man. If she chose to alter the household it would be to suit her own damn pleasure, not an attempt to coax her way into his life. And as for fussing over him, well . . . he was not entirely certain she was more than passingly aware of his presence most of the time.

Highly reasonable excuses. Unfortunately, they did not explain his sense of ease as they had shared the private luncheon, or the undeniable pleasure he found in simply having her near.

"This is odd," she murmured.

Hawksley leaned forward. "What is odd?"

"The paper."

Turning his attention to the vowels in her hand, Hawksley frowned in puzzlement. "No doubt it is just a scrap that Lord Doulton had lying about. There is no need for a formal contract between gentlemen."

"This is not a scrap." Without warning she rose to her feet and moved toward a nearby window. With a flick of her hand she pulled the curtain aside and held the vowels against the windowpane. "It is old. Very old."

Undeniably curious Hawksley rose to join her at the window.

"What is it?"

"There is writing on the back."

Ignoring the tingling awareness of her slender form, he leaned close to study the faded ink.

"Some sort of scribbling?"

"No, it is script," she corrected. "Some sort of formal document, I believe."

He shrugged, not quite so entranced by the long-forgotten letter as his companion seemed to be.

"It is not that unusual to use old bits of paper or even manuscripts for such purposes, Miss Dawson. Not all of us possess a fascination with the past."

She turned to regard him with a searching gaze. "What of your brother?"

"I beg your pardon?"

"Was he a scholar?"

Hawksley blinked. God, she was uncanny. "Yes. A very devoted scholar."

"Then he would have taken notice of such writing."

He caught his breath. Bloody hell. He had been so occupied with the vowels and Lord Doulton's signature that he never even taken note of the paper.

But then, who would?

No one but the peculiar Miss Dawson . . . and very possibly his brother.

"You think this important?"

She wrinkled her slender nose. "I think that anything out of the ordinary should be explained before dismissing it."

He gave a slow nod of his head, reaching to take the vowels and tucking them back into his pocket. He might not possess Miss Dawson's obvious brilliance, but he did have something she lacked. The dark, seedy connections to discover the sort of information he needed.

"You are right, of course."

She tilted her head to one side. "What are you going to do?"

"I am going to meet with someone who can assist me in translating these scribblings."

"You have to meet with someone?" She gave a lift of her brows. "Surely you must have studied Latin while attending school?"

His lips twitched at her goading. Minx. With a swift motion he had her pinned next to the wall. He did not want her to think he was somehow lacking.

At least not in matters of importance.

Besides which, he had forced himself to behave as a gentleman throughout lunch. Surely he deserved some reward for all that tediously proper conduct?

Twirling a curl about his finger, he smiled into her widened eyes.

"I was far too busy with more practical lessons to be troubled with such nonsense."

She attempted to appear disapproving, but she could not disguise the leap of her pulse at the base of her throat.

"I can imagine."

He chuckled, his lips softly brushing her forehead. "There is no need to imagine when I would be happy to demonstrate."

Her hands abruptly clutched at his arms. "Hawksley."

"I like the sound of my name upon your lips."

"I . . . I thought you were leaving?"

"I could be convinced to stay," he murmured huskily.

"Sir . . . ?" she breathed.

His lips trailed over her temple before he was sucking in a deep breath. Damn. He pulled back to regard her with a brooding intensity. My God, what was it about this woman? She seduced and disturbed him in a manner he was not entirely certain he cared for.

Well, there were some parts he cared for, he acknowledged as his body quickened.

Too much.

"You are right, I must go." He forced himself to step back, his gaze lingering on the faint flush on her cheeks before sending her a stern frown. "One thing before I go."

"What?"

"If I discover you have spent the afternoon doing dishes I shall be very displeased," he warned. "You are not a servant here."

She met his gaze squarely. "What am I?"

His smile twisted ruefully.

"Perhaps my salvation." He ran a finger along the line of her jaw. "I shall return as soon as I am able."

Despite the stern warning that she was not to be a servant, Clara could not thwart her instinctive need to set the small house to rights.

And why should she, she reassured herself, bustling through the rooms to polish the furniture and demand that Dillon have the carpets thoroughly beaten.

If she was expected to remain at the Hawk's Nest, then she would have it suitable for a woman of fastidious taste.

Her burst of cleaning, however, did halt outside Hawksley's private chambers. She might not know much of the devilishly handsome pirate, but she was certain he was not a man to take such an intrusion lightly.

Whatever his ready charm, Clara was perceptive enough to sense the nearly indiscernible distance he kept about himself. It was as if he harbored a secret deep within him that he refused to share with anyone.

Perhaps even with himself.

Dusk was falling when she was at last satisfied that

the rooms had been properly scrubbed, polished, aired, and arranged in precise order.

Taking a tray of tea and sandwiches to her chambers, she requested that a bath be brought up and devoted herself to washing the lingering traces of the road from her body. It was only when she was in her sensible robe and brushing her hair by the fire in her room that she turned her thoughts to the troubles at hand.

She had not missed Hawksley's deep, biting grief at the death of his brother, nor his fierce determination to lay blame for the murder at the feet of Lord Doulton. Such strong emotions rarely allowed for logical thought, she had discovered, but she could not wholly dismiss the notion that he might very well have something to his vague suspicions.

After all, the journal did suggest his brother had broken habits of a lifetime after meeting with Lord Doulton. And then there was the unexplainable fact that his lordship had commanded her own death.

Seemingly unconnected events, but enough to earn Lord Doulton a closer inspection.

If nothing else, she had a personal need to discover more of the wretched man. Until she learned why he would send a murderous fiend to ambush her, she would be forced to keep herself hidden away.

Not an entirely unpleasant task at the moment, she had to wryly concede, but one that could not continue for long.

Soon enough she would be expected back in her cottage. She could not risk having questions raised at her absence. Not when it might jeopardize her reputation.

Setting aside her brush, Clara restlessly raised herself to her feet. Although she was weary, she knew it would be some time before she would fall asleep.

She might as well find herself something to read, she decided. It would keep her occupied until Hawksley's return.

Not bothering with a candle, she carried her tray back to the kitchen and tidied the dishes before heading to the small library she had discovered earlier in the day. Moving down the hall, she passed the small parlor, pausing as a faint tingle of awareness feathered over her skin.

Someone was in the darkened room. Of that she was certain.

Stepping over the threshold, she scanned the darkness until she noted the darker shadow near the bay window.

"Hawksley?" she questioned softly, only to stiffen in wariness as the shadow turned in her direction. "Who are you?"

There was a moment's pause. "How did you know I was not Hawksley?" a rich, faintly accented voice demanded.

Unafraid, Clara took another step forward. She already suspected the identity of the intruder.

"You do not smell as he does."

A startled chuckle echoed through the heavy silence. "I beg your pardon?"

"Hawksley does not wear sandalwood, nor does he smoke cheroots."

"Ah, you are very observant, Miss Dawson," the gentleman murmured.

"You were at the cottage."

"Santos. At your service."

He stepped into the slanting moonlight to perform an elegant bow. Clara was once again struck by his sheer beauty. It was not the powerful, smoldering attraction of Hawksley, but instead an aloof perfection that was more than a tad intimidating.

"The smuggler."

A dark brow flicked upward at her unwitting words. "So some claim, although rarely to my face."

Clara grimaced. "Forgive me, I did not intend to insult you."

He shrugged. "It takes a great deal to insult me, *anjo.*"

"It is just that you do not look like a smuggler."

"Hmm. I wonder if I should take that as a compliment?" A faint smile curved his lips. "I suppose my vanity must insist that I do."

Clara swallowed a sigh. She should no doubt have herself muzzled.

"Are you searching for Hawksley?"

"No, I spoke with him earlier."

She was caught off guard by his ready response. "You spoke with him? Where is he?"

"At Hellion's Den."

"Hellion's Den?"

"A gambling establishment not far from here."

"He is gambling?" She did not bother to hide her confusion. "I thought he was meeting with a scholar?"

Santos' lips twitched. "If anyone can assist in acquiring obscure information, it is Biddles. He is rather a legend around London. Hawksley requested that I come here until he was finished."

"I see." Her brows drew together as she considered his smooth explanation. Then abruptly she stiffened in outrage. "Oh. Why, that . . . toad. He sent you here to ensure that I did not slip away."

The man's amusement only deepened at her accusation. "Actually, I believe he was more concerned with keeping you safe. This neighborhood is not the most suitable place for a young and innocent maiden."

"Fah." Her hands landed upon her hips. "Dillon is here, as well as two other servants who appear quite capable of dealing with a French invasion if need be, let alone any stray criminal who might be about. Why would he believe I would have need for more protection?"

He elegantly strolled forward, his hand reaching out to touch a still-damp curl that lay against her cheek.

"I would presume it was for the same reason he felt the need to threaten me with a very nasty retribution if I dared to offer you so much as a smile."

"What?" She frowned. "But that is absurd."

"My thought precisely. Gentlemen, however, are rarely reasonable when a beautiful woman is involved."

Although admiration shimmered in his gaze, Clara was too accustomed to being thought an oddity to accept his interest could be genuine. No doubt he was simply playing one of those sophisticated games that always baffled her.

"I begin to believe that London gentlemen are either blind or daft," she said dryly.

He gently twirled the curl about his finger. "I

should say that we simply possess a more refined appreciation for the rare and unique."

Oh my. Clara blinked in astonishment. The gentleman's charm was lethal.

"Do you work for Hawksley?" she abruptly demanded.

His gaze narrowed, as if he disliked the implication he might answer to anyone.

"I work only for myself."

"Oh." She wrinkled her nose in an apologetic manner. "But you are assisting him in the search for his brother's murderer?"

"Yes."

"Do you believe Lord Doulton is involved?"

She was pleased when he considered her question for a long moment. Clearly he was a man given to thought before action. His assistance would serve Hawksley well.

"I believe he has far more of a fortune than he should have. And that he would kill to keep his newfound wealth."

She gave a slow nod, ignoring his lingering touch as her mind was consumed with the riddle of Lord Doulton.

"There are not a great many means of gaining a fortune, illegal or otherwise," she murmured.

"True."

She met his gaze squarely. "I suppose you would know if he were involved in criminal opportunities?"

His lips twitched, his countenance revealing he was not offended by her delicate question.

"He has no connection to any known smugglers, thieves, or counterfeiters."

"Ah." She absently nibbled her bottom lip as she shifted through various possibilities. "Blackmail?"

"A possibility."

"Yes . . . It does not, however, explain murder," she had to concede. "You would be far more likely to do whatever necessary to keep your victims alive. They can hardly pay your demands from the grave." Abruptly Clara became aware of Santos's soft laughter. "What is it?"

His fingers moved beneath her chin to tilt her face upward for his inspection.

"Hawksley warned me you were most unexpected."

"Unexpected?" She rolled her eyes upward. "I would rather say he warned you I was completely mad. I have a tendency to become rather fixated when I am working upon a riddle."

He leaned closer, his eyes smoldering in the moonlight. "A most charming tendency."

There was the sound of a footfall near the door, and a dangerously soft male voice sliced through the room.

"A step closer, Santos, and I shall have you drawn and quartered."

Chapter Seven

Hawksley should no doubt have been shocked by the force of his emotions when he entered the room to find Clara practically in Santos's arms.

He was not one of those ridiculous buffoons who allowed a woman to toy with his affection or play him for a fool. Indeed, more than one mistress had bemoaned his lack of proper sentimental feelings.

Oddly, however, he was not at all startled by the dark anger that could only be jealousy tensing his muscles. Nor by the urge to march across the room and knock the handsome Santos onto his arse.

From the moment this woman had dropped into his arms he had been plagued by a host of unfamiliar emotions. Why should tonight be any different?

With an effort, Hawksley squashed his more violent urges and conjured his nearly forgotten sense of humor. For all his sins, perhaps he deserved to be undone by a tiny angel who preferred mathematical equations to seduction.

Besides which, it had been his own daft notion to send Santos to his house. Whatever the gentleman's danger to poor Miss Dawson's heart, he would protect her with his very life.

Strolling forward, he watched as Santos stepped away from Miss Dawson with a lazy smile.

"Ah, Hawksley. I wish I could claim it is a pleasure to see you," Santos drawled.

Hawksley smiled, but there was no doubting the warning in his expression. "Am I intruding, old friend?"

"If I say aye will you leave?"

Hawksley came to a halt directly in front of the smuggler. "Not even with a pistol held to my head."

Santos chuckled. "Something that could be arranged."

"I see that I shall have to be more specific when I request that you refrain from seducing my guests, Santos."

"I have not seduced her." The dark eyes slanted toward the frowning Clara. "Yet."

Hawksley's features hardened. He was well aware that Miss Dawson appeared a delectable morsel in that damnable sheer robe and silken curls tumbled about her shoulders. What male would not wish to devour her?

The sooner he rid himself of Santos, the better.

"Miss Dawson, will you excuse us a moment?" he murmured, his gaze never straying from his companion. "I wish to have a word with our guest."

With a laugh Santos clapped his hand on Hawksley's stiff shoulder. "I fear you shall have to save your dire threats for later, Hawksley. I have a pressing appointment that I dare not miss." He captured Miss Dawson's fingers and lifted them to his lips in a practiced motion. "Until later, *meu anjo*."

"Santos," Hawksley threatened as his friend swept toward the door, "we *will* finish this conversation."

The smuggler offered a mocking bow. "I await your convenience with breathless anticipation, old friend."

Hawksley smiled wryly as Santos vanished in the darkness. As much as it annoyed him to admit it, he possessed a liking for the audacious smuggler. They might come from differing social classes, but they were much alike.

Too much alike, that jealous voice in the back of his mind whispered. At least when it came to a taste for beautiful females.

Turning back to Miss Dawson, he reached out to stroke his hand over her soft curls.

"Santos is a dangerous rake, kitten, and one that will devour you if you do not have a care," he murmured.

She regarded him with a hint of surprise. "Really, Hawksley, I am not so foolish as to have my head turned by his ridiculous flattery. 'Tis obvious his interest is more in aggravating you than in seducing me."

As always, Hawksley discovered himself caught off guard by her utter lack of vanity. Was the woman demented?

"By all that is holy, have you never seen yourself in a looking glass, Miss Dawson?" he demanded in exasperation. "You are exquisite. There is not a man who would not wish to seduce you. Myself included."

She abruptly stepped backward, her hands clutching the folds of her robes together.

"Please, Hawksley, do not tease. It is not at all kind. I am well aware that gentlemen do not find me appealing."

"Not appealing?"

"One does not reach the great age of six-and-twenty without a suitor and not be aware she is lacking in the sort of attractions men prefer."

Hawksley felt a flare of fury at the buffoons who had dared to treat her with such disregard. He did not doubt for a moment that she was worth a dozen of them.

"I have heard that every village must have its idiot; it seems that your particular village possesses an epidemic of them," he growled in annoyance.

She considered a moment before giving a slow shake of her head. "No, 'tis the simple fact that I am . . . not like others."

"Which is something to be admired."

A reluctant smile tugged at her lips. "You sound like my father."

"Obviously a wise man." Of their own violation his hands curled about her shoulders, pulling her close enough for him to feel the enticing heat of her body. He gritted his teeth as his body readily responded. Unlike the fools she was accustomed to, Hawksley was painfully aware of just how desirable she was. "I am certain he must have told you that you are quite special."

"Oh yes." Blithely unaware of the tension sizzling in the air, she gave a faint shrug. "He assured me that being intelligent and unique was something to take pride in. Easy enough for him to claim. He enjoyed the life of a recluse."

He scanned her pale features. "But you did not?"

She paused a long moment before heaving a sigh. "There is nothing pleasant in sitting in your room and listening to the distant sound of a party you were not invited to. Nor knowing the next morning that some hostess would appear to claim that your invitation must have been lost or overlooked."

He flinched at the unexpected jolt of pain that clutched at his heart.

"I was right. You live in a village of idiots."

"No, it was not their fault. Or at least, not entirely."

His brows snapped together. "What the blazes do you mean?"

"You said yourself that I am an eccentric," she reminded him simply. "I believe you even claimed me a lunatic. And you were not wrong."

His hands tightened upon her. By gads, he had never intended to hurt her.

"Kitten . . ."

"You were right," she overrode his soft protest, her eyes shimmering in the moonlight. "I have never managed to mix easily with others. I do not comprehend the jests that others find so amusing, or possess the talent to dazzle gentlemen with my wit. I even manage to annoy the servants who wait upon me." She gave a faint sigh. "'Tis not that I have not tried to change. I practice before mirrors and even memorize precisely what I should say when at a party. Unfortunately, it never comes out right. I am like a dancer who is always one step out of beat."

A voice of foreboding whispered in the back of Hawksley's mind as he shifted his hands to frame her countenance.

Her words had been calmly spoken, her demeanor more of bewilderment than a plea for sympathy, but they managed to stir wounds long forgotten.

He knew what it was to feel unappreciated and

unwanted. To struggle to please only to fail despite his best efforts.

It was a vulnerability within him that he kept sternly protected. Not even Fredrick had been allowed to see into his heart. His brother, like everyone, had believed in Hawksley's magnificent air of wicked disdain.

For once, however, he ignored the prickling unease that warned of impending danger.

He would not pull away from this woman who had so readily laid her heart bare to him.

"Why should you desire to mix with such obvious dolts? You are better served without them," he assured her gently.

A hint of sadness settled about her. "Perhaps, but I cannot deny that there are times I wish I were not quite so alone."

Alone. His eyes slid closed. He was intimately familiar with the sensation.

Or he was as a rule.

Rather to his surprise he discovered that he did not feel alone at the moment.

Not with this woman held in his arms.

He leaned his forehead against hers, breathing in deeply of her feminine scent.

"You are not alone now, kitten, you are with me, and I assure you that I possess the good sense to appreciate your fine qualities."

She slowly tilted back her head to regard him with wide eyes. No doubt at last sensing the awareness thick in the air.

"Hawksley . . ." she breathed.

A shudder wracked through him. He had warned himself a dozen times on his way back to the

Hawk's Nest that he must remember he was a gentleman. Holding a proper lady against her will was
scandalous enough without adding her seduction
to his sins.

But no amount of honor could halt the searing
urge to know her touch, to feel her lips beneath his
own.

"Clara . . . my sweet angel . . . I want to taste of
you," he husked, holding her gaze with smoldering
need. "Will you allow me?"

She touched the tip of her tongue to her lips, the
unwitting motion clenching the muscles of his
thighs.

"Taste?"

"I want to kiss you."

"Oh." She gave his plea a moment of consideration. "Why?"

Despite his aching urgency Hawksley could not
halt a small laugh. "Not everything has a reasonable
explanation, Miss Dawson. Indeed, there are some
things that should be left a mystery."

She regarded him with a somber expression.
"Such as kisses?"

"Such as kisses." He stepped until her soft curves
were pressed to his own. Still holding her face in his
hands, he lowered his head until he was a breath
from her lips. "Give me leave, kitten. I will not steal
what should be offered freely."

Her hesitation could not have lasted more than a
heartbeat, but to Hawksley it seemed as if it were an
eternity.

"Yes," she at last whispered.

"Yes."

With a groan he softly touched her lips, fiercely

reminding himself she was an innocent. Certainly there was passion enough beneath her proper manner, but she had no experience with the darker desires. He must take care not to startle her with his hunger.

Unfortunately his silent lecture did nothing to prepare him for the satin sweetness of her mouth. Barely sweeping over her lips, he gasped as a flood of gut-wrenching pleasure surged through his body.

Holy hell. He had expected to enjoy her. A lot. The truth had simmered between them from their first glance.

But this . . . this was magic.

Sliding his fingers into her hair he tilted her head back, allowing himself to slowly savor the taste and feel of her. Over and over he kissed her, outlining her lips with the tip of his tongue and nuzzling the corner of her mouth.

In the darkness she gave a low moan, her body arching instinctively closer to the growing hardness of his own. His breath caught as her arms lifted to encircle his neck, and all too easily he allowed himself to forget the danger to be had in her ready capitulation.

Instead his caresses deepened.

Urging her lips apart, he teased her tongue with his and swept his hands gently down the curve of her neck. *By gads, this must be heaven,* he fuzzily acknowledged, feeling the softness of her warm skin beneath his fingers.

Heaven complete with his own angel.

The robe proved to be a meaningless barrier as he impatiently tugged it open to allow his hands greater freedom to explore her curves. He growled

as he encountered the soft thrust of her breasts.
They were as sweet and delicate as the rest of her.
And utterly perfect.

He cupped them gently, allowing his thumbs to
brush over the puckered nipples.

She murmured restlessly against his lips but
made no move to pull away. Indeed, her arms tightened about his neck in obvious approval.

Bloody hell, he was on fire. His erection strained
painfully against the tight breeches and his hands
trembled as if he were an overeager youth rather
than a man of sophistication.

More, he needed more. More, more, more.

The word drummed like a litany through his blood
as he tore his lips from her mouth and branded an
urgent path of kisses down her neck, his arms encircling her waist to raise her off the floor.

With swift strides he was across the room and lowering her onto the narrow sofa. For a breathless
moment he simply regarded her with astonishment. In the moonlight her curls shimmered like
priceless silver, her features the purest ivory. And
most enticing of all were the emerald eyes that
shimmered with an invitation as old as time.

Careful to keep from crushing her, he lowered
himself on top of her body, giving a groan of satisfaction as his swollen muscles pressed into the
curve of her hip.

"Perfect . . . You are so perfect . . ." he muttered,
his mouth moving down the line of her collarbone
and at last to the softness he craved.

"Hawksley . . ." she breathed in shock as his lips
at last closed about the straining tip of her breast.

It was the sound of her voice that made him

pause and allowed his niggling conscience to be heard over his pounding heart.

He had only meant to kiss her, it reminded him. Just a taste. Not to take the innocence that did not belong to him.

With a savage curse he battled to gain control of his biting lust. Not an easy task when he knew with a few swift movements he could have himself free of his breeches and thrust deep into her heat.

And it most certainly did not help matters to have her hands clinging to his shoulders as if she possessed not the slightest sense of self-preservation.

What woman with the least amount of wits would trust him to be the one to halt matters before they tumbled beyond control?

A woman utterly unfamiliar with her own passions, a voice reminded him in the back of his mind.

Damn and blast, it was no wonder chivalry had died out.

It was a ghastly business.

Sucking in deep, rasping breaths, Hawksley pressed himself onto his elbows, his body threatening open mutiny.

"Holy hell . . . This is where you are supposed to slap my face and tell me that I go too far, kitten," he muttered in the thick silence.

Below him she blinked in confusion, as if she had been rudely interrupted from a particularly pleasant dream.

"But I do not wish to slap you. I very much enjoy your kisses." She stilled, a sudden concern darkening her eyes. "Do I not please you?"

Not please him? A groan was wrenched from his

throat. He was so hard he was damn well near to exploding and she asked if she did not please him?

"My God, if you knew precisely how much you please me, you would be locked in your rooms and hidden beneath your bed."

Pleasantly floating within the warm sensations that shimmered through her body, Clara regarded the man poised above her with a hint of impatience.

Everything had been going along splendidly. At least as far as she had been concerned.

His kisses had been just as glorious as she had suspected they would be. Tender and yet demanding a response she was quite eager to offer.

And as for those hands . . .

Well, she had feared she might actually catch fire as they had so skillfully smoothed over her body.

She had wanted nothing more than for him to continue with his intoxicating seduction. It seemed somehow a crime to halt so abruptly.

"I do not understand, Hawksley," she whispered. "If I please you, then what is the matter?"

His jaw locked as he took stock of her disappointed expression.

"Do you desire to be my mistress, Miss Dawson?"

She faltered at his blunt question.

"I . . ."

"A few moments more and I will be inside you and any claim to innocence you might possess will be lost forever," he pressed with grim determination, obviously determined to make her realize that the cost of such pleasure was higher than any respectable lady should be willing to pay.

Unfortunately for him, Clara was not like any other lady. Instead her eyes widened in astonishment.

"You wish to make love to me?"

"Make love to you?" He gave a disbelieving blink, as if he wondered if she was jesting. "I wish to carry you upstairs and drown in your heat. I wish to take you over and over and listen to you scream in pleasure. In truth, if I had my way I would tie you to my bed so that you could never leave. Does that not shock you?"

She met his blazing gaze squarely, still not able to accept such a man could ever find her desirable. For so long she had convinced herself that she must be somehow repulsive to men. It was little wonder her notorious logic was decidedly absent.

"It should, of course," she conceded ruefully.

"But . . . ?"

"But I discover I must be shameless as well as eccentric. I find your kisses far too thrilling for an innocent maiden."

His eyes squeezed shut as if he were in actual pain. "Bloody hell, kitten, you shall surely be the death of me." Sucking in a rasping breath, he fluidly pushed off her willing body and held out an imperious hand. "Come, it is time you were safely tucked in your bed."

Allowing herself to be lifted to her feet, Clara absently tugged the belt about her robe tighter, her brow furrowed at his abrupt dismissal.

"But you have not yet told me of your meeting," she reminded him. "Did you discover anything of value?"

"We shall discuss what I learned on the morrow," he said, his voice strained.

"But I wish to—"

Her words ended in a squeak as he easily reached out to pluck her from the floor and lifted her until they were eye to eye. Only then did she become fully aware of the torment shimmering in the indigo gaze.

"Miss Dawson . . . Clara . . . I beg if you have any compassion for me at all, you will return to your chambers and lock your door."

"Oh." Her heart gave a tiny flutter. Perhaps it would be best to speak in the morning, she had to concede. At the moment her thoughts possessed the most disturbing tendency to stray in forbidden directions. Not surprising when pressed against a very handsome, very wicked pirate. "Very well."

Chapter Eight

Hawksley awoke with a curse, the slanting morning sunlight revealing that he had managed to oversleep.

Not that he couldn't be excused for his rare indulgence, he grouchily acknowledged. He had paced the floor for hours as he had battled the urge to toss nobility into the midden heap and give in to the passion pulsing through his body.

Why should he not?

He was a rake, a scoundrel, and a perpetual disappointment to his family and the world in general. Why should he balk at seducing a female who was clearly as eager as himself to explore the smoldering desire?

He would ensure she was well pleased, both in bed and out. Hell, he would lavish her as if she were a princess.

In the end, however, he had forced himself to splash his face with cold water and crawl beneath the blankets to fantasize what he would be doing with Clara if only he were not such a fool.

There was something about the woman that

brought out a sense of honor he barely knew he possessed. And made him long for her . . . what?

Her respect, he at last concluded with a hint of embarrassment.

Absurd, but there it was.

With a shake of his head he plunged himself in the bath that had been left for him and shaved without assistance. Once clean he attired himself in the plain black garb that he had donned since his brother's death and pulled his still-damp hair into a ribbon at his neck.

The house was silent as he made his way down the stairs, and a frown touched his brow as he searched through the parlor and dining room to no avail.

He began to suspect where his missing guest might be discovered.

Angling toward the back of the house he entered the kitchens, halting at the doorway in sudden amazement.

Oh, not at the sight of his angel dusted with flour and her silver curls already tumbling from her tidy knot. That was a sight he fully expected to discover.

It was the squat, pug-nose man standing beside her that made him choke back a sudden laugh.

Covered in a large apron with his countenance red with exertion, the one-time thief was busily pummeling a lump of dough with obvious relish.

At his side Clara gave a light laugh, reaching out to pull back his large fists. Hawksley's heart gave an odd leap at her engaging smile, and suddenly the morning seemed a bit brighter.

"No, no, Dillon, you are not attempting to murder the dough," she corrected the burly servant, taking the dough into her slender hands to knead it with a rolling motion. "You must fold it gently and wait for it to tell you when it is done. You see?"

Dillon regarded her in understandable horror. "The devil I will. I am an Englishman, not some bloody French chef. The day I fondle a lump of dough is the day you might as well have me neutered and tossed into the gutter."

Hawksley bit his lip as Clara slanted the man a wide-eyed glance. "Well, if you wish your crust to be a charred, tasteless lump, then by all means continue to pummel it like a proper Englishman."

For a moment Dillon merely glared at her, and then clearly no more immune to those beautiful green eyes than Hawksley, he moved forward to snatch the dough from her hands.

"Blast it all . . . Give it here."

Watching with the eye of a master chef, Clara at last gave a satisfied nod of her head.

"Much better, Dillon. I shall turn you into a proper cook yet."

The servant merely snorted, although Hawksley did not miss the covert smile of pleasure that touched his lips.

"If you tell anyone of this I shall . . . Well, I cannot think of anything horrible enough to threaten you with that Hawksley wouldn't have me flayed for, but I assure you it will be dire."

Unperturbed by the gruff warning, Clara gently patted his arm. "My lips are sealed. Now while you finish that, I shall take Hawksley his tray."

With those concise, deliberate motions that fascinated him, Clara plucked a heavy tray from the counter and moved toward the door.

Swiftly Hawksley backed into the corridor and awaited her in the shadows. What he had to say to her would be best said in private.

Holding still until she was nearly level with him, Hawksley reached out to firmly snatch the tray from her hands.

"On how many occasions must I remind you that you are not a servant in my home?"

Stifling a gasp, she clutched her hands to her heart. "I was merely bringing you your breakfast."

His features hardened at her defensive words. It was not that he was offended by the knowledge that she had already taken firm control of his household. Or that she had clearly bewitched his staff.

It was quite simply a deep offense at the thought of her waiting upon him as if she were a lowly servant.

"I am well aware of what you were doing and I assure you that it is utterly unnecessary. If I desire breakfast I am perfectly capable of entering the kitchen and retrieving it for myself."

She blinked at the edge in his voice. "Are you angry?"

"Yes."

She bit her lip, her gaze wary. "I suppose I have rather taken over your home . . ."

"'Tis not that." With a hint of impatience he balanced the tray on one hand and reached out to grasp her arm with the other. "Come in here."

Too startled to properly argue, Clara allowed herself to be tugged into the small morning parlor where Hawksley set aside the tray and turned to regard her with his arms folded.

"What is the matter, Hawksley?" she demanded.

"You are my guest here," he said in stern tones. "If the house or food is not pleasing to you, then I shall hire servants to have it made suitable. You are not to tire yourself working as a common scullery maid."

Surprisingly, a small flush touched her cheeks, although he could not be certain if it was pleasure at his insistence or anger that inspired the delicate color.

"I told you I enjoy such work."

"Be that as it may, I will not have you playing maid beneath my roof. Here you are to be waited upon, as is only fitting for a lady."

This time there was no mistaking the faint twinkle of amusement in the emerald eyes.

"I suppose you will insist upon having your own way?"

"I fear I must." Reaching out, he touched her cheek. "I have great need of that astonishing mind of yours. I cannot have you distracted by stray battles against dust and lumpy crust. Agreed?"

She eyed him squarely, as if easily sensing she was being manipulated, but much to his relief she at last gave a decisive nod.

"Very well."

"Good. Now will you join me while I eat?"

Together they settled at the small table, and Hawksley hid a smile as she reached out to straighten the plate of toast and perfectly center the sugar and cream upon the tray.

He was quite certain she did not even realize her instinctive need to keep all in tidy order.

Placing the napkin in his lap, Hawksley allowed

himself to thoroughly enjoy the plates of smoked ham and warm toast with marmalade.

Since leaving his family estate he had lived the life of a bachelor. What did it matter if his home was tidy or his food cooked to perfection? All he needed was a roof over his head and a place to store his meager belongings.

Now he realized that he had unwittingly missed all the small comforts that made a house a home. The touches only a woman could provide.

With a soothing calm Clara waited for him to polish off the last of his tea before at last leaning forward.

"Did you manage to have the paper translated?"

Hawksley pushed aside the tray before reaching beneath his jacket to pull out the vowels and arrange them in the center of the table. Carefully he placed them together as if they were pieces of a puzzle.

"What there was to translate. Even together they only complete a portion of the page."

"Did you learn anything at all from them?"

Hawksley's lips twitched as he recalled his meeting with Biddles. As always, the little ferret had been a font of information.

"A bit. The writing is old Latin, as you suspected. And more fascinating, it appears to be some sort of petition."

"A petition?" She regarded him with a curious expression. "A royal petition?"

"Papal."

"Papal," Clara murmured, mulling over his revelation before her eyes abruptly widened and she was on her feet. "Dear God . . ."

Hawksley regarded her with a lift of his brows. He

had expected a measure of surprise at his revelation, but not this blatant amazement.

"What is it?"

"Mr. Chesterfield," she breathed.

A flare of possessive annoyance hardened Hawksley's expression. He found that he deeply disliked the man's name upon Clara's lips.

"Now is hardly an appropriate moment to be worrying over your mathematical genius."

She gave an impatient shake of her head. "Mathematics was only a hobby for him, as they are for me. His profession was that of a church historian, specifically translating ancient manuscripts," she said, leaning her hands on the table as she stabbed him with a glittering gaze. "If your brother managed to suspect that this paper was religious in nature, he most certainly would have sought out Mr. Chesterfield if he desired more information." She allowed herself a dramatic pause. "And just as importantly, it would explain the mysterious appointment with MC he noted in his journal."

Hellfire. Hawksley rose to his feet, belatedly realizing what had captured her interest.

"MC. Mr. Chesterfield."

"Precisely."

"Yes." He gave a slow nod. "It certainly fits. Like you, my brother could not possibly allow a mystery to go unsolved. Especially not if it included some musty bit of history."

"And perhaps he would have begun to question how Lord Doulton could possibly have come to possess a petition to the pope," she muttered. "Such a document is not something that is commonly lying about a gentleman's home."

A slow smile curved his lips. God, it had been so long since he had managed to uncover the faintest trail that might lead to his brother's murderer. He had begun to fear that he was beating his head against an impregnable wall.

Now he wanted to shout in happiness. Or better yet, grab Clara in his arms and soundly kiss her for her assistance.

Very, very soundly.

Instead he contented himself with grasping her fingers and squeezing them in silent appreciation.

"I think it time I pay a visit to this Mr. Chesterfield."

The green eyes sparkled with excitement. "Allow me to change my gown. I will not be a moment."

She would have slipped away if he had not tightened his grasp to keep her standing before him.

"Hold a moment, kitten."

She frowned at his stern tone. "What?"

Hawksley was wise enough to consider his words carefully. Miss Clara Dawson was not a woman who meekly accepted a gentleman's commands. No matter who that gentleman might be.

If he wished to keep her safe he would have to use logic, not male intimidation.

"You cannot simply go dashing about London," he pointed out in smooth tones. "For now we can hope that Doulton believes you to be dead. I have no intention of disabusing him of that notion."

"How would he possibly recognize me?"

Hawksley shrugged. "We cannot be certain he does not somehow know you and what you look like."

The delicate features tightened. "You intend to hold me prisoner in this house?"

His lips twitched at the mere thought of attempting to hold her captive. So far she had chosen to remain with him of her own will. Should she change her mind he did not doubt for a moment that she would be away before he could blink.

Still, he could not resist a bit of teasing.

"Well, there is that lingering fantasy of tying you to my bed."

An enchanting blush touched her cheeks, but it did nothing to ease her annoyance.

"Hawksley."

"Be at ease, kitten," he murmured, pressing a swift kiss to her forehead. "I have no intention of holding you prisoner. As delightful the thought, not even I am that brave. I do think, however, that we must see about some sort of disguise before you go about town."

"Oh." She mulled over his words before giving a nod of her head. "I suppose that is reasonable."

"I do have my moments."

She offered a grudging smile. "A few."

"Mmm." He gently dusted the flour from her cheek, his fingers lingering before he sternly pulled them away. "Allow me to go speak with Dillon and we will make our plans."

On this occasion it was her turn to reach out and halt his retreat.

"You do not intend to sneak out behind my back?"

He gave a lift of his brows. "Why would I do such a thing?"

"Out of some misguided need to protect me."

His features softened as he met her searching gaze. "I have every intention of protecting you, but I am honest enough to admit that I have need of your assistance. Whatever my varied talents, they do not include your unique ability to notice those niggling details the rest of us overlook. I promise I shall return in a moment."

Her expression of gratitude warmed his heart far more than was reasonable, but distracted with his thoughts, Hawksley missed the dangerous sensation.

With swift steps he returned to the kitchen, discovering his manservant muttering beneath his breath as he carefully chopped a mound of vegetables.

"Dillon, I have need of you," he commanded.

"Thank God," Dillon breathed, yanking off the offending apron with obvious relief. "Do I get to hit someone?"

Hawksley gave a chuckle. "I fear not. I desire you to discover a housekeeper who can not only be discreet but possesses the skills to keep this house in the sort of order that Miss Dawson prefers."

A rare smile touched the battered face. "Ach, t'will not be easy. Miss Dawson is right particular."

"So I have discovered," Hawksley retorted dryly.

"Mayhap I can convince my sister to come and lend a hand for a few weeks. Before she was pensioned off she was the housekeeper for Lord Tierney, and you know how fussy he was."

Hawksley gave a swift nod. He was familiar with Lord Tierney and his notable obsessions.

"Perfect. Tell her that we shall have need of her as soon as possible."

"I'll go fetch her now."

"While you are out I shall also need you to procure two gowns for Miss Dawson."

Surprisingly, Dillon's features abruptly hardened with a grim expression.

"She ain't the sort of woman to be accepting gowns from gentlemen," he growled.

Hawksley grimaced wryly at the unmistakable warning. How the devil could Clara claim she possessed no ability to charm the opposite sex? Since he had taken her from the carriage, she had managed to bewitch every man foolish enough to cross her path.

"I am well aware that Miss Dawson is a lady," he assured his servant. "But if she is to leave this house, she will need to be suitably disguised. I would suggest a few of those black crepe gowns that widows always feel the need to drape themselves in and a heavy veil."

"Oh . . . aye. I shall see what I can discover."

With a rueful shake of his head, Hawksley turned to retrace his steps back to the woman who had already managed to storm her way into his life.

Gads, first he was playing the cavalier and now he was hiring servants to please her finicky nature.

If he did not watch himself, he would end up with a leash about his neck.

His steps briefly faltered as the disturbing thought flared through his mind. Then just as swiftly he was dismissing it as ridiculous.

Fah. He was in absolute control of the entire situation.

Absolute control.

* * *

Clara squirmed uncomfortably on the leather seat of the carriage.

She had never considered what those poor Egyptian mummies must suffer through. Of course, they at least were dead before they were put through such torture.

She, on the other hand, was very much alive and swathed from head to foot in enough black crepe to encircle a woman three times her size, not to mention a wide bonnet with a thick veil that made breathing far from a certain thing.

At least she would not be traveling far enough to test her stomach in the closed carriage. And better yet, Hawksley had not broken his promise, she acknowledged, stealing a pleased glance at the man seated at her side.

Most gentlemen in his position would no doubt have insisted that a lady had no business being part of a murder investigation. They would claim that they were only attempting to protect her when in the back of their minds they would be certain she would only be a nuisance.

But not Hawksley.

He believed in her strange talents.

He believed in her.

The knowledge sent a warm flutter through her stomach.

Regarding the fiercely beautiful profile, Clara barely noted when the carriage rolled to a halt. It was only when Hawksley turned to consider her with a tight smile that she realized they had arrived.

"This is the address. Are you ready?"

"Yes."

"Remember, you are my cousin from Devonshire

who has recently suffered the loss of your husband and are in town to settle his affairs."

Her lips curled into a smile. He had drilled her on her part for the past hour.

"I shall not forget."

"And you are not to lift your veil for any reason."

She rolled her eyes heavenward. "How many times must I promise you I will not?"

Clearly realizing he was being a tad ridiculous, he offered a rueful grimace. "Very well."

Pushing open the door to the carriage, he stepped onto the road and lowered the stairs. Eager to at last discover something of Mr. Chesterfield, Clara twitched aside her heavy skirts and hurried down the stairs.

Unfortunately, she had neglected to take into account the thick veil and predictably missed the first step. With a cry she discovered herself plunging into Hawksley's waiting arms.

For a moment she simply leaned into his chest, breathing deeply of his intoxicating scent as he held her close. Despite the urgency of their task, it seemed a very nice place to linger. Hawksley seemed to agree as his arms briefly tightened, then with obvious reluctance he steadied her and dropped his arms.

"Careful, kitten."

She gave an impatient tug on the veil. "Blast. I can barely see through this ridiculous thing."

"Which means that no one else can see through it either."

"That will certainly ease my mind when I break my neck," she said dryly.

He gave a soft chuckle as he firmly pulled her

arm through his. "Just hold on to me, I won't let you fall."

Together they stepped through the narrow gate and approached the townhouse.

Although respectably situated in Cheapside, the residence possessed little to recommend it. The gardens were shabby, the shutters peeling, and the front knob unpolished. Not at all what she had expected from her intelligent, methodical Mr. Chesterfield.

Perhaps sensing her surprise, Hawksley cast her a sideways glance as they stepped onto the stoop and he used the knocker. Clara shrugged, forcing herself to concentrate upon matters at hand as the door was pulled open to reveal a wiry, nearly bald butler with a sour expression.

"Yes?"

"We are here to see Mr. Chesterfield," Hawksley announced.

The butler narrowed his beady eyes. "Mr. Chesterfield ain't at home."

"We do not mind waiting." Hawksley took a smooth step forward. "If you will show us to—"

With a surprisingly swift motion the servant shifted to block the doorway. "I fear you misunderstand, sir. Mr. Chesterfield has left London."

Beneath her fingers Clara could feel Hawksley's muscles tense. "Left London, you say? Where has he gone?"

"He had family business to attend in the north. If you would like to leave a card, I will see that—"

Realizing that the butler was on the point of shutting the door in their face, Clara rapidly searched her mind for a means of entering the house. Not only was her concern for poor Mr. Chesterfield increasing by the moment, but she knew that Hawksley was desperate to discover some connection to his brother within.

If she did not take matters in hand, the dangerous pirate was quite capable of forcing his way in.

"No, that will not do at all," she stated in tones that would have done a duchess proud. "I traveled a great distance to meet with your master. He was transcribing a rare manuscript for my lately departed husband. His mother and I are anxious to have it returned."

The sour expression soured further. "Manuscript? I ain't knowing of any manuscript."

"It must be within." Clara allowed herself a strategic pause before clutching at Hawksley's arm. "Unless . . . dear Lord, what if he has taken off with it? We must go to Bow Street at once. That is my only inheritance."

Something that might have been amusement flashed in the blue eyes, but with a readiness that Clara admired, he swiftly followed her lead.

"Of course, dear cousin. We shall inform the authorities immediately."

"Here now, there's no call to do anything rash," the servant blustered. "Mayhap I can search the master's study and find the manuscript."

Clara met his offer with a disdainful sniff. "Fah. You are merely providing your master with more time to escape with his ill-gotten treasure."

"Quite right." Hawksley leaned forward in a threatening fashion. "I must insist that we be allowed to search the study for ourselves."

There was a tense moment as the servant grimly attempted to choose between the lesser of two evils.

It was no doubt the air of violence that shrouded

the looming Hawksley that at last swayed the balance. He was an intimidating beast under the best of circumstances. When he chose to use the full force of his will he was downright unnerving.

"Come in, then." Turning on his heel, the man led them through a small foyer and up a flight of stairs. Stopping at the first door on the left, he threw it open and regarded them with a petulant impatience. "This be it."

Both Hawksley and Clara paused in distaste upon the threshold. The narrow chamber was quite simply a mess.

Books, papers, magazines, and a healthy dose of pure rubbish managed to clutter every shelf and table. Clara might have thought that someone had broken in and created the destruction if not for the thick layer of dust that coated the clutter.

Her stomach clenched at the mere thought of entering the room, let alone touching anything. There could be anything under the grime.

Bugs, mold, creepy ancient creatures.

Glancing down at her horrified expression, Hawksley gave her fingers a sympathetic squeeze before pulling her across the threshold.

"I will begin with the desk, my dear, if you wish to sort through the piles near the window."

With grudging steps she crossed toward the stacks of books on the window seat. Once there, however, she could not force herself to touch the crumbling manuscripts.

She would as soon put her hand in a viper pit.

Holding her skirts off the floor, she gave a loud cough in the butler's direction. "Mr. Chesterfield is not a very tidy gentleman, is he?"

The servant stiffened in offense. "True genius rarely concerns itself with such mundane matters."

Hawksley gave a bark of laughter as he rummaged among the papers. "Clearly you have never been in the companionship of true genius. I assure you that tidiness is a matter of utter necessity."

"Sir—" the butler began to protest, only to be interrupted by Clara.

"Good heavens, I shall be a mess," she muttered, stiffening her spine. If she could not assist Hawksley in one manner she would find another. "I must have an apron if I am to work among such filth. Kindly collect me one from the kitchen."

"Nay, I'll not be leaving strangers alone in my master's study."

"Very well, I shall go and fetch one myself."

With firm steps Clara marched back toward the door, meeting Hawksley's warning frown with a reassuring smile.

"Hold on here." The butler wavered as she neared the door, clearly debating whether to chase after her or keep a suspicious watch upon the threatening form by the desk. Like most men he concluded that a mere woman could not poise any true danger, and he threw up his arms in defeat. "Damnation."

Heading down the hall, Clara reached the stairs and with a furtive glance over her shoulders turned to head up the steps. Mr. Chesterfield might very well have taken leave of London to deal with family matters, but her instincts refused to accept that it was anything so simple. She very much feared that the man was in danger.

Finding the private bedchamber by the process

of elimination, Clara sucked in a deep breath and shoved open the door.

She discovered that the cramped room was passingly tidy with an attempt to hold back the encroaching dust; still, she was relieved that she had on a pair of thick gloves as she gingerly began her search.

Near a quarter of an hour later she acknowledged that she had pressed her luck as far as she dared, and slipping from the chamber, she hurried down the stairs and back into the study. She had barely stepped over the threshold when the butler came hurrying toward her, his expression suspicious.

"I thought you had gone to get an apron?"

"I could not find one that was not as filthy as the rest of the household," she informed him coldly.

Strolling from the desk, Hawksley placed her hand upon his arm. "It does not matter, my dear. I can find no evidence of your manuscript."

"It seems that we shall have to go to the authorities after all."

The butler paled at the threat. "Nay . . . I . . . I will find your bloody manuscript."

"And how could we possibly trust you?" Clara demanded.

"Perhaps we should give him the opportunity to search, my dear," Hawksley murmured, his gaze holding hers. "It would be a pity to make a fuss if it is simply misplaced."

Easily sensing what he desired of her, Clara gave a slow nod. "I suppose I can wait a day or two."

"When you find the manuscript, you may send word to the Hawk's Nest," Hawksley commanded.

The butler did not bother to hide his relief. "Aye."

With an arrogant nod of his head, Hawksley led her out of the gloomy townhouse into the pale spring sunlight. In silence they crawled back into the carriage.

Only when the door was shut and they were clamoring down the cobbled road did Hawksley abruptly tilt back his head to laugh with rich enjoyment.

"Bloody hell, kitten, you were brilliant."

Chapter Nine

"I must say, I surprised myself," she admitted.

He reached out to grasp her hand, his smile warm. "Biddles himself could not have done better, and that is saying something."

Clara felt her countenance warm with startled pleasure. She was not at all accustomed to such praise.

"Did you learn anything in the study?"

"I discovered that before he left London, Mr. Chesterfield was researching papal records and the history of the Vatican."

"Perhaps not utterly surprising for a church historian, but still intriguing," she murmured.

"My thoughts precisely." Tossing his hat on the opposite seat, he turned to face her squarely, his diamond earring flashing in the dim shadows. "Now tell me where you disappeared to."

"I went to Mr. Chesterfield's bedchamber to be certain that he had truly left London."

"What did you find?"

"Much of his clothing has been taken from the

room, as well as his shaving kit, which indicates that he did indeed leave on a trip, but I found these on his desk." Digging into the pocket of her voluminous skirts, she produced a fine gold pocket watch and a pair of wire-rimmed glasses.

Taking them from her hand, Hawksley gave a lift of his brows. "Glasses and a pocket watch? Hardly unusual objects to find in a bedchamber."

"Yes, but a gentleman leaving town for several weeks would never leave them behind."

He pondered the objects in his hand a long moment, clearly attempting not to leap to conclusions.

"It could be that he possesses more than one pocket watch and pair of glasses."

The thought had crossed Clara's mind as well, only to be dismissed when she noted the undoubted craftsmanship of the watch.

"Mr. Chesterfield did not appear to have the sort of funds that would lend itself to having several gold pocket watches. And even if he did have more than one, he would surely have taken care to place this one in a safe rather than leaving it lying upon his desk where a servant might take off with it."

"Perhaps his trip was unexpected." His fingers slowly closed about the watch and glasses as he stabbed her with a glittering gaze. "Or someone decided to make him disappear."

A pang shot through her heart at the mere thought. From what she knew of Mr. Chesterfield he had been a quiet, scholarly gentleman. He would be no match for someone wishing him violence.

"But surely the servants would have reported to the authorities if he had gone missing?" she protested.

He grimaced, his expression revealing he was all too familiar with darker side of human nature.

"Not if they were paid well enough by someone who wished his absence to remain a secret. If Mr. Chesterfield did not have close family, it might be weeks or even months before his absence was noted."

"That butler did seem quite uneasy at having us poking around." She bit her lip, her stomach rolling with dread. "Dear Lord."

Pocketing the objects she had taken from Mr. Chesterfield's chambers, he gave her fingers a reassuring squeeze.

"We know nothing yet, kitten. For now I think it best we assume he is still alive."

Sucking in a deep breath, she gave a nod of her head. He was right. It would not help Mr. Chesterfield to leap to conclusions.

Until they had positive information they must presume that he was still alive. And perhaps in need of their assistance.

"What do we do now?"

He silently considered their options as the carriage swayed and rattled its way through the crowded London streets. With the windows shut and the heavy curtains firmly pulled, they might have been utterly alone in the world.

As the silence lingered, Clara discovered herself becoming disturbingly aware of the warmth of his thigh pressed close to her own and the sheer power of his presence. She knew that there were far more important matters to concentrate upon. Her body, however, seemed determined to play traitor.

"I believe I will call upon Biddles and see if he will

be kind enough to have Mr. Chesterfield's servants followed," he at last murmured.

Clara licked her lips, which seemed strangely dry. "Why?"

"I wish to know where they might be going and who they might be meeting with. If Mr. Chesterfield is in hiding, they might very well be carrying him supplies and information. Then again, if they are in league with Lord Doulton, then they might lead us to the bastard."

"An excellent plan," she agreed, albeit in strained tones. It *was* an excellent plan. Unfortunately, her brain was not functioning nearly so well as she might wish.

Reaching up, he deliberately grasped the end of her veil and pushed it back, his eyes darkening.

He slowly stilled, as if he could actually sense her tingling awareness. And perhaps he could, she wryly acknowledged. She was quite certain she had raised the temperature in the carriage by several degrees.

"Why, thank you, Miss Dawson, I did assure you that I have my moments."

"You told me I was not to raise my veil," she reminded him softly.

Yanking off his gloves, he tossed them aside and reached to remove hers. Only then did he lift his hand to trace the line of her jaw.

"But you did not raise your veil . . . I did."

The tingles became more pronounced. "That hardly seems fair."

His nose flared as his gaze lowered to her mouth. A nerve in his jaw twitched, as if he were waging a mighty battle.

"Neither is the manner you have bewitched me, kitten," he husked. "'Tis monstrously unfair."

His tension brought a faint frown to her brow. "Hawksley?"

"Ah, Clara, I promised myself I would not do this."

"Do what?"

"This . . ."

Framing her face, Hawksley slowly lowered his head. Clara's heart came to a perfect halt as the lips neared. Oh, thank God. Thank God.

Then, a breath away he paused, and she instinctively realized he was offering her the opportunity to pull away.

It was what she should do, no doubt. After last eve she could no longer plead ignorance as to what a mere kiss could lead to. But even her much vaulted logic was impervious to the fierce pleasure his touch could offer.

And why should she deny herself, she silently demanded?

For six-and-twenty years she had quietly endured the rude slights and direct cuts by gentlemen. She had pretended that she did not yearn to feel the warmth of a man's arms about her or to experience the secret delights that other women took for granted.

Now, this beautiful, wonderful pirate desired her. Her. Miss Clara Dawson, aging spinster and village oddity.

Logic and common sense be damned.

She wanted him. He wanted her.

What else mattered?

Suddenly frightened he might come to his senses

and turn away, Clara threw her arms about his neck and tugged his head downward.

Just for a moment she thought he might resist her silent plea, and a familiar sinking sensation rushed through Clara's stomach. No, not again. Surely she was not to be rejected yet again.

She had thought Hawksley different.

Special.

Then with a rasping sigh Hawksley dropped his head downward and claimed her mouth in a kiss that seared away any lingering doubt as to his willingness. Catching her breath at the jolt of sizzling excitement, she clutched at his neck, her eyes sliding shut as she savored his demanding touch.

This was what she wanted. What she had wanted since the first moment she had laid eyes upon him.

His kiss deepened, his tongue stroking over her mouth.

"Let me taste of you, kitten," he whispered.

Uncertain what he desired, Clara tentatively parted her lips and stiffened in surprise when his tongue plunged into her mouth.

Oh my. This was . . . delicious.

With a moan she arched forward, her tongue touching his to match the slow, steady rhythm. If someone had told her about such a thing she would have shuddered in horror. And she did shudder, only horror had nothing to do with it. Instead an intense flare of anticipation clutched at her.

She wanted to be closer to him. To feel the heat of his bare skin next to her own.

Once again seeming to read her mind, he shifted to wrap his arms tightly about her. She heard him growl deep in his throat and then suddenly he was plucking her off the seat.

Never breaking the kiss, he turned her in his arms, tugging her until she was straddling his legs, her knees bent and the thick dress hiked up well past her knees.

Clara abruptly pulled back to meet the smoldering blue gaze. In such an intimate position she could easily feel the thrust of his hardened erection. It pressed firmly against her cleft, creating a rash of thrilling sensations.

Holding her gaze Hawksley allowed his fingers to trail down her spine, easily slipping the buttons loose from their hooks.

"Am I frightening you?" he whispered in ragged tones.

"No." Her fingers trailed through the raven hair, delighting in the satin tresses. He was so unbearably gorgeous. So perfect. "I like your touch."

He gave a husky chuckle. "A good thing, considering that I cannot seem to keep my hands off you."

As if to prove his point he gave her gown a sudden tug, pulling it off her shoulders along with the thin shift beneath. He seemed to freeze as he regarded her bared breasts, an odd expression upon his countenance. Then with exquisite care he cupped the small mounds in his hands, simply holding them for a long moment before his head dipped and his lips closed over one tip.

Clara's eyes slid shut as she felt his tongue rasp over the sensitive nipple, coaxing it to a hard peak. Dear Lord, the pleasure was nearly unbearable. It was a struggle to recall to breathe as he tugged and teased her with merciless expertise.

"Does this please you?" he murmured, stroking his mouth to tantalize her other breast.

She moaned, besieged by a dark longing she did not understand. Shifting on his lap, she pressed herself against the jut of his manhood.

"Do not stop," she pleaded.

"Do you wish more? Shall I teach you of passion?" he muttered, his voice thick.

She clutched at his shoulders. "I am not certain I can bear more. I feel as if I might shatter."

He leaned back, his lids half lowered and a dark flush upon his cheeks.

"Will you trust me?" he demanded, easily holding her bewildered gaze.

She gave a slow nod, rather surprised to discover that she did trust him. Perhaps it was not utterly logical, but there was something about him that assured her that he would never deliberately harm her.

"Yes."

He smiled as he lifted a hand to lightly trace the line of her swollen lips. Distracted by his touch, she barely noted his other hand slipping beneath the heavy folds of her skirts. It was not until his fingers brushed the bare skin of her thigh that she gave a sudden jump.

"Hawksley?"

His eyes flared as he cupped the back of her head and drew her head downward to accept his fiercely hungry kiss.

Clara paused before eagerly returning his kiss, her momentary unease forgotten. He obviously knew what he was about, she acknowledged fuzzily. Indeed, he seemed quite an expert. And she was wise enough to always concede to an expert. No matter what the subject.

Running her hands over the hard planes of his chest, she felt his fingers continue their soft journey. Aimlessly tracing patterns on her tingling skin, he moved ever higher. And higher.

And . . . dear heavens.

He easily swallowed her scream as his fingers swept the line of her cleft, pressing between the lips to seek her damp heat.

Her fingers dug into his chest as he gently stroked her, tiny bursts of fire shimmering through her as he brushed over the very source of her pleasure.

Wrenching her lips free she buried her face in the curve of his neck, her breath coming in short gasps.

"Hawksley . . . there is something . . ."

"I know, my sweet," he murmured, his lips brushing her temple.

"I do not know what to do," she muttered.

He chuckled softly. "For once you need do nothing. Allow me to pleasure you."

Unable to help herself, she asked the question trembling on her lips.

"Why?"

He paused in surprise. "Why what?"

"Why me?"

Thankfully, he did not laugh at her absurdity. Instead his lips softly nuzzled her cheek.

"There is no logic to such things, kitten. I desire you because I desire you." She moaned as his finger resumed its steady caress, his thumb pressing against her tender nub as his finger slid into her with infinite care. "You. Just you."

"Oh." A sharp-edged pleasure was spiraling through her, tensing her muscles. She had to move. She could not halt the instinct to tilt her hips forward to meet his steady stroke. There was something awaiting her. Something beckoning just out of reach. "I can bear no more," she gasped.

"Trust me," he whispered, his head dipping to capture a straining nipple in his mouth.

Her entire body went rigid as her body posed at the edge of a chasm. The world receded as she arched backward and gasped. Then with an explosive force the tension fragmented into a hundred shards of pleasure.

Utterly stunned by powerful climax, Clara flopped onto Hawksley's broad chest.

"Oh . . . my."

"Oh my, indeed." Gently removing his hand, Hawksley smoothed the skirts over her legs and wrapped his arms about her.

Unable to help herself, Clara snuggled against his warmth. She felt sated. Wondrously sated. But there was more. She felt a connection to this man. As if when she was near him, she was not so terribly alone.

It was something she had not felt in a very long time, and a small ache clutched at her heart.

The sensation would not last, of course. Everyone she had ever been attached to had left her. But for the moment she intended to cling firmly to the illusion that she possessed someone she cared for.

A friend.

A lover.

A man who stirred emotions she had buried years before.

Breathing deeply of his scent, she smiled. "Thank you."

He became motionless before his chest rumbled with a startled chuckle.

"Good Lord. You never fail to amaze me."

With an effort she leaned back to meet his amused gaze. "What?"

"Most females would be slapping my face, regardless of whether they had enjoyed my touch or not. They certainly would not be thanking me."

She grimaced ruefully. "I never seem capable of doing what is expected of me."

"Which is no doubt why I find you so fascinating," he murmured. "There is nothing coy or deceptive about you. There is a purity in your soul that is all too rare."

She laid her head back on his chest with a sigh. Unlike her, he always knew precisely what to say.

"This has been a most unusual trip to London."

He kissed the top of her head. "Most unusual."

For the next two days Hawksley barely rested as he scoured London for information on Mr. Chesterfield and ancient papal records.

He spoke to the handful of gentlemen who could claim an acquaintanceship with the reclusive scholar. He approached church officials, renowned scholars, and a number of collectors who specialized in religious artifacts.

He even spent hours rummaging through his brother's library, all to no avail.

He told himself that his sudden burst of energy was

merely the result of having a new path to investigate after weeks of being thwarted at every turn.

In truth, however, he knew at least a portion of his restlessness was due more to the young woman currently seated across the table from him than his conviction that he would learn anything of value.

Damn and blast, but she had him twisted in knots.

The moment he entered the Hawk's Nest he was aware of her presence. It was in the lingering scent of vanilla in the air, the sound of her graceful footfalls as she directed the newly acquired maids to a flurry of constant cleaning, and the sweet laughter that echoed through the house.

She even haunted his private chambers despite her careful habit not to intrude into his sanctuary.

Lying in his bed at night, he was plagued with the memories as he had held her in his arms and tasted of her sweetness.

Hellfire. It had been bad enough when he could only imagine what she might look like as he coaxed her to her climax. Now that he knew precisely how her face would flush and her eyes darken with pleasure, it was near torture to keep his hands off her.

He wanted her. He wanted to thrust himself deep in her heat and listen to her cry out in fulfillment.

And he very much feared that no matter how noble he might attempt to be, sooner or later temptation would overcome chivalry.

Obviously it was imperative that he bring Lord Doulton to justice without delay.

Only then would Clara be safe from his evil, and Hawksley would be able to return her to her tidy cottage.

And he would be allowed to seek relief from his aching passions.

Please, God, allow him to find relief. He was quite certain that his sanity depended upon it.

Glancing up from the perfectly poached salmon and potatoes in cream, Hawksley met the emerald gaze that was openly regarding him in a speculative manner.

It was not the first time he had caught her gaze upon him during the meal, and he wondered if he was about to be lectured for having abandoned her over the past two days.

It would be what most women would do. Of course, this was Miss Clara Dawson. Which meant he didn't have a bloody clue what she might say or do.

"I have not grown horns, have I?" he murmured, setting aside his fork.

She frowned at his odd words. "I beg your pardon?"

"You were staring at me in a rather alarming manner. I feared perhaps my cloven hoofs and tail were showing."

Her lips twitched although her gaze remained steady. "Not as yet."

"Thank goodness." He lounged comfortably back in his seat. For all his aching desires, he could not deny there was a distinct pleasure in sharing his meals with Clara. It was a treat he refused to deny himself. "Dare I ask what is upon your mind?"

"I am merely curious." Placing her elbow on the table, she cupped her chin in her palm. "I know very little about you."

His brows lifted. "I would say you are rather intimately acquainted with me, kitten."

"I do not mean . . ." A delicious blush stole to her

cheeks before she was sternly gathering her composure. "What of your family?"

Despite his best efforts Hawksley felt his muscles
tense. Oh, he understood her curiosity. Even sym-
pathized with her need to know more of the man
who for all practical purposes held her captive. Still,
he had devoted nearly twelve years to forgetting he
even possessed a family. It was not easy to pretend
indifference.

"What of them?" he demanded in clipped tone.

She absently blew a stray silver curl from her
brow. It was a habit that Hawksley found oddly
charming.

"Do you have any?"

"Too damnably many. Thankfully, we are estranged."

"Thankfully?" She did not bother to hide her
shock. "But that is horrible."

"You say that only because you are not familiar
with them."

She gave a slow shake of her head, her eyes darkening with remembered pain. "No, I say that
because I have lost everyone I love. I am alone because of fate, not out of choice."

Hawksley's chest tightened with regret. Damn.
He was an insensitive lout.

"Forgive me, I did not mean to be flippant," he
murmured. Then, with a grimace, he forced himself to swallow his pride. "I assure you that I did not
turn my back on my family by choice. I was requested by my father to leave his home the day I
celebrated my eighteenth birthday."

"Oh." A shocked sympathy softened her features.
"Hawksley, I am sorry."

He shrugged, as always discomforted by any hint of pity. It was not what he desired from this woman.

"No doubt he felt he possessed reason," he confessed wryly. "I have never found it particularly easy to bend to another's will."

Her brows lifted. "Really? You shock me."

"Minx," he chastised her teasing. "Very well. I am stubborn and opinionated and far too frivolous of mind to suit Lor—" He abruptly bit off his words. He was not quite certain why, but he had no desire to reveal the identity of his father, or the fact that he now had been burdened with a title he had never desired. Perhaps it was a fear that Clara would suddenly treat him as something he was not. Or that she would become uncomfortable in his presence. Or perhaps it was something he did not want to ponder. In any event, he was not yet prepared to share all his secrets. "My father."

She had no doubt noted his hesitation and tucked it in the back of her peculiar mind. Thankfully, however, she did not press him with tedious questions.

"He truly requested you leave your home?" she demanded softly, clearly unable to conceive that any father would toss his own child from his house.

Hawksley had no such trouble. He had been a disappointment to his father for as long as he could remember. It had only been a matter of time before the pompous old prig had rid himself of such a constant irritation.

"Oh yes. He claimed my wicked ways would never be tamed as long as he was there to haul me out of trouble. He presumed I would soon tire of living upon my own wits and come crawling back for his forgiveness."

She pondered his words for a long moment before a small smile touched her lips. Hawksley felt his heart perform that unexplainable flop in his chest. Even attired in a plain blue gown with her hair pulled into a simple knot, she was still the most beautiful woman he had ever laid eyes upon.

"Obviously your wits proved more tenacious than he suspected," she retorted.

"I would say it was my pride, not my wits, that was tenacious."

"What of your brother? Did the two of you remain close?"

"In truth we were not that close when we were young. He is . . ." Hawksley painfully corrected himself. "He was eight years my senior, a vast difference in age when we were children. It was not until I arrived in London that we at last came to know one another."

Without warning she reached out to softly touch his hand. "And then you lost him."

His fingers clasped hers in a tight grip. Her warmth helped to ease the chill that had haunted him for too long.

"Yes."

"'Tis no wonder you are so determined to find his killer."

Hawksley gave an inelegant snort. For all his rushing about, he had achieved very little.

"Determined, perhaps. But thus far spectacularly unsuccessful."

"You have not managed to have the servants followed?"

"Only upon mundane tasks. If they are meeting with anyone they are sly enough to conceal it from Biddles's prying eyes." He gave an impatient shake of his head. "Most unlikely."

She leaned forward, her eyes glittering with a sudden excitement.

"Perhaps I can be of assistance," she informed him. "I think I have reasoned out why Lord Doulton wishes me dead."

Chapter Ten

Hawksley regarded her with that blank stare that was all too familiar to Clara. It often accompanied what she considered to be a brilliant deduction, but what others seemed to find as gibberish.

"You have reasoned out . . . have you received some new information?"

She gave him a steady glance. They both knew that she had not been allowed to step a foot outside the house without Dillon hovering like a rabid guard dog at her side. Nor did anyone know where to reach her even if they did wish to send her a missive.

Not that she had felt in any way imprisoned, she had to concede. She had no desire to flaunt her presence in London when someone wished her dead. Nor did she feel like indulging in the various entertainments when Mr. Chesterfield was missing and poor Hawksley's brother murdered.

Perhaps there had been a few occasions when she had been restlessly aware of Hawksley's absence. And a sense of regret that he seemed to have lost all interest in kissing her after their delicious interlude in the carriage, but she was swift to squash such selfish emotions.

Hawksley was naturally consumed with the need to capture his brother's murderer. She more than anyone understood such an intense distraction. She often forgot everyone and everything when puzzling a mystery.

And so she had devoted her time to more productive means than fretting over the strange yearning for Hawksley's company.

"No. I just took the time to consider the facts."

"What facts?"

"So far as we know, the only connection between myself and Lord Doulton is Mr. Chesterfield," she explained. "So we must begin with that."

His head tilted to one side as he regarded her with a curious intensity.

"We still have no evidence that Lord Doulton had anything to do with Mr. Chesterfield."

"True, but we must start somewhere," she pointed out.

"Very well."

Clara carefully organized her thoughts. Her conclusions called for a great deal of supposition, but she believed the logic to be sound. Now she had to convince Hawksley.

"If we may suppose that your brother took the manuscript to Mr. Chesterfield and learned something nefarious about the document, then it might be that your brother returned to Lord Doulton to question him on how he came to possess such an artifact."

His lips twisted. "It is possible. His curiosity would have been roused as to why a gentleman without the least interest in things scholarly would have an ancient papal petition lying about his house." His hand abruptly hit the table. "God, for such an intelligent gentleman he could be so bloody naïve."

Clara ignored the pang in her heart. Hawksley was in need of her intellect at the moment, not her emotions.

"And in approaching Lord Doulton he might have revealed Mr. Chesterfield's assistance."

"Ah." Comprehension dawned in the blue eyes. "Which would explain why Lord Doulton would turn his attention to the church historian." There was a short pause as he followed her line of reasoning. "But I still do not comprehend how you became involved."

"What if Lord Doulton did manage to either frighten Mr. Chesterfield away from London or . . . worse?" She stumbled over the mere mention of Mr. Chesterfield lying dead in some shallow grave. The thought was simply too unbearable. "He might have searched his home to discover if there was anyone to whom Mr. Chesterfield might have revealed his knowledge of any disreputable dealings."

He conceded her logic with a nod of his head. "It is what I would do."

"If he did so, he might very well have come across a letter Mr. Chesterfield was writing to me. His disappearance did occur at the same time he would be expected to send his monthly correspondence."

His fingers abruptly tightened upon hers. "You believe Chesterfield wrote to you of his suspicions?"

She grimaced, not yet prepared to take that great a leap of faith. For all her belief that her intellectual connection with Mr. Chesterfield was somehow superior to an emotional connection, she was beginning to suspect that it revealed very little of the true nature of the man.

In just a few days she knew far more of Hawksley than she had learned in an entire year of correspondence with Mr. Chesterfield.

"That is impossible to say, but in any event the letter would have been composed of mathematical equations," she reminded him. "Lord Doulton would have been unable to read it."

"Then . . . ah, he would have presumed it was some sort of code."

She smiled at his ready understanding. "Precisely."

Absently he stroked her fingers, his brow furrowed. "But if he stole the letter and knew you never received it, why would he consider you a threat?"

Clara gave a small shrug. "I can only suppose that he sent someone to keep watch on me. After all, he could not be certain that Mr. Chesterfield had not written more than one letter to me."

"And when you made plans to travel to London . . ."

"His worst fears were confirmed."

His eyes darkened with a suppressed fury. "Damn."

Sucking in a deep breath, she prepared herself for the next hurdle to overcome. Convincing Hawksley of her theory was one thing. Convincing him that she was the best suited to prove her theory was quite another story.

Men were rarely reasonable when they were being . . . well, men.

"'Tis still all speculation, but I do believe it would be worthwhile to see if we can discover whether or not Lord Doulton has my letter or anything of Mr. Chesterfield's in his possession," she murmured cautiously. "If nothing else, it would assist to confirm we are on the right path. And there is always the hope that Mr. Chesterfield did mention something of your brother or the manuscript in his missive to me."

A grim determination clenched his features, reminding her forcibly of the first time she had laid eyes upon him. He was a man who desired action. A means to strike at his enemy, not to lurk about in the shadows.

"I think you are right." With a smooth motion he was on his feet. "I shall contact Santos and Biddles. I will need their assistance if I am to search Lord Doulton's house."

Realizing he was preparing to charge off into the dark, Clara abruptly stepped directly before him, her hands on her hips.

"*We* shall need their assistance."

"We?" He gave a startled frown before his gaze narrowed. "Oh no, Clara. I absolutely refuse to allow you to put yourself in such danger."

Quite prepared for his typical reaction, Clara maintained her air of calm certainty.

"Actually, Hawksley, 'tis not your place to forbid me anything," she stated in firm tones. "If I choose to search through Lord Doulton's home, I am perfectly free to do so."

The diamond earring winked in the candlelight as he slowly leaned forward, no doubt believing he could somehow intimidate her.

Ridiculous, of course. Most females might shrivel beneath a forbidding male. She only found it a reason to dig in her heels with greater effort.

"I could force you to remain here."

"You could." She smiled slowly. "But you would not."

He glared at her for a long moment, then with a low curse he tossed his hands in the air.

"Bloody hell. It is what I would do if I had the least amount of sense."

Moving forward, she lightly touched his arm. "Consider, Hawksley, you shall need me to transcribe the letter, if there is one, since we dare not take it and alert Lord Doulton of our interest in it. And you cannot deny that I am far more likely to take note of anything unusual."

He was silent a long moment, a muscle in his jaw jerking as he gritted his teeth. At last he gave a sharp laugh as he reached out to tilt her chin upward.

"Will you tell me one thing, kitten?" he murmured.

"What?"

"Do you happen to notice whether or not I have suddenly acquired a ring through my nose?"

On this occasion it was Clara's turn to appear bewildered by his enigmatic words.

"A ring?"

"Never mind." With a faint shake of his head, he lowered his head to claim her mouth in a swift, demanding kiss. "I must speak with Biddles. I shall return later."

Clara watched his retreat with a sigh.

His ready belief in her skills deeply touched parts of her that were perhaps best left untouched.

And worse, that kiss had stirred dark needs that most certainly were best left unstirred.

Blast and blast. She was beginning to suspect that this adventure might be more costly than she had ever anticipated.

Biddles leaned back in his chair, his pointed nose twitching as he watched Hawksley toss back the finely aged whiskey.

Even in the shadows of the cramped office above Hellion's Den, the dandy managed to be near blinding in a canary coat and jade waistcoat. With a froth of lace at his neck and cuffs, he should have appeared ridiculous. There was nothing ridiculous, however, in the narrowed eyes that held a disconcerting glint of sly amusement.

It was a glint that would have been worrisome to Hawksley under normal circumstances. Biddles possessed a rather wicked ability to see more than he should. And a habit of using that advantage to manipulate those about him.

At the moment, however, Hawksley was impervious to everything but his dark thoughts.

What the devil had he been thinking?

Or more to the point, why had he not been thinking?

He knew quite well that it was beyond foolish to

allow Clara to put herself in such danger. Hell, she should not even step outside his door, let alone waltz into the home of the gentleman who desired her dead.

Anything could happen. They could be spotted by a nosy neighbor. A servant could stumble upon them. For God's sake, Lord Doulton himself might make a sudden appearance.

It was enough to make him break out in a cold sweat. A breathless panic. An itchy rash.

And yet, he had gazed down in those pleading, magnificent emerald eyes and his brain had turned to mush.

Idiot.

He was a spectacular idiot. There simply was no other explanation.

At last Biddles cleared his throat. "I will have you know, Hawk, that I pride myself on serving only the finest and most rare of spirits. However, if you insist on guzzling it as if it were no more than swill, I shall send to the kitchens for a bottle of Blue Ruin."

With a blink Hawksley realized he was standing in the middle of the office with an empty glass clenched in his hands. He grimaced as he set aside the glass and sucked in a deep breath.

"Forgive me, Biddles. I fear that I am rather distracted."

"Understandable, old friend. You have endured much." The thin face hardened. "Lord Doulton shall pay, that I assure you."

Hawksley gave a short laugh. "'Tis not Lord Doulton who has my nerves twisted into knots. That honor can solely be laid at the feet of Miss Clara Dawson."

"Miss Dawson? You intrigue me." Biddles abruptly leaned forward, his sly smile returning. "Tell me, Hawk, what has she done that has you in such a twit?"

Hawksley folded his arms over his chest. "Do not smile at me in that manner, Biddles."

"What manner would that be?"

"A condemned man who is pleased to have a partner in his misery."

"Is that how you feel? Condemned?"

"That all depends upon the hour."

The pointed nose twitched in avid curiosity. "Beg pardon?"

Hawksley blew out a sigh. He was not particularly comfortable in revealing his emotions. Hell, under normal circumstances, boiling tar and feathers could not have wrenched a confession from him.

But Miss Clara Dawson had ensured these were not normal circumstances, and he possessed a near-overwhelming urge to discover if he had completely lost his mind.

"I haven't a clue what I shall feel from one moment to another," he growled. "In one breath I desire to toss Miss Dawson into the nearest carriage and have her sent back to that damnable village so that she will no longer be a plague to me, and the next I want her flat on her back in my bed."

Far from appearing shocked by his words, Biddles tilted his head to one side with a smirk.

"I should choose the bed if I were you. According to Santos, this Miss Dawson is not only beautiful but extraordinarily intelligent."

Hawksley's teeth snapped together. A pox on the dashing smuggler. "Santos plays a dangerous game."

"He is not happy unless he is walking the edge of disaster." Biddles shrugged. "Still, his taste in women is impeccable. If I were you I would make her my mistress before he can seduce her away."

Hawksley was not even aware he was moving until his hands slapped loudly onto the desk. "Damn you, Miss Dawson is a lady, not a light skirt."

The little rat did not even blink. Instead he leaned back in his seat and templed his fingers beneath his chin.

"Then make her your wife."

"Wife?" Hawksley jerked back as if he had taken a roundhouse to the chin. "Have you taken leave of your senses?"

"Why not?"

Why not? Good God, there were a dozen, nay, a hundred reasons why not. The fact that he could not think of one was simply because he was so utterly stunned by the absurd suggestion.

"What the blazes would I do with a wife?" he at last blustered.

"If I need tell you, Hawk, then perhaps you should give up on women altogether," Biddles drawled.

His gaze narrowed. He did not need anyone to tell him what could be done with Clara, a wedding ring, and a bed. It was seared into his mind.

"There is more to a wife than bedding her."

"Quite a bit more," Biddles readily agreed. "Should you be fortunate enough, she will also be a friend, a helpmate, and the one person in the world whom you will trust above all others."

Hawksley's chest tightened in a frightening manner before he forced himself to frown. Helpmate . . . fah.

"You sound like a ghastly poet."

"No, merely like a happily married man."

"Not all men can claim such satisfaction," he swiftly pointed out. "Indeed, the clubs are littered with husbands seeking solitude from their nagging wives."

Biddles gave a superior lift of his brow. "That is because they sought a wife they believed would suit their needs. One who was beautiful, or wealthy, or from the proper family."

"And you think I should seek a bride who does not suit my needs? Rather absurd logic, even for you, Biddles."

"I do not think you should seek one at all," he corrected smoothly. "I believe that fate will ensure you stumble across the true woman for you. Or sometimes fate just tosses her straight at your head."

Just for a heartbeat Hawksley recalled the moment he had opened the door to the carriage. There had been a jolt of recognition. As if he had been waiting for the lovely angel. Perhaps all his life.

No. God, no.

He shoved his hands through the long strands of his hair. "Enough. I have no interest in acquiring a wife."

Biddles's expression became suddenly somber. "'Tis unfortunate, but there is no escaping the fact that you now possess responsibilities that cannot be ignored forever, Hawk. One of which is to marry and produce children."

Hawksley froze, his countenance grim.

"Responsibilities that I will not consider until after I have caught Fredrick's murderer." He squared his shoulders. "Now can we please turn our attention to the reason I sought you out this evening?"

Chapter Eleven

It was nearly a week later when the plan was at last put into place. Throughout the long days Clara had remained patient, although she had chafed at the knowledge that she was unable to offer assistance in the actual details of the scheme.

In truth it had been Hawksley's friend Lord Bidwell who had taken charge of arranging the high-stakes hazard game that was perfectly suited to lure Lord Doulton to Hellion's Den for the evening, and Santos who had devoted several evenings to covertly watching the servants' routines so there would be no unpleasant surprises.

As for Hawksley, he had disappeared each afternoon only to return when the dawn was breaking.

At first Clara had feared he was avoiding her.

He certainly would not be the first man to go to extraordinary lengths to flee her presence. Some even went so far as to leap behind bushes when they spotted her walking down a lane.

Why should he be any different?

Fortunately, the horrid notion barely had time

to slice through her heart before she discovered the truth.

Returning her breakfast tray to the kitchen, she had heard Dillon speaking to his sister, who had recently arrived to take over the housekeeping duties. He had confessed that Hawksley had been forced to return to the gambling hells to earn enough money to pay for the wages of the increased staff.

Her fear had shifted to guilt.

Oh . . . blast.

She knew perfectly well that Hawksley had only hired the housekeeper and maids to please her.

Servants he could ill afford.

Still, there seemed no simple means of confronting him with her knowledge. Even *she* knew better than to offer him the funds she had brought with her, as meager as they might be, or to suggest that he allow her to care for the house without assistance.

Gentlemen were astonishingly sensitive when it came to such matters. And the less money they possessed, the more sensitive they became.

It was all a mystery to Clara. But then, most things that had to do with the opposite sex were a mystery to her. Such strange creatures.

It seemed best to hold her tongue until she could consider a means of easing his burden without harming his pride.

At last the days passed and the plans were in place and Clara discovered herself rattling through London in the closed carriage with a clearly tense Hawksley.

She allowed his ceaseless lectures to wash over her as she smoothed her hands over the pants and

shabby coat Dillon had procured for her. It felt odd to
be dressed as a man, but she had to admit Hawksley had been right. Such attire gave her much more
freedom than that blasted crepe dress from the nether-
world. And best of all, her hair had been shoved
beneath a hat rather than concealed behind a
heavy veil.

She was fully prepared for her life of crime.

Shrouded in the darkness of the mews, the carriage came to a silent halt and Hawksley assisted
her into the narrow alley. Still without speaking, she
discovered herself being hoisted over the high wall.
She stifled a squeak as she was swung over the top
to land awkwardly on the other side.

She was quick, however, to have herself upright
and dusted off before Hawksley landed softly
beside her. He would use any excuse, no matter
how trifling, to force her to remain in the carriage.

As if to prove her point, he regarded her with a
searching gaze before reluctantly pulling her
toward the looming stone structure.

"Here we are," he whispered.

Clara's eyes widened as she counted the arched
windows that glinted in the moonlight. She did not
doubt her cottage could fit in the kitchens alone.

"Good heavens. It is quite . . . lavish, is it not?"

Hawksley gave an inelegant snort. "Lord Doulton
possesses a taste, or many would say a lack of taste,
for the large and gaudy. The question is how he has
managed to acquire the fortune to pander to his
expensive habits."

Clara nodded. To purchase such a home and
staff would require an enormous fortune.

"Hopefully we shall soon discover."

"Clara."

His hand landed upon her arm, and Clara heaved a sigh. "Yes, Hawksley, I know. I am to remain at your side at all times, keep my mouth shut, and leap through the nearest window at the first hint of danger."

The blue eyes flashed in the darkness, his other hand reaching up to gently cup her face. "If something were to happen to you . . ."

A tiny thrill of pleasure shot down her spine. It had been far too long since he had touched her, she inanely realized. She had missed the feel of his warmth.

"It will not. I am not a courageous sort. If something occurs, I assure you that I will scamper away in the most cowardly fashion."

His lips twisted into a humorless smile. "I would feel much better if I truly believed that." There was a faint whistle in the distance and Hawksley sucked in a deep breath. "That will be Santos. Are you ready?"

"Yes."

"Then let us be done with this," he muttered, grasping her fingers in a tight grip as he led her toward the back of the house. They had reached a pair of French doors when a tall form suddenly detached from the shadows and Santos joined them. Dressed in black, as were Clara and Hawksley, he was tall and beautiful, and when he flashed her a seductive smile she could not help but smile back. He was not Hawksley, but there was not a woman alive who would not go a bit weak in the knees when near the man. A frown abruptly marred Hawksley's brow, and the glance he shot toward his friend seemed unnecessarily fierce. "You have searched the house?"

Santos chuckled with a strange hint of satisfaction.

"Yes. The staff have all retired to the servant quarters except for a footman and Lord Doulton's valet."

"You will keep watch upon them?"

"Of course. Biddles is already within the library awaiting you." Stepping forward, he grasped Clara's hand and lifted it to his lips. "Be careful, *meu anjo*."

He disappeared through the French doors as Hawksley muttered beneath his breath. They waited a long moment before following him within, both moving with a slow caution that had Clara's nerves on edge. She discovered it was one thing to logically plot stealing into a house, and quite another to actually do the deed.

Thankfully, she managed to make it to the library without stumbling, sneezing, fainting, or even breaking her neck. Slipping into the vast room, they shut the door behind them and there was a rustle of movement. In moments a small gentleman with a pointed nose and shrewd eyes had lit a candle.

"So glad you could make it, Hawk," the gentleman drawled, walking forward to regard Clara with a disturbingly perceptive gaze. "Ah, and the intriguing Miss Dawson. My very great pleasure." Lifting the candle, he studied her flushed countenance. "Egads. Santos did not exaggeraté."

Hawksley gave a low growl at her side. "Not now, Biddles. Have you discovered anything of interest?"

Lord Bidwell turned that unnerving gaze upon Hawksley for a long moment before waving his hand about the room.

"The usual collection of the vulgar. Really, it is astonishing how many who seek to claim the position of gentlemen retain the soul of the bourgeoisie." They all took a moment to grimace. Although there were a handful of obligatory books upon shelves, it was the artwork that held and captured the attention. Paintings, sculptures, and figurines were hung, crammed, and stuffed into every available space. All of them of dubious quality, and all of them of naked women. "There is one thing of interest, however."

"What is it?" Hawksley demanded.

Leading them to a distant alcove, Lord Bidwell halted before a life-sized statue of a woman with a bosom that made Clara wonder how it could possibly remain upright.

"If I do not miss my guess, I believe it to be a safe," Biddles murmured.

Hawksley gave a raise of his brows. "Vulgar, indeed."

The thin gentleman was busily running his fingers over the statue, giving a faint sniff as he reached the tip of one breast.

"How depressingly predictable," he drawled, pressing a hidden lever so that the front torso swung open.

Taking the candle from his friend, Hawksley leaned forward to peer into the murky darkness that ran down both legs.

"There is something within. Ah."

He pulled out a neatly folded paper, and Clara reached out to pluck it from his grasp. "Good heavens, it is my letter."

"Indeed." Hawksley narrowed his gaze before returning his attention to the safe. "There is something else."

"More letters?" Biddles demanded.

"No." He pulled out what appeared to be several squares of canvas tidily rolled together. "What the devil?"

Clara gave a sudden gasp. Her father had taught her well.

"Hawksley, be careful," she warned.

He regarded her in surprise. "Do you know what it is?"

"Paintings." Taking the bundle from him, she moved to a nearby table where she smoothed the canvases flat with exquisite care. "Dear heavens, not just paintings. Titian, Valentino Baroccio . . . and what I suspect might be a Raphael." Something niggled in the back of Clara's mind, but at the moment she was too stunned at actually having her hands upon such masterpieces to give it much note. "These are priceless."

The two gentlemen crowded behind her, peering over her shoulder.

"She is quite right, Hawk," Biddles said. "These are masterpieces. They cannot be left here and allowed to disappear."

"Damn." Hawksley blew out a frustrated sigh. "I was not yet prepared to tip my hand, but it appears we shall have no choice."

Clara breathed a sigh of relief as she carefully rolled the canvases and handed them to Lord Bidwell. As an art scholar, her father had firmly believed that such works should be offered for all the world to enjoy, from kings to the lowliest servant. He would have thought it no less than sacrilege to leave the paintings in the hands of a scoundrel.

Taking the paintings with obvious reverence, the

thin gentleman glanced toward Hawksley. "Shall we continue with our search?"

Hawksley moved to shut the now-empty safe. "Not this eve. I prefer not to press our luck."

"My thought as well," Biddles swiftly agreed.

Together they moved across the room, Hawksley cautiously peering out the door before waving them through. Santos appeared next to them as they slipped through the silent house and out the French windows.

It was a distinct relief to Clara when they at last approached the wall and no disaster had befallen them. Logic might assure her that they had taken the necessary precautions to ensure a successful campaign, but she was discovering that adventures were not always about logic and strategy. There was far too much luck involved for her peace of mind.

On this occasion she was prepared for the feel of Hawksley's strong hands encircling her waist and hoisting her upward. She scrambled over the wall and managed to land upon her feet.

Turning, she awaited Hawksley to join her. Oddly, only silence greeted her and she frowned. What the devil were they doing?

No doubt some stupid male battle over who would go over the fence last, she told herself with a roll of her eyes.

It was then that she heard the sound of footsteps stomping through the garden and the call of a rough male voice.

"I heard ye sneaking about, ye rotten thieves. Show yerself or I'll blast a hole in yer head."

Clara's perfect brain froze in horror. Blessed Saints, they had been caught. And worse, the angry servant sounded more than a little eager to begin firing lead balls about the garden.

Think, Clara, think, she grimly commanded herself. If she did not do something swiftly, then Hawksley would take matters into his own hands. A thought that was enough to make her eye twitch.

She had to do something. But what?

A distraction, the voice of reason whispered in the back of her mind. That was what was needed.

Swiftly, she bent down and searched until she found two stones that fitted comfortably in her hands and darted down the alley. Along the way she managed to drop one of the stones painfully upon her toe but she never faltered. Reaching the corner of the property, she drew her arm back and tossed the remaining stone over the wall.

Luck for once was on her side and the stone landed with a loud splash in a nearby fountain.

"Hah, yer mine now, ye bloody sod," the servant growled as he barreled toward the fountain.

Clara silently moved back down the alley, not at all surprised to discover the three gentlemen vaulting over the wall by the time she returned.

None of them spoke as they skirted the stables and headed down the block to where Hawksley's carriage awaited them. They clambered within and Hawksley gave a rap on the ceiling to set the vehicle into motion.

Only when they were well away from the expensive townhouse did Biddles suddenly lean forward to where she sat next to Hawksley to grasp her fingers and lift them to his lips.

"We are in your debt, my dear," he murmured, his gaze slanting toward the tense gentleman at her side. "I admire a woman with such quick wits. You are fortunate I am already wed, Hawk."

Not about to be outdone, Santos snatched her fingers from Biddles's grasp and brushed his lips over them in a lingering kiss.

"I am fortunate that I am not."

There was a growl of irritation as Hawksley grabbed her wrist and tugged her fingers free. Then possessively he tucked her in the crook of his arm and glared at his two companions.

"You will both keep your lips to yourself unless you wish to be tossed from this carriage."

Santos merely chuckled as he lounged carelessly in his seat. "You cannot keep her hidden away forever, Hawksley."

Clara felt herself tugged even closer. Not that she was about to protest. As far as she was concerned, he could hold her in his arms for the rest of eternity.

"Actually, Santos, that has yet to be decided," he warned in dangerous tones.

It was nearly an hour later when Hawksley escorted Clara to her dark chambers in the Hawk's Nest.

The priceless canvases had been left in Biddles's care with the hope that Lord Doulton would have no means of connecting him to the theft, and Santos had been charged with the task of planting rumors that the artwork had been smuggled out of England by an unknown band of cutthroats.

Such a flimsy tale would not fool Lord Doulton for long, but it might keep him from turning his suspicions toward Hawksley for at least a few days.

Halting in the shadows of the upper hall, Hawksley glanced down at the woman at his side.

As always when she was near, he felt that potent mixture of exasperation, pride, and gut-wrenching tenderness.

And of course, that damnable lust that clawed at him with ruthless determination.

Bloody hell, he had been a fool to insist she dress as a young lad. At the time his thought had only been to ensure that a casual observer would mistake her for a young male servant.

How the devil was he to know that the soft breeches would cling to her sweet bottom with such tenacious perfection? Or that the masculine coat would reveal the enticing curve of her breasts?

Or that the knowledge that Santos and Biddles were enjoying the same erotic view was enough to make him smolder with possessive anger?

Ignoring the small voice in the back of his mind that warned it was dangerous to linger here in the dark, he reached out to pluck the hat from her head and tossed it aside. In a heartbeat her satin hair tumbled about her shoulders.

"Biddles was right, you know," he said softly, his fingers lingering of their own accord to toy with a silver curl. "You were magnificent."

She grimaced, the emerald eyes still shimmering from her night of adventure.

"Actually, I was terrified," she confessed. "I dropped the first rock upon my toe, and to be honest, the second barely made it over the wall."

"You did what was necessary even though you were terrified. That is the true measure of courage."

She shivered. "It was a near thing, was it not?"

His expression abruptly hardened. The fear he had experienced when he thought they might be exposed was still too fresh to be shrugged aside.

"Too near," he muttered.

She regarded him a moment before she stepped close enough for her soft, feminine scent to weave about him.

"Oh no, Hawksley. Do not even consider it," she warned.

"Consider what?"

"Locking me in this house."

Against his will Hawksley discovered his lips twitching in amusement. It was a wonder that this woman had not yet been burned as a witch.

"Actually, I was considering an offer Santos made to have you tucked away in one of his cottages." He fingers shifted to brush over the lush curve of her lips. His muscles hardened with a swift arousal. Damn. It had been days since he had allowed himself to be near her. And with good reason, he reminded himself sternly. He was not a chivalrous man. He was a rogue, a rake, and a pirate. He took what he wanted. And he wanted this woman with a force that was nearly blinding. "It would be far safer."

Indifferent to the sudden danger shimmering in the air, she reached up to grasp the lapels of his coat. The movement brought her body next to his, and Hawksley bit back a groan of torment.

"You cannot send me away. I will not allow it."

"Not allow?" he rasped.

"You have need of me, Hawksley. You know that."

His hands cupped her face with a flare of compulsive desire. Damn and blast, but he had need of her.

Shrouded in her sweet heat and feeling the brush of her soft curves against him, Hawksley could barely breathe. He wanted this woman. He wanted her enticing innocence, her heat, her ready passion.

More than anything, he wanted to hold her in his arms and not feel alone for the first night in more nights than he cared to remember.

"Yes, I have need of you."

A shudder raced through him and she regarded him with darkened eyes.

"Hawksley?"

"Damn," he cursed his unfamiliar weakness.

"What is it?"

He briefly closed his eyes, battling the fierce urge to pick her up in his arms and carry her off to his chambers.

"'Tis not only Lord Doulton you need fear, kitten," he warned her in a thick voice. "I am not at all certain that you may trust me."

She pulled back to frown at him with obvious disbelief. "That is absurd. I would trust you with my life."

His smile was without humor. "And what of your virtue? Do you trust me with that?"

She grew motionless as she considered his stark words. At first Hawksley feared he might have frightened her with his honesty, and a pain clenched his heart. The last thing he would ever desire was for this woman to lose her faith in him. Astonishingly enough, he realized that her trust was more important to him than her passion.

Just another assurance that this woman had him utterly daft.

"Do you wish me to be honest?" she whispered.

Oh Lord. Even as he struggled to breathe, her eyes began to smolder with a dangerous fire. A fire that seared straight through him.

"Of course."

"I have begun to suspect that virtue is highly over-rated for a female of my age and temperament," she murmured, deliberately pressing herself against his hard body.

Hawksley's heart halted at her stunning confession. A confession that he did not need to be hearing. At least not when they were all alone in the dark with nothing to prevent him from claiming her. Nothing but his own badly battered chivalry.

"Clara . . ."

"You once asked me if I wished to be your mistress, and I have given the matter a great deal of thought."

Actually feeling his control slipping from his grasp, he gazed helplessly into those beautiful emerald eyes.

"You have?"

"Yes."

He groaned, his fingers tightening upon her cheeks. "Bloody hell. I need to—"

Without warning Clara tossed her arms about his neck. "Do you not wish to know what I have concluded?"

Feeling her pressed tightly against his stirring body, Hawksley clenched his teeth in agony. Hell-fire. Surely he had done nothing to deserve such torture? Well, perhaps he had. Still, it did not seem entirely fair considering there were any number of gentlemen who had no doubt done far worse.

And then, without warning, he remembered Biddles' simple words.

"*Then make her your wife . . .*"

At the time Hawksley had been too shocked to even consider the ridiculous suggestion. Not in all his thirty years had he given serious thought to binding his life irrevocably with a woman's.

Why should he?

His brother held the title and responsibilities of producing the necessary heir. And of course, Fredrick also held the family fortune that would ensure that his bride was not forced to live in a shabby house on the edge of the stews.

Hawksley had no need for a bride and nothing to offer even if he did desire one.

Now, however, he could not entirely scrub the tantalizing thought from his mind.

Married. To his angel.

Why not?

She fascinated him in a manner he had never before experienced. Her swift wits, her unique intelligence, her kind heart, and her breathtaking beauty. She certainly would never bore him.

And perhaps most importantly, she had accepted him precisely as he was.

From the beginning, she had seen him at his very worst. And yet in all their time together, she had done nothing to try and mold him into something he could never be.

It was a hell of a lot more than most people who claimed to love him had ever given.

Just for a moment the image of his father's face rose to mind. He grimaced at the thought of informing the proud, pompous nobleman that his unwanted heir was determined to marry a woman with no wealth, no position, and none of the usual social graces.

No doubt he would be horrified.

His grimaced turned to a slow, satisfied smile.

There might not be any means of turning his back upon the responsibilities that had been thrust onto him, but there was no reason he could not thoroughly enjoy his father's utter fury when he discovered Hawksley had wed a woman he would consider thoroughly unworthy to eventually become the Countess of Chadwick.

Aye . . . He gazed down at her sweet, beautiful countenance. His wife, his future countess. Suddenly he felt as if a heavy burden had been lifted from his shoulders.

There would be no more aching battles to contain the desire that gnawed within him. No more nights spent alone in his bed. No more facing life without a partner at his side.

It all seemed astonishingly simple. And right.

With a groan he wrapped his arms about her and buried his head in the scented softness of her hair.

"Clara, you are certain this is what you want?" he muttered.

Her arms tightened about his neck, nearly strangling him in the process.

"Yes, Hawksley, I am certain."

Chapter Twelve

The words had barely tumbled from Clara's lips when she discovered herself scooped up in a pair of strong male arms and carried down the short hall.

With the same swift movements, Hawksley had her in his shadowed chambers and tumbled onto his bed.

Despite her sharp anticipation, she could not help but chuckle as she heard him muttering low curses while he struggled out of his clothing.

"Hawksley?"

"You would not be laughing if you knew how desperately I desire you, Miss Dawson," he growled, the sound of ripping fabric echoing through the darkness before he was abruptly upon the bed beside her and gathering her into his arms. "God, at last."

All amusement faded as Clara felt the naked heat sear through her thin clothing.

Dear heavens, he was hard. Hard . . . everywhere.

A blush touched her cheeks as his erection pressed into her thigh. She had never so much as caught a glimpse of a naked man, let alone had one sprawled half on top of her.

Oddly, however, she experienced no fear as she allowed her hands to tentatively stroke down the curve of his back. The satin heat of his skin made her breath catch in her throat. Who could have known the feel of a man could be so incredible?

"I am not certain what I should do," she murmured.

"Mmm . . ." His breath brushed her temple as he nuzzled her skin. "Just touch me, kitten. I have dreamed of your hands upon me since I first saw you."

Emboldened by the husky need in his voice, she skimmed her hands lower, smiling at the sensation of his rippling muscles that clenched beneath her fingers. He moaned as she reached the lean hips, thrusting his swollen staff against her leg.

"This is about to end before it begins," he muttered, abruptly flipping on top of her and pinning her hands above her head.

Her protest at having her delicious exploration brought to an end was halted as he covered her mouth with a fierce, demanding kiss.

Clara closed her eyes, nearly overwhelmed by the raw hunger she could feel humming through him.

Suddenly the barrier she had always felt in his touch was gone. There was no hesitation as he swept the clothing from her body with experienced ease, no hesitation as his lips brushed down the line of her neck and latched onto the aching tip of her breast. No hesitation as a hair-roughened leg pressed between her thighs to rub at her sensitive cleft.

Clara gasped as she arched upward, assaulted by a flood of unfamiliar sensations.

"Hawksley," she breathed, tugging her hands loose so that her fingers could tangle in his hair.

He suddenly stilled, a groan wrenched from his throat.

"Forgive me, Clara," he muttered, his lips brushing the curve of her breast. "I do not mean to frighten you."

"I am not frightened," she denied, shivering as his hot breath stroked over her skin. And she was not. The feel of his warm body pressed to her own was sending a wave of tingling pleasure through her blood, the stroke of his lips making her forget the importance of breathing. Still, for a woman accustomed to a strictly predictable life, she had to admit that it was difficult to plunge into the unknown without a few qualms. "I suppose I might be a bit . . . nervous."

He pulled back to regard her with a searching gaze. "I wish you to be absolutely sure, kitten. There must be no regrets."

Her heart faltered at his tender expression. Oh my, for the moment he was hers. All hers.

"I am sure," she whispered, her fingers softly stroking the aquiline planes of his countenance. "'Tis only that I would feel more at ease if I knew what was to occur."

He remained silent a long moment, as if searching to assure himself that she did indeed wish to be in his arms, and then a slow smile curved his lips.

"Very well, my logical Miss Dawson, we shall do this your way," he murmured. "You will know precisely what is about to occur."

"Hawksley . . ."

"Shh." He pressed his mouth lightly to hers.

"First, kitten, I am going to taste that delectable skin of yours. I am going to kiss and lick and nibble you from the top of your head to the tip of your toes. And then I shall make my way back to your soft lips."

Without giving her time to consider his husky words, his mouth was already in motion. He stroked over her cheek, nipping gently at the line of her jaw and then down the curve of her neck. He paused at the base of her neck to kiss the frantic pulse that beat there, his tongue brushing over the spot before he was trailing ever lower.

Clara sucked in a hissing breath, her eyes squeezing shut.

Sweet saints.

She had thought that there could be nothing beyond the pleasure Hawksley had given to her in the carriage. To be honest, she was not certain a woman could survive anything more pleasurable.

Now she realized that there was something incredibly sensuous in having a handsome pirate devouring her with such methodical care.

Dropping soft kisses upon the curve of her breasts, he gave each aching nipple a lick of his tongue before moving down to her stomach. Clara arched upward, unable to hold still as a sharp burst of excitement clutched deep within her.

"So sweet . . ." Hawksley murmured as he tasted the curve of her hip and then down the tense muscles of her thigh. "So soft."

"Oh my." Her hands clutched at the blanket beneath her. "This is . . ."

"Yes, kitten?" he demanded, slipping off the bed as he ran his tongue down the inside of her leg.

"This is wondrous."

His chuckle tickled over the arch of her foot. "You are wondrous. As delicate as the rarest flower."

She swallowed a moan as he shifted to torment her other foot, lazily exploring her toes and then her ankle before moving on to her knee. She would not survive, she thought as she clenched her teeth.

Already she could feel that damp heat between her legs. Could feel the glorious pressure beginning to build. And those demonic lips were only adding to the fierce ache.

Using his teeth he nipped at the inside of her thigh, making her hips lift off the mattress as the sharp pleasure speared through her.

"Hawksley, I am uncertain I can bear much more," she rasped.

"Kitten, I have only begun," he warned her, his hands grasping her legs and tugging them apart.

Feeling oddly vulnerable as he lay between her thighs, she lifted herself onto her elbows and gazed at his shadowed countenance.

"What are you doing?"

"I am going to taste you," he murmured, holding her gaze as one slender finger slipped into her slick heat. "I am going to taste you here."

"Hawksley, no . . ." she began to protest, only to have her words stolen as he shifted upward and she felt his tongue part her tender flesh to discover the tiny nub of pleasure. "Oh, yes."

She flopped back onto the bed, her head tilted back as she bowed beneath the intense sensations.

His tongue was relentless as it teased and stroked her need to the very edge of explosion. At the same time his finger was pushing steadily into her, smoothing in and out with a rhythm her hips instinctively matched.

The bliss was so near. The shattering pleasure beaconing with desperate force.

Her teeth gritted as she gave a strangled groan. "Please, Hawksley, I need you," she pleaded.

With a last soft kiss upon her thigh he slowly surged back over her, his eyes stark with a need that sent a shiver through her body.

"Clara, I am going to enter you," he prepared her in rough tones. "I shall try to take care, but I cannot be certain it will not hurt you."

She framed his face with her hands. "I am ready."

His eyes slid shut as his brow furrowed with concentration, clearly determined to hold himself in check. Settling more firmly between her spread legs, he nudged the tip of his shaft into her.

Clara instinctively tensed as he slid deeper, stretching her with his steady thrust.

Above her Hawksley pressed his forehead to hers. "I am no expert, kitten, but I believe this will go easier for you if you try to relax."

Her fingers dug into his shoulders. There was no pain, but she could not deny a measure of discomfort.

"You must recall, Hawksley, I am a rather small person," she said. "You do not seem to fit properly."

She felt his shoulders shake beneath her fingers. "Perhaps not at the moment; still, I promise this will work just fine."

Shifting beneath him, Clara opened her mouth to suggest he make an attempt at reducing his size when he gave a low groan and with one swift motion lodged himself deep within her.

Clara gasped at the brief stab of pain. Thankfully

it was short lived, and as it receded all that was left was the sensation of him filling her. Utterly and completely.

"Forgive me, Clara," he whispered against her temple.

"It is all right," she murmured, her fingers unclenching from his shoulders to run a soft path down the curve of his spine. "The pain is gone."

"Then let us see if we can make this a night to remember," he murmured, claiming her lips in a demanding kiss.

Lost in the pleasure of his kiss, Clara was barely aware of the shallow thrust of his hips, not until she discovered herself moving in harmony with his rhythm as the sweet pressure began to build again.

Wrapping her legs about him, she tangled her fingers in his hair. With every stroke his chest brushed over her sensitive nipples, increasing her pleasure until she could barely breathe.

Oh yes, this was what she had longed for, she acknowledged as she groaned in approval. This was what she had secretly fantasized during the long hours of the night.

Someone to desire her. To hold her. To keep the aching loneliness at bay.

She heard him growl as his thrusts became more insistent, his pace quickening.

"Dear God . . . Clara . . . I cannot . . ."

She unwittingly pulled at his hair, her back arching as she hovered on the edge of bliss.

"Please do not halt," she pleaded.

His hands shifted beneath her thighs, spreading her wide as he pumped himself ever deeper within. Clara became rigid as a cry was wrenched from her throat.

Then that glorious delight exploded through her, making her shake uncontrollably as she tumbled over the edge.

"Hawksley," she breathed, wrapping her arms about him as he gave a shout and the feel of his warm seed poured into her.

Slowly her shaking subsided as Hawksley rolled to his side, pulling her firmly into his arms. Her hand rested on his chest, feeling the thunderous beat of his heart as he kissed the top of her curls.

"I did promise, kitten, that it would work just fine," he murmured.

She snuggled closer. The feel of his arms about her was something she wished to brand into her memories. It would be all she had to keep her warm during the long nights to come.

"So you did."

"And you are . . . pleased?"

She was surprised by the hesitancy in his voice. As if the proud pirate was actually worried she might possess regrets.

With a smile she tilted back her head to meet his searching gaze.

"Are you searching for compliments, sir?" she demanded.

A wicked glint entered the indigo eyes. "If you wish to offer compliments, I am quite willing to accept them."

Clara wrinkled her nose in regret. "I fear compliments are yet another social skill I have never managed to master. I always manage to make a muck of it."

"Ah. Then let me assist you, my angel." His hands slipped down to intimately cup her bottom in his hands. "You should tell me that you are captivated by my kisses and enthralled by my touch. You should tell me that you will never forget this night together. And course, you must assure me that I am the very best lover you have ever had."

Her heart flopped over in her chest. Not so much at the tantalizing exploration of his hands, although that was delightful. But more at the casual teasing in his tone.

Suddenly she understood why women battled so desperately to gain the attention of a gentleman.

With Hawksley there was none of the awkward uncertainty she always endured. None of the fear that she was about to make a fool of herself. None of the sickening realization that her companion was desperately seeking some polite means of fleeing her company.

Instead there was a sense of absolute comfort. Of belonging.

And that meant more to her than anything else he could possibly offer.

Her fingers reached up to trace the line of his sculpted lips.

"Very fine compliments, Hawksley, but I do feel duty bound to point out that I can hardly claim you as the best lover since you are my first lover."

Abruptly Clara discovered herself rolled onto her back, Hawksley poised above her as his eyes darkened to a blue mist.

"No, Clara, not your first lover," he corrected, his voice oddly tight as his head lowered with sensuous intent. "Your *only* lover."

* * *

For the first time since his brother's murder, Hawksley was not plagued with ruthless nightmares that marred his nights. Nor did he awaken at the crack of dawn battling the restless need to be upon the hunt.

Perhaps not so surprising, he drowsily acknowledged as he breathed deeply of the feminine scent still clinging to his skin. He had devoted hours to teaching his bride-to-be the delights of desire. Wondrous hours that had revealed Clara's passionate nature and ready wish to please and be pleased.

Even after she had fallen asleep, he had remained awake to watch her.

She appeared so delicate, so fragile. And yet, he was discovering that she possessed more strength and courage than any woman he had ever encountered.

No, not any *woman*, he had corrected himself. Any person he had ever encountered.

He had chosen well.

Near dawn he had gathered her into his arms and had at last fallen into a deep, peaceful sleep.

Now an unwitting smile curved his lips as he reached out to touch the woman who had banished the demons of the night.

"Clara . . ."

His smile faded and his eyes opened as he realized he was alone in the bed. Abruptly sitting up, he glanced about his chamber, belatedly noting the shaft of late-morning sunlight peeking between the curtains.

Damn.

Tossing aside the covers, Hawksley plunged himself into the bath that had long since cooled to a tepid temperature and shaved his heavy whiskers. With the same swift efficiency he pulled on his attire and tugged his damp hair into a queue at his neck.

Why the devil had she not awakened him?

Bloody hell, he had taken her innocence. Surely she must realize they needed to discuss what had occurred last night? To come to an understanding of their future together?

In the process of tying a simple knot in his cravat, Hawksley abruptly grimaced.

What the devil was he thinking?

He knew better by now than to expect the expected from Miss Clara Dawson.

While any other woman might be clamoring for promises of a wedding, or at the very least the assurance that he would take care of her, Clara was no doubt off baking a cake or polishing the silver.

It would never occur to her that he might possess a responsibility for her now.

She had been too long on her own. Too long forced to fend for herself. And too long surrounded by buffoons who had no appreciation for her rare qualities.

Well, no longer.

From this day forward she would have someone to take care of her. Someone who would ensure that she need never be alone again.

Feeling an unfamiliar sense of anticipation, Hawksley let himself out of his chambers and went in search of his bride. It was time she realized that her future was very much settled.

He at last discovered her in his small library, seated at his desk. She was occupied with a paper upon the blotter, and for a moment he simply allowed himself to drink in the sight of her.

With the sunlight slanting through the window, her hair shimmered with a silver halo and the purity of her profile was thrown into relief.

His angel, indeed.

All his.

Feeling a ridiculous urge to strut about like a puffed-up rooster, Hawksley crossed the room to stand directly behind her chair. He brushed a kiss over her bare nape before leaning toward her ear.

"Good morning, kitten."

With a startled squeak Clara was on her feet and whirling about. At the sight of him her expression abruptly softened.

"Oh, Hawksley, you are awake."

"So it would seem," he murmured, pushing the chair out of his way as he stepped toward her.

"I am so glad. I have been working upon . . . oh." Her eyes widened as his arms lashed about her and hoisted her against his chest. "Good heavens."

Hawksley smiled with wicked enjoyment as her eyes darkened with pleasure. With ready case he recalled the memory of her lying beneath him as she cried out her pleasure. Slowly he allowed his hands to trace down the slender curve of her spine, lingering upon the softness of her hips before skimming their way back up. He breathed deeply of her clean scent. She smelled of soap and vanilla and sweet feminine heat. It intoxicated him in a manner he had never before experienced.

Intoxicated and bewildered him, he had to acknowledge.

Lust he understood. It was as familiar as hunger and thirst and pain.

And the reason his manhood was rapidly hardening with determined intent. But he did not understand the tenderness that ached deep in his heart whenever she was near.

There was no urge to roughly conquer and brand this woman as his own as he lowered his head. Instead, with exquisite care he tasted of her lips, savoring her softness as if she were a rare nectar. She shivered even as her arms lifted to wrap about his neck.

He moved to drop light kisses over her cheeks, her temples, and her wide brow. He memorized every plane, every angle of her countenance from the fullness of her mouth to the sweep of her lashes before burying his face in the curve of her neck.

"This is the proper way to greet your lover in the morning," he murmured against her skin.

He could feel her heart racing. "It is?"

"Most certainly."

"What of the servants?"

He pulled back to regard her with a lift of his brow. "If you imagine I am about to kiss Dillon or his sister like this, you have lost your wits."

Her eyes sparkled with amusement and a passion that warmed him to his very heart.

"I meant what if they happen upon us?"

"Then I shall send them away. Or better yet, we could return to my chambers where we will be certain of privacy." Hawksley stole a lingering kiss. "Why did you leave me?"

"Oh." Pressing her hands to his chest, she leaned back to regard him with a sudden expression of excitement. "When I wakened I recalled Mr. Chesterfield's letter."

Hawksley froze in disbelief. After spending the most incredible night of his life in the arms of this woman, the last thing he desired to hear was the name of another gentleman upon her lips.

"You awoke in my bed thinking of another man?" he demanded in dangerous tones.

Gloriously indifferent to the prickles of danger in the air, she offered a charming smile.

"I wished to discover what he had written."

His teeth clenched. By the fires of hell. There was something gnawing in the pit of his stomach. Something that he did not care for the least bit.

"It seems that I am not giving you the proper attention if you are able to consider anything but me when you are in my arms," he growled.

At last sensing his stiff annoyance, Clara regarded him with a faint frown.

"Hawksley, is something the matter?"

"Beyond your fascination with that damnable Mr. Chesterfield?"

Her eyes widened. "Good Lord, are you . . . jealous?"

"Yes, I damn well am."

She appeared stunned by his blunt confession. He did not know why, he grumpily told himself. He had already physically threatened his two best friends for simply kissing her hand.

"But that is absurd. You know very well I have never even met Mr. Chesterfield."

He gave a restless shrug. "What does that have to say to anything? You were one to claim to have some mystical, intellectual connection with the man. You were even willing to endure being physically ill so that you could rush to London and be at his side."

"I was naturally concerned."

"Now you leave my bed to come and moon over his letter."

She gave a slow shake of her head as her hand lifted to gently touch his tight jaw.

"Hawksley, I wanted to assist you in your search for your brother's murderer. I thought the letter might hold a clue."

"And Mr. Chesterfield?"

"I am worried for him and certainly hope that he is well," she confessed, her gaze holding his. "But you were right when you said I did not know him as a woman should know a man."

The tightness in his chest began to ease. "As you know me?"

"Yes."

With a low moan he kissed her with stark relief. The sooner this woman belonged to him, the better.

"Hawksley?"

Busily nuzzling the curve of her neck, Hawksley silently cursed the prim neckline of the dowdy gray gown. Once they were wed he would ensure that she possessed the sort of elegant wardrobe suitable for a lady of Quality, he assured himself. The sort of gowns that every woman desired.

"Mmm?"

"Do you not wish to know what I have discovered?"

Battling the urge to sweep her in his arms and haul her back upstairs, Hawksley reluctantly dropped his arms and stepped back. The next occasion he had her in his bed, it would be as his fiancée.

"First I believe we should discuss something of rather more importance."

She did not bother to hide her surprise. "What could be more important than your brother?"

A fortnight ago nothing would have been more important than Fredrick and discovering his murderer. Now, however, Hawksley realized that the beautiful woman had reminded him that he possessed a life of his own. And a future that suddenly seemed worth looking forward to.

"You."

"Me?"

"More precisely . . . us."

"I do not understand," she began, and then strangely her face seemed to pale and something that might have been panic flared through her eyes. "Oh no. No, Hawksley. Do not even think it."

"I beg your pardon?"

She poked him in the chest with her finger. "You are not going to do something wretchedly noble such as ask me to marry you because of last night. I will not allow it."

Well.

Hawksley swallowed a rueful laugh.

He had not precisely expected her to flutter or swoon at the thought of becoming his wife. That would be far too predictable. But he certainly had not anticipated the irritation that smoldered about her slender form.

Not about to be put off, he gave a lift of his brows. "Fortunately, I do not take orders from you, Miss Dawson. At least not yet," he said in firm tones. "As for asking you to marry me . . . well, there is no question that we will wed. I would never have taken your innocence if that was not what I intended."

If anything her annoyance only deepened. "You did not take my innocence, Hawksley, I gave it to you. And it was not with the notion of manipulating you into marriage."

His expression softened. "I am well aware of that, Clara. You are incapable of such treachery."

Her hands landed on her hips, pulling the gray material tantalizingly over the swell of her breasts. Breasts that had fit perfectly in his hands and tasted of . . .

"Then why?"

His mouth became dry. No, Hawksley, he sternly chastised himself. Not now. Later. Definitely later.

"Why what?" he muttered.

"Why do you wish to marry me?"

His lips twisted; she had only to glance down to know at least one reason that he desired to haul her to the nearest vicar.

"Well, there is the rather obvious fact that I desire you to the point of madness."

A delicate color touched her cheeks. "Marriage is more than desire."

"You also fascinate me." He stepped forward to tuck a curl behind her ear, allowing his fingers to trail along the line of her jaw. "I have never before met a woman like you."

"That I can well believe," she breathed.

He gazed deep into her eyes. "And you have given me a reason to live again."

Her breath caught as she gazed helplessly into his countenance. At last he had touched her vulnerability. She might not wed to ease her own lonely existence or to ensure the security of her future, but she could not ignore her instinctive yearning to be needed by another.

"Hawksley . . ." she husked, her hand touching his cheek before she was sucking in a deep breath and stepping backward. "No."

He blinked at her abrupt withdrawal. "What?"

"It is not possible."

"What is not possible?"

"I cannot be your wife."

Hawksley studied her set expression. What the devil was going through that peculiar brain now?

"Why? I will admit that it does not appear that I have much to offer a bride, but I assure you that you will not want for anything."

She gave a sudden snort. "Good heavens, it is not that. As if I would care for such a thing. I have no desire for wealth or position. Indeed, I should not accept them if they were offered."

A faint twinge of unease touched his heart at her disdainful tone. Surely she would not be disappointed when she discovered that her soon-to-be husband was not the penniless gambler she believed but rather a viscount of enormous wealth?

No. It was not possible, he hastily reassured himself. No matter how eccentric, there was no woman who would prefer to beg and scrape for existence when she could have luxury offered on a silver platter.

"Then what is it, Clara?" he demanded, his voice revealing a hint of impatience. "Do you fear I will not make a suitable husband? I may not possess the charm of Santos or the intellect of Mr. Chesterfield, but—"

"Hawksley, I cannot be your bride simply because

I could not bear to have you loathe me," she abruptly announced.

Silence descended as he regarded her in disbelief.

Was she mad? Had her mother managed to drop her upon her head when she was just a babe? Or perhaps the strain of the past few days had made her plunge into insanity.

There had to be some reason she could believe a gentleman who had not only made desperate love to her for hours, but had turned his household upside down to please her, could ever possibly loathe her.

With a determined motion he reached out to take her hands in a firm grasp. He was startled to discover they were actually shaking.

"That is the most ridiculous thing I have ever heard," he said, holding her gaze as he steadily pulled her toward him. "Why would you even think such a thing?"

She bit her bottom lip at his soft question. "Because I always manage to annoy and irritate those about me. I do not mean to do so. Indeed, I rarely even realize that I am doing so until they are angry."

He gave a slow shake of his head, silently cursing those who had so wounded this poor woman.

"Clara, there are none of us who do not annoy and irritate others upon occasion."

Her lashes lowered to hide the beauty of her eyes. "Not as I do, Hawksley. You claim to find me fascinating, but soon enough my eccentricities will have you wishing me in Hades. It is inevitable, and I do not intend to remain here long enough for that to occur."

His lips thinned. "For God's sake, my father

found me so annoying he demanded I leave his home. Not even you can make that claim, kitten. Obviously we are perfectly suited."

He heard her catch her breath at his brutal confession, her expression abruptly softening. "Oh, Hawksley."

Always swift to take advantage of the slightest weakness in his opponent, Hawksley had her in his arms and pressed to the rapid beat of his heart.

"Marry me, Clara. Be my wife."

He watched the play of emotion over her sweet countenance. Longing, uncertainty . . . and fear.

"I think it would be best if we discuss this after we have discovered the truth of your brother's murder," she at last muttered.

Hawksley squashed his fierce surge of impatience. He wanted her agreement to his proposal. Hell, he wanted to haul her to the nearest church and be done with the business.

Unfortunately, he knew enough of Clara to realize that she could not be coerced or bullied. Until she accepted that she was all he desired in a bride, she would balk.

Obviously, it was his duty to prove to her that they were meant to be together.

A notion that, now he considered it, held a certain amount of appeal, he accepted with a slow smile. There were many means of convincing a passionate young lady just how desperately he was in need of her.

Cupping her chin in his hand, he tugged her face upward to meet his smoldering gaze. "You will not leave? You promise to stay here with me?"

There was a tense pause before she gave a slow nod of her head. "I promise."

Hawksley released the breath that he did not even realize he was holding. She would stay. She would never break such a promise.

And in the end she would be his wife.

With an effort he lowered his arms and stepped back.

"Very well, tell me what it is you have discovered."

Chapter Thirteen

Clara moved to the desk to retrieve the letter she had been studying for the past three hours. Outwardly she managed to appear her usual efficient self, while silently she recited the multiplication table, forward and then backward, in an effort to calm her rattled nerves.

Wife.

Hawksley's wife.

Cripes. What the devil was he thinking? She had not yet accustomed herself to the earth-shattering notion that she was his mistress. And now he flummoxed her with a marriage proposal.

A warm, aching pleasure flared through her before she was sternly squashing the sensation.

No.

Hawksley was simply not thinking clearly. He saw her as a lonely spinster with no family and no one to care for her. And there was the added guilt of having taken her innocence.

It was his nature to rescue her.

She would never allow him to make such a sacrifice. Not when it would in the end make him miserable.

All too soon he would come to his senses. And then he would thank her for having refused his proposal.

In the meantime, it was vital that she hide her own foolish emotions. Emotions that she refused to contemplate. Not when they were perilously close to love.

Swallowing back the most ridiculous urge to cry, Clara firmly squared her shoulders and returned to Hawksley's side. She was relieved to discover her hands were steady as she held up the sheets of paper.

"As you see, I have made the calculations," she said, pointing toward the tidy line of formulas and sums.

Hawksley grimaced. "Bloody hell, it makes my brain ache to even look upon them."

She wrinkled her nose at his obvious horror. It was a common enough reaction. There were few who shared her love for complicated equations.

"Actually they are quite simple. You see, the formula for the first is—"

"Please, I beg of you, kitten, no mathematics or calculations before breakfast. Or for that matter, before luncheon or dinner," he pleaded.

"Very well," she conceded with a low chuckle. Shuffling the papers, she revealed the poem she had discovered hidden within the numbers. "This is the translation:

> *'A man must take risk and even harm*
> *When seeking a bride of wit and charm,*

*If you will have me, my precious love,
I shall bring you riches from heaven above.'"*

Hawksley made a strangled sound deep in his throat. "Hellfire, what drivel. You cannot mean to tell me you had your head turned by such rubbish?"

A blush touched Clara's cheeks. She had to admit she was rather shocked by the strange poem. Mr. Chesterfield had on occasion complimented her intelligence or offered suggestions that they someday meet.

This, however, was something quite different.

"He never before sent such a thing," she confessed. "I cannot imagine what he was thinking."

His expression hardened as he glared at the paper. "I can tell you precisely what he was thinking. I should know, after all. He was asking you to marry him."

Her blush deepened. "Ridiculous."

The blue gaze lifted to stab her with a sardonic glitter. "I will allow you to be the expert when it comes to equations. I, however, must insist on being the expert when it comes to a man who is desperate to take a wife," he retorted dryly. "You are clearly the *bride of wit and charm.*"

She grimly ignored the pain that stabbed through her heart. Not long ago she might have dared to hope that Mr. Chesterfield would make her a suitable husband. Now she very much feared she would never be satisfied with less than a wicked pirate.

"Even if that is true, what of the rest of the poem? It makes no sense."

He gave a lift of his shoulder. "Does any poetry?"

"Mr. Chesterfield was a very . . . literal sort of

gentleman," she pointed out, giving a shake of her head as her gaze skimmed over the strange words. "'A man must take risk and harm.' It must have some meaning."

She sensed his tension, as if he longed to snatch the papers from her and toss them into the nearest fire. Then, with an obvious effort, he plucked the poem from her fingers and forced himself to study the peculiar lines.

"Perhaps it does," he grudgingly conceded, his brow furrowing in concentration. Clara remained silent, covertly allowing her gaze to wander over the chiseled profile. A faint shiver raced through her as she recalled the feel of his slender fingers smoothing over her skin, and the tender demand of his lips . . . "Damn."

Jerked out of her pleasant daydreams, Clara met the startled blue gaze.

"Hawksley?"

"By God, I think you were right when you suggested that my brother went to Mr. Chesterfield with his vowels. I also think that Mr. Chesterfield must have recognized the scraps of paper as something important."

Unaccountably pleased, but still confused, she glanced toward the paper clenched in his fingers. "Why do you say that?"

"'Risk and harm,'" he quoted the poem. "Mr. Chesterfield was clearly a gentleman of strained means. One who suddenly possessed a desire to wed the woman who had caught his fancy. No doubt he would be eager to grasp at any opportunity to improve his dubious resources."

She stiffened. Really, for such an intelligent,

handsome, sophisticated gentleman, he could be remarkably foolish, not to mention stubborn.

"You cannot think that Mr. Chesterfield would harm your brother?"

"No, but I do believe that he might attempt to blackmail Lord Doulton," he said slowly. "What easier means of acquiring a tidy fortune?"

Clara opened her mouth to argue. Mr. Chesterfield would never do anything so nefarious. He was a scholar and a gentleman, was he not? Then she abruptly paused.

She had already acknowledged that she knew precious little of Mr. Chesterfield. Certainly she could not attest to his character from a handful of letters.

And logic did indeed suggest that he had involved himself in something beyond his control.

"Goodness," she breathed.

He regarded her with a somber expression. "It would explain how Lord Doulton learned of Fredrick's suspicions."

"And it might very well account for Mr. Chesterfield's disappearance."

"Yes. Either he has been wise enough to hide his presence until receiving the funds he demanded, or else . . ."

"Lord Doulton has already ended his threat," she completed his thought in tight tones.

"Rather costly riches from heaven."

She blinked at his words. "What did you say?"

He shrugged. "I was merely quoting from the poem."

"Heaven above," she muttered, that niggling she had experienced the night before returning with a vengeance.

"Hardly original; still, he no doubt considered the thought of sudden wealth as a gift from God."

"There is something . . ." Barely aware of moving, Clara began to pace about the room, absently straightening the books upon the shelves and arranging the handful of snuffboxes into a precise line.

Hawksley gently cleared his throat. "Clara?"

"There is a pattern." She continued her pacing, her skirts twitching in agitation. "One strand leading to another."

"Are we discussing Mr. Chesterfield or weaving?" he demanded in wry amusement.

"Heaven."

"Heaven?"

Consumed with her broodings, Clara circled the room, not even noting when her very large companion was forced to leap out of the way or be run over.

"More precisely, religion. The papal petition, Mr. Chesterfield, the poem, the paintings . . ." She caught her breath as she at last realized the source of that niggling. "Of course. The paintings."

Abruptly stepping before her, Hawksley grasped her shoulders in a firm grip, his expression bemused.

"Please hold still, kitten. You are making me dizzy. What is this about the paintings?"

"Last eve when I saw the paintings, I sensed there was something I should recall about them, but I could not put my finger upon it."

"And now?"

She gave a disgusted shake of her head. "And

now I wonder how I could be so stupid. My father would have been very disappointed in me."

His gaze narrowed as his fingers tightened upon her shoulders. "No, kitten, that I refuse to believe. Your father could never have been anything but extraordinarily proud of you."

A warmth flared through her as her lips curved in a small smile. Gads, but he always seemed to know exactly what to say.

"Thank you."

"Now, what is it about the paintings? You said they were priceless?"

"Priceless, and many would claim, the property of God."

"What?"

"The Vatican."

Feeling the tender bewilderment that was becoming all too familiar when in the presence of Clara, Hawksley watched as she resumed her pacing.

He wanted to demand that she explain her cryptic comments. Or at least give him some indication of what the devil was going through her mind. But he was becoming wise enough not to intrude when she was in the midst of her deep thoughts.

He might as well bang his head against the nearest wall.

A rather ironic situation for a man who had always taken for granted his irresistible appeal to women.

There was a slight rustle at his side and he jerked about to discover that Biddles had slipped silently into the room and was currently watching Clara with a faint smile.

"Really, Hawk, if the poor lady is in need of a morning stroll, the least you could do is take her to the park," the little rat drawled, smoothing his hand over the buttercup coat that was jarringly paired with a scarlet waistcoat.

Hawksley smiled as he leaned his shoulders against the paneled wall.

"And risk having her trample the helpless natives?" He gave a shake of his head. "Take my advice, old friend, protect your toes and any vital organ when she nears. She can be an unstoppable force when she is in the throes of pondering."

"And what, may I inquire, is she pondering?"

Hawksley shrugged. "Something of paintings and the Vatican."

Much to his surprise, his companion gave a choked cough of shock.

"How did she . . . ? Egads."

Hawksley narrowed his gaze. Dammit all, enough was enough. Was he the only one in England who had not yet managed to deduce what the hell was going on?

"What is it?"

"I made a few discreet inquiries this morning concerning the paintings we discovered."

Hawksley froze. The last thing he desired was Lord Doulton suspecting that Biddles was involved in the hunt for his brother's murderer.

"How discreet?"

Biddles held up a hand. "Do not fret, I merely mentioned in passing that a wealthy patron of Hellion's had a desire to collect some of the more unattainable masterpieces, especially Titian's *Pope*

Alexander. A collector who did not particularly care to await the usual auctions."

"And?"

Biddles smiled grimly. "And I was assured by one and all that my friend was wasting his time. The painting is in the hands of God."

Hawksley froze, his gaze turning toward the silver-haired angel who had just realized they were no longer alone.

"The Vatican," he muttered.

"Precisely."

Reaching their side, Clara gave an awkward curtsy. "Lord Bidwell."

"Please, Biddles." The slender man gave a delicate shiver. "Gads, Lord Bidwell reminds me that I am supposed to be a proper gentleman."

"Biddles," Clara readily agreed, obviously relieved to dispense with formality. "Did you say something of the Vatican?"

"Yes. I discovered that the paintings we took from the safe belong to the pope."

Clara grimaced as she heaved a sigh. "I should have recalled it last evening."

Biddles tilted back his head to laugh at her self-disgust. "Being in the midst of a burglary is not always the best occasion for coherent thought, my dear."

"Still . . ."

"You have done astonishingly well, Miss Dawson," Biddles assured her. "And now the question is how did Lord Doulton end up with the paintings?"

"Surely he could not have stolen them from the Vatican?" Clara demanded. "The place is a fortress."

Hawksley sucked in a sharp breath as realization hit. "He did not."

They both turned to stare at him in puzzlement.

"What?" Clara demanded.

"Napoleon stole them from the Vatican," he said softly.

"Of course." Biddles slapped his forehead, although Clara continued to frown in puzzlement.

"Napoleon?"

"It is well known that he hauled off wagon loads of priceless objects to take to Paris," he explained. "These paintings could easily be a part of his booty."

"But I thought the treasures were returned?"

Hawksley gave a slow shake of his head. Although he possessed little interest in moldy paintings and ancient frescos, he had heard Fredrick condemn their theft often enough. In great detail and tedious length.

"A portion only. There are countless objects still missing."

Clara accepted his assurance with a nod of her head. "That still does not explain how Lord Doulton managed to acquire them."

"No, but it gives us a place to begin searching," Biddles murmured, a sudden smile curving his lips. "I believe I shall call upon a few acquaintances in the War Office. There are always one or two in my debt."

Hawksley flicked a brow upward. Having known several gentlemen in the War Office, he was well aware that they would as soon have their privates chopped off as to place themselves at the mercy of Biddles.

"Gads, they must have been desperate indeed to have allowed themselves to be in your debt."

The pointed nose twitched. "Just one of the many pleasures of owning a gambling den."

Hawksley gave a low chuckle. "You are a dangerous little man, Biddles."

"I do try. Until later, my friends." With a flamboyant bow toward Clara, the nobleman turned on his heel and disappeared through the door.

Hawksley sensed when Clara moved to stand close to him. It was in the manner his skin suddenly prickled and his heart picked up speed. Just for a moment he closed his eyes and allowed her presence to soak into him. There was something quite satisfying in simply having her near, he discovered with a jolt of surprise. As if she completed him.

With a shake of his head at his odd fancy, he turned his gaze to discover her regarding him with a quizzical expression.

"Do you believe Biddles will discover anything of worth?"

He smiled wryly. "Trust me, if there is anything to be discovered, Biddles will soon have it ferreted out. No one can keep a secret when he is about."

There was a brief pause as she searched his countenance with a curious gaze.

"He seems a rather unique choice of companions," she at last admitted.

A wicked smile curved his lips as he reached out to tug a silver curl. "Surely by now you should know I prefer the unique and the unusual?"

Her eyes darkened, as if touched by his low words, but before Hawksley could take proper advantage of her momentary weakness, she was firmly stepping back.

"We must decide what we shall do next. Perhaps

we could find someone to take a look at your brother's vowels and—"

"Later," Hawksley firmly interrupted, his glance shifting toward the window. For the first time in a long time he wished to simply enjoy the day. With this woman. "For the moment there is something I desire you to see."

"What is it?"

"I shall show you." Hawksley held out his hand. "Will you join me?"

She hesitated just a moment, as if debating the wisdom of giving in to his request. And then with a rather odd smile she placed her fingers into his hand.

"Yes, Hawksley, I will join you."

With undeniable curiosity Clara allowed herself to be led into the kitchen, where Hawksley gathered a large basket of apples and oranges. Then with a mischievous grin he regained command of her hand and led her up the narrow staircase.

A part of her longed to protest at his secretive manner. She was a woman who disliked the unexpected. Indeed, she preferred a detailed schedule for every moment of her day. Structure, she had discovered, ensured that her life would remain steady and predictable without the tedious problems that seemed to plague those more impulsive souls.

"An ounce of prevention was worth a pound of cure" were words she took deeply to heart.

Still, she could not deny a sense of pleasure in watching Hawksley as he urged her to follow him.

He was far different from the grim pirate who had stolen her from her carriage. There was a new ease about him and a wicked playfulness that she would never have expected.

Against her will, a faint twinge of hope touched her heart. Was she responsible for the change in him? Was it possible that she truly had the ability to offer him happiness?

Reaching the last narrow flight of stairs that led to the attics, Clara sternly attempted to rein in her fanciful thoughts. She was a pragmatic woman. Wishing for something did not make it so.

Of course, a small voice whispered in the back of her mind, she was not utterly infallible. Perhaps she should not be so hasty to dismiss his claim that he needed her in his life.

She might not be the most beautiful, or charming, or wealthy woman in England. But there was surely no other who would be more devoted to ensuring his utter contentment.

"Here we are."

Rather thankful to have her tangled broodings interrupted, Clara firmly turned her attention to the gentleman who was standing beside the open door to the attic.

"Really, you are being most mysterious, Hawksley," she informed him with a faint smile. "Whatever are you about?"

"If you will remain patient a few more moments, you will see for yourself."

Allowing herself to be pulled over the threshold, Clara came to an instinctive halt, her hands reaching to pull up her skirts least they touch the dusty floor.

"Good heavens, what a mess," she muttered, glancing about the tumble of trunks and boxes that were stacked about the cramped space.

Hawksley chuckled softly as he slung an arm about her shoulders. "Not now, kitten. Later you may return to clean and scrub and arrange to your heart's content. This way."

Nearly itching with the need to charge off to gather a pail of soapy water and a rag, Clara instead forced herself to keep pace with the gentleman at her side. He had promised she could return later, she reassured herself. And it was not as if the disorder would disappear before she could get her hands upon it.

Instead she regarded what seemed to be a narrow door across the way.

"What an odd place for a door."

"The gentleman who built the house was an old sailor," Hawksley explained as he steered her to the door and pulled it open. "When he was at home he wished to keep a careful watch upon his ship. You are not afraid of heights, are you?"

She smiled wryly. "Surprisingly, no."

"Good." He stepped onto a small, square balcony with a wrought-iron railing before tugging her out to join him. "What do you think?"

Clara's lips parted in pleased surprise as she glanced over the bustling docks and the Thames that glittered in the distance. From such a height the unpleasant smells and raucous noise of the waterfront were undetectable, allowing Clara to thoroughly enjoy watching as the ships were loaded and unloaded with lively chaos.

"It is a beautiful view," she murmured, her gaze

shifting to the shallow boats and barges that drifted down the river.

"Quite beautiful," he agreed, his voice oddly husky.

Turning her head, she caught him regarding her with a smoldering gaze. A dangerous excitement slithered down her spine. Dear heavens. He was so absurdly handsome with his raven hair ruffled by the breeze and his perfect features silhouetted by the late-morning sunlight. And then there was that hard, muscular body. A body she knew more than lived up to the promise offered by the tailored black coat and breeches.

He was quite simply delectable.

Who could blame her for the sharp desire to tackle him to the ground and have her way with him?

Giving a choked cough at her outrageous imaginings, Clara hastily attempted to distract herself.

"I still do not understand why you insisted we bring a basket of apples and oranges to enjoy the view."

With a shake of his head, as if he had been as lost in his own thoughts, he leaned against the iron railing and pointed toward a dirt yard just beyond the hedge.

"Look there."

Much to Clara's amusement, she noted a dozen young urchins who were racing about the hard dirt, all of them scrambling to kick at a leather ball.

"What are they playing?" she demanded, her lips curving as they all suddenly piled upon one another with a loud whoop.

"Actually, I have come to the conclusion that it is a game they have invented all on their own. It seems to involve a great deal of rolling about in the dirt, shouting, and scraped knees."

The mob untangled from one another and Clara noted several lads who could not be more than five or six. Even at a distance it was obvious they were filthy, with ragged clothing and no shoes.

"Where do they all come from?"

Hawksley shrugged. "The East End is crawling with such imps. Most of them abandoned or simply forgotten by their families."

Her heart gave a twinge of sympathy. Having lived her life in the country where neighbors cared for one another, she was unaccustomed to such callous disregard.

"How sad."

"Yes, their lives will be a constant struggle for survival," he murmured, an odd expression upon his countenance. "But not for now. At the moment they are utterly happy."

Startled at his words, Clara turned to study his profile as he watched the children play.

"You sound almost envious."

"Listen."

"To what?"

"Their laughter," he murmured. "Have you ever visited an aristocratic estate and heard children enjoying themselves with such unabashed joy?"

"I have hardly spent a great deal of time upon any estate, aristocratic or not," she retorted dryly. "My invitations always seem to become misplaced."

"Consider yourself fortunate." Without warning, he turned to regard her with a glittering gaze. "There is nothing more stifling than a load of pompous fools all prancing about in an effort to prove that they are more important than one another."

About to agree with his sharp disdain for the upper orders, Clara felt a whisper of unease in her heart.

"You sound as if you have spent a great amount of time among the aristocracy. I did not presume your family would be so well connected."

Chapter Fourteen

Hawksley stiffened as he realized his unwitting revelation. Damn, damn, damn. When the devil would he learn that he need consider every word he uttered in the presence of this woman?

There was no such thing as casual conversation when it came to Miss Clara Dawson.

"My father possessed a highly developed sense of his own self-worth. One he was constantly determined to share with his sons," he hedged, not willing to outright lie to the woman he intended to wed. "Neither Fredrick nor I was allowed to associate with anyone that he considered beneath us. I was whipped more than once for having dared to join in games with the village children."

Thankfully, beyond her shrewd intelligence his angel also possessed a soft heart, and she was swiftly distracted at the thought of his father with a whip in his hand.

"That is horrid."

Hawksley smiled wryly. "He thought that he was saving me from myself."

"And instead he only drove you away," she said softly.

He made the mistake of glancing into her eyes and promptly found himself lost in the tender depths.

Hellfire, a man could spend an eternity gazing into those eyes.

"Yes," he murmured, his hand reaching to lightly touch her face.

In silence they stood close upon the sun-drenched balcony, each savoring the perfect moment as they simply appreciated being together.

And then, as with all perfect moments, they were rudely interrupted by a sudden chorus of whistles and calls.

"Oy, guv. Over here, guv."

Reluctantly returning to reality, Hawksley shifted his gaze to the herd of lads who had forgotten their game as they waved their arms in his direction.

"They seem to desire your attention," Clara murmured.

Hawksley smiled ruefully even as he silently damned their rotten timing.

"No, they desire these." Reaching down, he retrieved the forgotten basket and with practiced ease he began to toss the apples and oranges down to the boys below. The sound of excited whoops filled the air as the lads darted to catch the rare treats. Leaning against the railing, Clara chuckled at their antics and Hawksley handed her one of the oranges. "Would you care to join me?"

Taking the fruit, she carefully judged the distance to the barren yard.

"I am not certain I can toss an orange that far."

"You managed to toss that rock a goodly distance

last eve," he reminded her with a wicked grin. "Just try not to drop them on your toes."

Astonishingly she stuck out her tongue in a teasing manner. "Beast."

Hawksley tilted his head back to laugh as she reared back her arm and tossed the orange to the impatient imps, managing to skim it just beyond the hedge.

"There, I told you you could do it," he encouraged her, handing her an apple.

Together they swiftly dispensed the last of the fruit, and dropping the basket, Hawksley watched in pleasure as the older children carefully doled out the prizes, taking care to ensure that even the youngest of the lads received their bounty.

Their obvious concern for one another never failed to astound him. Despite the fact that many of them no doubt went to bed with empty stomachs, they possessed a natural instinct to protect what they considered their family.

Slowly becoming aware of Clara's steady gaze upon him, he turned to catch an odd expression upon her countenance.

"What is it?" he demanded.

"You."

He lifted his brow in puzzlement. "What about me?"

"You genuinely enjoy those children."

He pretended a nonchalance, but as usual she had read him with precise ease. He did enjoy coming to the balcony and watching their play. They reminded him of the child he had once been. The child that his father had never appreciated and always attempted to change.

"They are rather entertaining for filthy urchins."

"No, it is more than that," she said firmly, then tilting her head to one side, she met his gaze squarely. "You should be a father."

He gave a choked cough at her words. "Good god, kitten, tossing apples to stray children is considerably different from being a father."

She reached out to touch his arm. "I am not referring to your habit of tossing apples, Hawksley. I mean that you truly appreciate children. Most gentlemen in your position would call for the Watch to have them hauled away, but you come up here to simply listen to their laughter."

He lowered his gaze to where her pale fingers lay against the black material of his jacket. As always he was struck by her sheer delicacy. The force of her considerable will made it easy to forget just how tiny and fragile she truly was.

Unable to resist, his hand shifted to cover hers. A strange combination of tenderness and fierce desire surged through him at her nearness.

"I suppose I have never given much thought to having a child," he confessed.

Her expression softened with sympathy. "Not surprising after your experience with your own father."

He drew in a slow deep breath as he allowed his gaze to drift over her slender form. In his mind he imagined her growing thick with his child, her hands gently rubbing her rounded belly.

It was an image that should have terrified him, no doubt. But instead a sense of absolute wonder filled his heart.

A child. His child. With this woman.

Yes. It was right.

"Actually, I believe it has more to do with the fact I never met a woman whom I desired to be a mother to my children," he informed her, shifting to sweep her off her feet and cradle her close to his chest. "Not until now, that is."

Her eyes widened as her arms instinctively encircled his neck. "Good heavens, Hawksley, what are you doing?"

Stepping through the door to the shadowed attic, he paused to regard her with open yearning.

"I want you, Clara." He gave a slow shake of his head. "No, it is more than want. I need you," he admitted with stark honesty. "May I make love to you?"

Her eyes readily darkened, but she could not prevent a small grimace. "Here?"

He chuckled as he promptly headed for the nearby stairs. "Perhaps we could find someplace a little tidier."

She snuggled into his chest, her expression dreamy. "That would be nice . . ."

Nice? A smile tugged at his lips as he easily moved down the stairs and toward his nearby chamber. He had never thought of taking a woman to his bed as nice.

Pleasurable. Satisfying. And always transitory.

But with Clara it was nice. She offered more than a temporary ease to his sexual needs. When he touched her it filled him with a sense of wonder that no other woman had ever offered. And the desire to hold her close long after his needs were satisfied.

Entering his chamber, he firmly shut the door and carried her to the bed. With care he lowered her onto the blankets, his desire blazing to life at the sight of her tumbled silver hair and flushed cheeks.

She was so beautiful. So exquisite.

And his.

Reverently he settled himself beside her, stroking his fingers through her satin hair.

"I could lie here next to you forever," he husked in low tones.

She smiled faintly. "I fear you would soon become bored."

"Bored?" He offered a wicked chuckle as he shifted to tug free the ribbons on her bodice. "I assure you, kitten, becoming bored is the very last worry upon my mind."

Her breath caught as he tugged down the sleeves of her gown and then the thin shift beneath to reveal her beautiful breasts.

"This seems rather . . . decadent to be doing in the midst of the day," she murmured with a faint blush.

"Mmm . . . the decadence has only begun, kitten," he whispered as he dipped his head down to take a rosy nipple into his mouth.

Her sweet moans filled the room as he slid his tongue over the hardened nub, making his own blood race with sharp-edged excitement.

He wanted to make love to her for hours. To stretch out her pleasure until she was pleading for release.

Unfortunately, he had only to touch her for his own body to become as randy as a school lad in his first throes of passion. With a low groan he yanked down the bothersome clothing that impeded his touch, leaving her attired in nothing more than her stockings and sensible boots. Ridiculously, the sight only inflamed his desire, and trailing his lips down her stomach, he wrestled to rid himself of his own clothing.

Oh, Hawksley, you are in a bad way, he told himself, nibbling at the satin skin of her hips and thighs.

A woman's scent shouldn't make a hardened rake's head spin. Nor should his shaft be hard and aching with the need to thrust into her simply because she was near.

Lowering himself farther, Hawksley burrowed himself between her parted thighs, gently parting her folds to stroke his tongue into her damp heat.

"Hawksley."

Clara's soft cry echoed through the room as her fingers sank into his hair. He laughed softly as he continued his intimate caress, skimming his hands up her stomach to toy with her straining nipples.

Within moments she was arching off the bed as she moaned in pleasure.

"Oh . . . please . . . Hawksley . . ."

"Yes, kitten."

Finding her center of pleasure, Hawksley gently sucked and stroked the tender nub. He experienced a heady sense of satisfaction as she writhed beneath his touch, her fingers yanking at his hair. She made no effort to attempt and disguise her enjoyment of his touch. Or to make him plead for her favors. She was as sweetly honest about passion as she was about everything else in her life.

"Dear heavens," she gasped, then suddenly she stiffened, and with a rasping cry she reached her climax.

With a lingering kiss upon her inner thigh,

Hawksley pressed himself upward, entering her with one smooth thrust.

His teeth ground together as her tightness clamped about his erection. Oh . . . God. She felt so damnably good. As if she had been made just for him.

Burying his face in her hair, he greedily inhaled her female scent.

"I will never tire of you, kitten," he whispered in her ear. "Never."

Her arms wrapped about him as Hawksley steadily stroked himself into her heat. She was soft and welcoming and everything he desired in a woman.

Keeping his pace steady, he reached down his hand to find her pleasure point, teasing her back to full arousal. Her nails clenched his back and her breath quickened in response.

Pulling back, he reveled in the emotions playing over her delicate features. She had never appeared more lovely, with her lips slightly parted and her eyes smoldering with desire.

All too quickly the tension built within him. As much as he wanted to prolong the exquisite pleasure, he was unable to halt the gathering climax.

Lifting himself onto his hands, he pressed himself ever deeper, listening to her soft pants as her hips lifted to accept him. Her hands shifted to grip his surging hips, pulling him ever deeper as together they exploded in searing delight.

Sucking in a rasping breath, Hawksley collapsed on top of her, shuddering as a warm peace enfolded him.

This was how a man was meant to make love to a woman, he told himself with a contented smile.

It was how he intended to make love to this particular woman for the rest of his life.

Hours later, Clara absently toyed with the food
upon her plate.

In many ways she was utterly content. What
woman would not be, she wryly acknowledged. A
day spent in bed with Hawksley was surely the stuff
of dreams.

As a lover he was passionate, tender, and surprisingly playful. She could not recall when she had
laughed so much as she had lying in his arms.

But while she cherished the moments she spent
with Hawksley, she could not deny that there was a
growing restlessness in the back of her mind.

She could never be fully at ease when there was a
puzzle to be solved.

Certainly not with a puzzle as important as discovering the identity of Fredrick's murderer.

Unaware of the lazy blue gaze that kept close
track of her growing distraction, Clara was startled
when Hawksley abruptly broke the silence.

"Is there something wrong with your trout?"

With an effort she forced her thoughts back to
the small dining room, and more importantly back
to the handsome gentleman sprawled in the seat
opposite her.

A faint amusement raced through her as her gaze
lingered over the chiseled features and broad form.
With his raven hair pulled to his nape and his earring glinting in the candlelight, he looked
deliciously wicked.

Goodness, what woman in her right mind could

have taken her mind off him for a moment? Especially a woman who could never have dreamed in her wildest fantasies she could attract his attentions?

It was little wonder she had been left firmly upon the shelf.

"Oh no, it is perfect," she protested. "Mrs. Black has proven to be very skilled in the kitchen."

A raven brow flicked upward. "There must be some reason you are not eating."

She grimaced, well aware she could hide nothing from his piercing gaze.

"I was thinking of Lord Doulton."

"Yes, well, that is enough to make anyone lose their appetite," he growled, his features tightening at the mere mention of the man's name. "Were you thinking anything in particular?"

She blew out a frustrated sigh. "I was simply attempting to straighten things out in my mind."

"Were you successful?"

"Not particularly," she confessed. She hated the feeling that she had overlooked something important. Something that might very well help Hawksley. "What I need is paper and a pen."

There was a short pause as he regarded her in a searching manner. Then with an elegant motion he was on his feet and pulling out her chair for her.

"Very well, we can retire to the library." In silence they left the room and moved down the short hall to the book-lined room. Clara waited while Hawksley lit the candles upon his desk and pulled out a piece of parchment and a pen. "Here you are."

Taking a seat at the desk, she pulled the writing implements toward her and gathered her thoughts.

A lesser woman might very well have been distracted by the large pirate who leaned over the back of the chair with his hand flat upon the desk. Not only did his close presence send a rash of prickled awareness over her skin, but his scent cloaked her with potent force.

Even worse, the desire to pull his head down and kiss those talented lips suddenly seemed like a much better notion than hashing through Lord Doulton's nefarious dealings.

Thankfully, Clara was well aware that she would have no peace until she had sorted through the unease plaguing her, and she managed to resist tossing herself at Hawksley like some common tart.

"Let us begin at the beginning," she muttered, scratching the number one upon the paper.

"Which beginning?" he demanded, his breath tickling her ear.

"The beginning of what we know of Lord Doulton. Now, according to your brother's journal, he played cards with the gentleman and received the vowels that you found hidden."

"Yes."

She wrote *card game* on the paper. "We assume that he noticed the writing on the back of the vowels and became curious."

"Which led him to Mr. Chesterfield."

"Precisely." She wrote *vowels* followed by *Mr. Chesterfield*. "From there we think that Mr. Chesterfield approached Lord Doulton and demanded some sort of payment for keeping his silence."

She could feel Hawksley stiffen behind her. If he were a dog, his hair would be bristled and his teeth bared.

"And ensured Fredrick's death," he growled.

Neatly scratching the number four on the paper, Clara paused. This was the source of her unease, she abruptly realized. Number four.

"It is missing," she muttered.

"What is missing?" he demanded in confusion.

"Number four."

"Number . . . ?" Hawksley shifted to lean against the desk, his arms folded over his broad chest. "I presume you are now speaking in the obscure 'Clara tongue' only you understand. You will have to translate for me, I fear."

She wrinkled her nose at his teasing. "Number four should be the manner that Mr. Chesterfield blackmailed Lord Doulton. But how did Mr. Chesterfield know that Lord Doulton was involved in anything nefarious?"

A frown tugged at his brows. "The vowels . . ."

"Revealed a petition to the pope," she said, warming to her subject. "On its own it is meaningless. There are no doubt thousands of such petitions. It might have been peculiar, but it would not have revealed that Lord Doulton possessed stolen artwork from the Vatican. There is still something we are missing."

He gave a slow nod of his head, easily following her logic. "Perhaps you are right. Still, it is impossible to know unless we find the missing Mr. Chesterfield."

"May I see your brother's journal?" she abruptly demanded.

"Of course." Reaching beneath his jacket, he pulled out the leather book and vowels that he still kept close to his heart. A gesture that revealed just how deeply he still mourned his brother's death.

Giving his fingers a tender squeeze, she took the journal and flipped through the pages.

Arriving at the date of the infamous card game, she studied the tidy handwriting. *Speak to me, Fredrick*, she silently willed, *tell me your secrets.*

Coming to the bottom of the page, she pointed toward the meticulous numbers at the corner.

"What are these?"

Hawksley leaned forward. "It is the tally of what he won during the evening. Fredrick was always careful to keep careful account of such matters."

Clara carefully smoothed out the vowels on the desk. "But the vowels do not equal this number."

Hawksley shrugged. "That means very little. No doubt some of his winnings were from other gentlemen who possessed the funds to pay him that evening. Not all gamblers depend upon vowels."

He had a point, of course. Still, Clara felt a tiny flare of excitement.

"Or there might have been other vowels."

Hawksley appeared more confused than excited. "If there had been other vowels, they would have been with these."

"Not if Mr. Chesterfield kept them to examine more closely."

"Why would he keep only a portion of the vowels?"

A reasonable question, she had to concede. Closing her eyes, she attempted to imagine what had occurred. She could see Fredrick bent over the vowels, piecing them together as he realized there was something written on the back. As a scholar he would have been curious and of course determined to unravel the mystery. He must have managed to decipher that it was of a religious nature for his thoughts to turn to Mr. Chesterfield, a religious historian.

And then what?

The brain that she took such pride in seemed to flounder.

Why would he have taken only half the vowels to Mr. Chesterfield? It was hardly the swiftest means to uncovering the truth of the document. And as a scholar . . .

A scholar.

Of course. He was a scholar just like her father.

What would he have done in such a situation?

Briefly she recalled the quiet, studious man who always had a smile for his only daughter. A sweet-tempered man with a gentle soul.

But one who could become as rabid and secretive as any scholar when it came to his research.

"If Fredrick believed the petition to be of historic value, he would have been careful with what he was willing to share. With anyone," she said slowly, lifting her head to meet his watchful gaze. "True scholars are notoriously fearful of having others steal their research and claim it as their own."

He stilled at her words. "Are you implying that the petition itself is somehow valuable?"

Clara grimaced. It all made sense, but she was well aware that it was little more than a leap of faith. The logic involved would fit in a thimble.

"It is only a theory," she warned. "And a rather far-fetched one at that."

He did not seem to hear her words of caution as

he lifted himself from the desk to pace across the worn carpet.

"Why would Lord Doulton use a valuable document as scrap paper?"

"Perhaps he did not realize the value. If it was stuffed among the paintings, it might easily have been dismissed and tossed aside."

"Until Chesterfield approached him and blackmailed him for the return of the petition," he said slowly.

"Lord Doulton would realize that he was in more danger than simply being blackmailed for a forgotten piece of parchment. He had brought unwanted attention upon himself, and worse, there was now a connection to him and the Vatican."

He moved to grip the mantle above the fireplace, his knuckles turning white with strain.

"And so he took the necessary steps to rid himself of those who might stir up unwanted questions. Including my brother."

Leaving the desk, Clara moved to lay a hand upon his tense arm. Too often she allowed herself to forget just how difficult this must be for Hawksley.

"We will find the evidence we need, Hawksley," she promised. "Lord Doulton will pay for what he has done."

The blue eyes flashed with frustrated pain. "That is all I have thought of for months. All I wanted . . ."

She shifted to lay her hands upon his chest, her expression troubled. "What is it?"

His eyes briefly closed. "I suppose I am at last realizing that even should Doulton be punished, it will not bring my brother back to me. He will still be dead and I . . . I will be completely alone."

Her heart twisted. He sounded so lost. So terribly frightened of the future. It was a feeling she knew all too well.

And one she could not bear the thought of this wonderful man enduring.

Not giving herself time to consider the wisdom of her words, she laid her head upon his chest and wrapped her arms about him.

"No, Hawksley, not alone," she whispered. "I will be with you."

She felt him stiffen beneath her. "Clara, what are you saying?"

Tilting back her head, she was startled to discover his expression guarded, as if he feared she was playing some horrid jest upon him.

"I think you know perfectly well what I am saying," she whispered, a blush staining her cheeks.

His fingers lifted to brush over her lips, his eyes glowing with a hectic glitter.

"Since I quite often am at a loss when you speak, kitten, I think it best if you tell me in simple words so that my poor brain can comprehend what you mean."

Regarding the fiercely handsome countenance, Clara nearly faltered. How she possibly hope to please such a man? He could have any woman he desired. All of them more beautiful, more charming, and more wealthy than herself.

But none of them capable of loving him with more devotion, her heart whispered.

She swallowed heavily, and for the first time in her six-and-twenty years, tossed caution to the wind.

She would take a chance.

A chance that would either bring her happiness beyond her wildest imaginings or break her heart utterly.

"I will be your wife, Hawksley," she said simply.

There was a brief, terrifying pause when Clara was suddenly certain that he must be regretting his impulsive proposal. Then, before she could guess his intention, she discovered herself lifted off the floor as Hawksley planted a burst of heated kisses over her countenance.

"You will not be sorry, kitten," he muttered, his lips brushing her mouth. "I promise I will make you happy."

Squeezed by his tight grip to the point she could barely breathe, Clara slowly smiled.

Her father had promised that someday she would meet a man who could appreciate her just as she was. A man who would see beyond her annoying eccentricities and peculiar habits.

Who the devil would have suspected he would be a dangerous, wicked pirate?

Chapter Fifteen

Hawksley awoke to a loud clatter of pails and pouring water as his bath was being prepared. Instinctively he reached out for Clara, only to heave a sigh as he recalled her slipping from his arms to return to her own bed before dawn.

Damn, but he needed to get her before a vicar. The sooner the better. He did not like awakening alone. Not when he might begin the day with an angel in his arms.

His dark thoughts were interrupted by another loud clatter, followed by a string of hair-raising curses.

Dillon, of course, he acknowledged even before he opened his reluctant eyes to regard the grizzled servant. And in an even fouler mood than usual, if his grim expression and rigid movements were anything to go by.

"Good God, Dillon, there have been French invasions less deafening than you pouring a simple bath," he groaned as he pushed himself upright and scrubbed a hand over his face. "I presume you are in some sort of a twit?"

"A twit?" Dillon allowed an empty pail to clank loudly onto the floor. "Should have strangled you in your sleep when I had the opportunity."

Hawksley lifted his brows at the muttered threat. "I do hope that I have done something to annoy you, you cantankerous old goat. I should hate to think I have harbored you beneath my roof for all these years while you plotted my demise."

The gnarled servant kicked a stray pail, wincing as he obviously hurt his toe. "If I'd been plotting you'd already be cold in the ground."

"Why do you not just tell me why you are so perturbed before you do injury to yourself?" Hawksley retorted.

"Very well." His chest swelling with indignation, Dillon turned to stab Hawksley with a withering glare. "I thought you to be a gentleman."

Hawksley lifted his brows even higher. "Hellfire, that is a stretch even for you, Dillon. Why the blazes would you ever presume a poverty-stricken rake with nothing more than a talent for gambling could claim the title of gentleman? I certainly have never done so."

"Even a hardened rake should recognize a lady when he encounters one," Dillon muttered.

Ah. So that was it. Hawksley heaved a deep sigh. He should have known he could hide nothing from his loyal servant. The man possessed an uncanny ability to know precisely what was upon his employer's mind. Hawksley had often depended upon that talent over the years.

Attempting to hide his amusement, Hawksley settled himself more comfortably upon the pillows. There was no reason he could not have a bit of fun.

Dillon had often enough played some prank or another upon him.

"May I hazard a wild guess and say that you are referring to Miss Dawson?" he drawled.

The battered features hardened. "I am not blind. I have seen how you look upon her."

"And how is that?"

"Like a starving hound sniffing about a bone."

Hawksley wrinkled his nose. Gads, it was a fortunate thing he had never been forced to rely upon his acting skills to keep a roof over his head. They would all be living in the gutter.

"Hardly the most flattering comparison, but no doubt accurate."

"You should be ashamed of yourself," Dillon growled.

"Actually I am inordinately proud of myself."

The servant took a sharp step forward. "Why, you randy—"

"'Tis not often that I realize what is good for me and what is not," Hawksley overrode the angry words. "In truth, I have always possessed a tedious habit of preferring dross to gold. On this occasion, however, I was quite wise enough to comprehend that Miss Dawson is by far the best thing that has ever entered my life."

Perhaps sensing he was being roasted, Dillon regarded him with suspicion. "That she is."

"Which is why I am to make her my wife."

A suitably shocked expression touched the lined countenance. "Wife?"

"Shocking, is it not?" Tossing aside the covers, Hawksley rose to his feet and pulled on his brocade robe. "She is clearly daft to have agreed to my proposal, but there it is. It seems even eccentric angels prefer a rogue to a gentleman."

Without warning Dillon had crossed the room to enfold him in a tight hug. "You worthless scoundrel. Ach, you have done well for yourself."

Hawksley struggled to free himself before several ribs were sacrificed to Dillon's enthusiasm.

"Good Lord, Dillon, you are not about to get sentimental on me, are you?"

Coming to his senses, the elderly servant gave an embarrassed tug upon his coat as he stepped back.

"Not bloody likely."

"Good. There will no doubt be enough tears, not to mention gnashing of teeth, once my family discovers their wastrel of a son has chosen to wed a penniless miss from the country," he said dryly.

Dillon grimaced. Although he had only met Hawksley's family during the funeral for Fredrick, that had been more than enough for the servant to take them into a rabid dislike. Especially after Lord Chadwick had demanded that the silver be locked away after catching sight of Dillon's battered countenance.

"The tears are more likely to be poor Miss Dawson's when she is forced to meet your puffed-up prig of a father," he groused.

"If she does not toss herself from the nearest roof," Hawksley agreed grimly. "In fact, I have decided that it is best simply to acquire a special license and be done with the business before she has an opportunity to change her mind."

Expecting full agreement with his rather brilliant notion, Hawksley was caught off guard by Dillon's abrupt frown.

"And deprive her of the lavish society wedding that all women dream of?"

"All women but my Clara," Hawksley corrected with an unwittingly tender smile. "She possesses a distinct distaste for drawing attention to herself. I believe she would rather be drawn and quartered as to subject herself to the fuss of a large wedding."

"She will have to become accustomed to being nobility eventually."

A vague flare of panic fluttered through his heart before he was sternly squashing it.

No.

He had just managed to convince Clara to be his wife. He was not about to risk driving her away. The proper moment to reveal his title and wealth would surely present itself. Until then, he intended to use his time binding Clara so tightly to him she could never let go.

"That is a worry for another day."

His fierce tone must have alerted his servant that there was something he was hiding.

"Hawk?"

"Yes?"

His gaze narrowed. "You have told her the truth of yourself, have you not?"

Hawksley shrugged, his expression guarded. "Perhaps not entirely."

"Good God almighty." The former thief muttered several colorful curses beneath his breath. "You asked a woman to wed you who does not even know your true name?"

"She knows all she needs to know for the moment."

"Fah. She has a—"

"What she has is enough to concern herself with,"

Hawksley said in tones that defied argument. "Not the least of which is a crazed nobleman who wishes her dead. Once Lord Doulton is properly dealt with, I will reveal everything to her."

Dillon threw his hands in the air. "You are courting trouble, Hawk."

"It is what I usually court, is it not?" he retorted in mocking tones. "Now, may I have my bath before the water ices over?"

Clearly realizing Hawksley would not be moved, Dillon moved to collect the empty pails.

"Do as you will," he muttered.

"I always do, old friend."

Pausing at the door, Dillon offered a sudden smile. "Oh, aye, that you do."

After slipping from Hawksley's bed, Clara had no thought of returning to sleep. Not when her entire body tingled with a restless energy that nearly made her hair stand on end.

So this was love.

A smile curved her lips as she attired herself in a faded blue gown and pulled her hair into a tidy braid. It was odd how the poets always portrayed love as a sweet and tender emotion.

They spoke nothing of the sharp-edged excitement that seemed to be permanently lodged in the pit of her stomach. Or the giddy urge to giggle at the most ridiculous moments. Or prance about as if she were a complete loon.

For a sensible woman it was all vastly confusing.

And vastly delightful, she conceded with a faint sigh.

Perhaps she was being a fool.

History was littered with the broken hearts of women who believed they had discovered true love, only to be betrayed. But at the moment she could not make herself care.

She was happy.

Completely and utterly happy.

And if she was blinding herself, well . . . so be it.

For once in her dull, predictable life she was going to take a risk. And damn the consequences.

Far too restive to simply remain in her chambers, Clara at last went in search of the housekeeper. She needed something to keep her occupied until Hawksley arose and they could make their plans for the day.

Nearly two hours later she had commanded the boxes in the attic to be neatly stacked to one side and began busily mopping years of grime from the wooden floor. Already she had dusted the rafters clean and scrubbed the walls, and there was a freshness to the air that would please the most fastidious soul.

Humming beneath her breath, she attacked the cobwebs hiding in a corner with her mop, her distraction great enough that she missed the sound of approaching footsteps. No distraction, however, was great enough, not even death itself, to prevent her from noticing the sudden prickle of awareness that feathered over her skin.

"I thought I should find you here," a warm male voice murmured from behind.

Dropping the mop, Clara turned to discover Hawksley a few feet away, his shoulder propped negligently against the wall and a mysterious smile playing about his lips.

Her heart did its familiar leap and her mouth went dry. Oh . . . my. Would she ever become accustomed to such potent male beauty?

She had to hope she would. People would begin to suspect she was touched in the noodle if she were always fluttering and swooning whenever her husband entered a room.

Husband . . .

Her heart took another leap.

"Hawksley," she at last managed to squeak.

He slowly glanced about the attic that was glowing in the slanting sunlight. "You really do enjoy this scrubbing business, do you not?"

Retrieving a dampened handkerchief from the pocket of her apron, Clara wiped her hands clean.

"Well, it is to be my house as well now, and you know I can not abide a mess." She smiled rather shyly. "Besides, I would not wish anyone to think that I was not being a proper wife to you."

His eyes oddly darkened, almost as if her soft words troubled him. Slowly pushing away from the wall, he moved to stand before her, taking her hands in a tight grip.

"Clara . . . I would not request you to live in such an establishment once we are wed."

She bit her lip at his hesitant tone. Blast. She had forgotten just how fragile his male pride could be. Obviously he was concerned that his home was not worthy of her.

Well, she would put a swift halt to such nonsense. She would not have him plunging into debt in an effort to keep her in a style that he believed suitable for a lady. Nor would she have him returning to those horrid gambling hells to provide for them.

She was a simple woman with simple taste. Somehow she had to convince him that all she needed to be happy was him.

"It does not bother me, Hawksley, truly it does not," she earnestly assured him. "It is very cozy."

"No." He gave a sharp shake of his head. "It is a crumbling pile of rubbish in a neighborhood not fit for the rats."

She could not halt her chuckle at his dramatic words. "It is not so bad."

"My wife deserves better." His hand cupped her cheek. "She will have better."

She swallowed a sigh at his adamant expression. She might not know much about men, but even she could sense a battle when it was brewing.

"If you prefer we could always live at my cottage," she hastily offered. "It is not much, but it is sturdy, and with my yearly allowance we should be quite comfortable."

Just for a moment she feared she had managed to say precisely the wrong thing.

Again.

But even as she wracked her mind for some means of undoing the damage, Hawksley was wrapping his arms firmly about her and resting his cheek atop her head.

"My God . . . You truly are a most remarkable woman, Clara Dawson."

Warm relief flooded through her as she snuggled against his firm chest. She had no notion why this man found her remarkable while all others considered her merely annoying, but she was not about to question her good fortune.

Especially not when his warm, male scent was making her knees weak and the feel of his arms about her was reminding her just how wondrous it was to have him so close.

Pulling back, she deliberately smoothed her hands over his broad chest and up to his shoulders, an alluring smile curving her lips.

"Mayhap I am a bit remarkable."

Beneath her hands she felt his heart jolt against his chest, his eyes darkening with a familiar smoldering heat.

"Clara, are you actually jesting with me?" he teased softly. "I am all astonishment."

She wet her lips, delighting as she could feel his stirring erection. She had never thought of herself as desirable before. She found it a rather heady sensation.

"I am not so very dreary, Hawksley," she murmured.

"No, you are beautiful, and intelligent, and incredibly tempting," he growled, cupping her hips to press them sharply against him. "Too tempting by half."

She chuckled softly, her hands slipping down the hard planes of his stomach with a daring she never knew she possessed.

"Hawksley. Are you always in this mood directly after breakfast?"

"After breakfast, luncheon, tea, dinner . . ."

His head lowered to nibble at the pulse pounding at the base of her neck, his fingers already busy with buttons at the back of her gown.

"The servants."

He brushed her mouth with a light kiss. "I locked the door when I entered."

"You are quite wicked."

Lifting his head he slowly, methodically pulled down the sleeves of her gown.

"Oh, I have not yet begun to show you precisely how wicked I can be," he assured her.

Holding his gaze, she allowed a mysterious smile to curve her lips. She had always been a swift student, and Hawksley had taught her a great deal of passion over the past few days.

She intended to prove just how much she had managed to learn.

"Perhaps it is my turn to be wicked," she murmured.

Brushing her hand downward, she tugged at the buttons already straining beneath the thrust of his arousal. Then, still holding his stunned gaze, she allowed her fingers to encircle his rigid erection.

Hawksley sucked in a sharp breath, his fingers grasping her shoulders as if to keep himself upright.

"Bloody hell."

"Do you not like this, Hawksley?" she teased, running a finger up to the moist tip.

He growled deep in his throat. "Hellfire, if I liked it any more I'm not sure I could bear it."

She ran her fingers back down to the base of his manhood, delighting in the feel of his violent shudder.

"And that? Do you like that?"

"God," he groaned, abruptly propelling her back against a newly scrubbed wall as he was hastily lifting her skirts to her waist. "One of these days, kitten, I intend to devote an entire day to seducing you."

Her eyes slid closed in pleasure as his clever fingers parted her thighs to employ his special brand of magic.

"But not today," she murmured on a sigh.

"No," he rasped, his lips brushing hungry kisses over her upturned countenance. "Most certainly not today."

Chapter Sixteen

Several hours later Hawksley was seated in his library, while Clara was happily training the maids in the proper method of cleaning the windows. He wanted to protest. It still pained him to think of her performing even the slightest household duty. But accepting that she preferred to feel as if she was accomplishing some task or another, he held his tongue.

Soon enough she would have a husband and children to keep her thoroughly occupied.

Children.

The most ridiculous thrill of anticipation raced down Hawksley's spine and he gave a disbelieving shake of his head.

Hellfire. When did this happen?

When did he become a gentleman who no longer thought of his evenings devoted to gambling and debauchery, but instead tingled at the thought of curling up on a sofa with his wife at his side and silver-haired children with emerald eyes playing upon the floor?

Madness was the only explanation. Utter madness.

Aimlessly crossing the room toward the desk, Hawksley abruptly stilled at the faint rustle outside the window. The noise might have been caused by anything. A curious cat. A branch scraping the window pane. A passing servant.

Hawksley did not pause, however, as he slid silently toward the desk to collect his loaded pistol and then moved to a shadowy corner that possessed a clear view of the window.

He did not have long to wait as the curtains billowed from a sudden draft and a small, decidedly human form appeared in the room.

Hawksley lifted the pistol quite prepared to shoot. He would hesitate to pull the trigger if it were his own life at risk, but not with Clara in the house. To keep her safe he would do whatever was necessary.

He aimed toward the narrow chest, his finger upon the trigger, when he was struck by the blinding pink coat. What sort of self-respecting thief would wear something so ridiculous?

The answer was, of course, no thief would be seen in such a travesty.

Only one man would dare.

Lowering the pistol, Hawksley forced himself to count to ten before stepping from the shadows and confronting his intruder.

"You do know, Biddles, that one day you will crawl through the wrong window and discover a bullet lodged in your arse?"

Dusting his hands with a lace handkerchief, Biddles offered him a sly smile.

"The danger, of course, is half the enjoyment. Windows are always so much more interesting than doors."

Crossing the room, Hawksley replaced his pistol in the drawer and leaned negligently against the corner of the desk.

"It must make it rather interesting when you escort your wife about town," he drawled.

"Oh, Anna is always up for a bit of sport."

Hawksley gave a bark of laughter. He did not doubt for a moment that the spirited Anna would readily crawl through a window if she chose.

"She would have to be up for a bit of sport, wed to you."

"True enough." Tossing aside the handkerchief, Biddles stabbed him with a knowing glance. "Let us hope Miss Dawson possesses an equal taste for dashing gentlemen."

Hawksley narrowed his gaze. "I beg your pardon?"

The pointed nose twitched. "You have asked her to wed you, have you not?"

"How the devil . . ."

Biddles tilted back his head to laugh with rich enjoyment.

"Really, Hawk, I am not blind. There are only two reasons for a gentleman to possess that look of vacant astonishment. Either you have just been run over by a carriage or you are in love."

"Love? Do not be . . ." The growling words trailed away as Hawksley encountered his friend's shrewd expression.

Blast. Who was he fooling? Of course he was in love.

Why else had he kept Clara with him even when he could easily have handed her over to the care of Santos? Why else had he used his last grout to hire servants to keep her happy? Why else had he been near sick with tension until she had at last agreed to become his wife?

At least his madness had a name.

Watching Hawksley grapple with the stunning truth, Biddles at last arched a brow.

"Well?"

"Bloody hell."

Biddles moved forward to clap him on the shoulder, a grin splitting his face.

"I fear that it happens to the best of us. And if it is any consolation, you have chosen well."

Hawksley's slowly smiled. "Yes, I have."

Biddles gave his shoulder a squeeze before stepping back. "Now, let us see if we can rid London of Lord Doulton so that you may wed in peace."

Hawksley gave a lift of his brows, knowing that smug tone all too well.

"Ah, you managed to speak with someone within the War Office."

Biddles produced a painted fan to waft it gently beneath his nose. "I did. And I happened to pick up a few very interesting details."

"What details?"

The pale eyes glittered. "Did you know that Lord Doulton had a young cousin who was an ensign in the ninety-second Foot?"

"No."

"A tragic story." Biddles assumed a sorrowful expression. "The poor boy served in both Spain and then France before he was lost during an ambush and his body never recovered."

France? Hawksley narrowed his gaze. He was beginning to suspect where Biddles was leading him.

"Tragic, indeed."

"And oddly enough, he was upon a secret mission when he and two other soldiers were attacked by bandits."

"What sort of secret mission?"

Biddles snapped his fan shut. "Guarding a very large wagon filled with priceless artwork bound from Paris to the Vatican."

Hawksley nearly choked. He had hoped for some sort of connection between Lord Doulton and the Vatican. He could not have ever have dreamed that it would be so tangible.

"Damnation," he breathed. "Do the officials know what happened?"

"The actual events seem to be suspiciously obscure. The soldiers set out from Paris, but they had only traveled a few days when it appears that they were attacked and the wagon went missing. Unfortunately, two of the soldiers were shot in the back of the head while they slept, and the third had completely disappeared after what appeared to be a terrible struggle."

Hawksley shuddered. By any standard it had been a brutal attack. Only the most heartless sort of bastard would shoot a man while he slept.

"Appeared to be a struggle?"

"The authorities have never been entirely satisfied with the notion that bandits could outwit three trained soldiers and make off with the bounty, not to mention the fact that none of the artwork has made an appearance upon the European auction blocks." Biddles's thin features abruptly hardened, putting paid to his usual air of frivolous indolence. Anyone who dismissed Lord Bidwell as a silly buffoon made a dangerous, and at times deadly, mistake. "Still, with no evidence to the contrary, they could hardly brand a soldier as a traitor and a thief. Not without considerable proof."

Hawksley slowly smiled. His friend had done well. Very well.

"We now possess a legitimate connection between Lord Doulton and the stolen artwork."

"Indeed," Biddles agreed without hesitation. "For a nefarious man it would have been a simple matter to await his turn at guard duty during the night and shoot his companions in the back of the head. Afterward he could have created the appearance of a struggle and taken off with the wagon."

Hawksley paced across the room, refusing to allow himself to be distracted by his instinctive hatred for a man capable of such cold-blooded murder. Instead he forced himself to consider what must have occurred once the treasure had been so brutally taken from the soldiers.

"From there he must have smuggled the goods to England."

Biddles gave a nod. "According to Santos, it would not have been a difficult task."

Hawksley abruptly halted his pacing, a frown marring his brow. "So what happened to the treacherous young cousin?"

Biddles gave a lift of his hands. "Either he is in hiding or . . ."

"Or he is yet another victim of Doulton's greed," Hawksley finished in hard tones.

"Yes."

Hawksley clenched his hands at his side. "It is time for the bastard to pay."

Biddles moved to stand before him, his expression uncommonly somber.

"I agree, but we must recall that for all his sins Lord Doulton is a peer of the realm," he pointed out. "We cannot have him simply hauled off by the magistrate."

Hawksley smiled without humor. He now had all the proof he needed. Lord Doulton was responsible for Fredrick's murder. And for that he would pay.

"Oh, I have no intention of bothering the magistrate with such tedious rubbish. A lead ball through the heart is much more efficient."

The pale eyes narrowed at Hawksley's grim tone. "And might very well have you transported. I do not believe that Miss Dawson would care overmuch for the climate in the colonies."

Hawksley regarded his companion in astonishment. There was a time when Biddles would not have hesitated to deal out justice. With his own hands, if necessary.

"You cannot be suggesting that Lord Doulton not be punished for his sins?" he gritted.

"Of course not." There was a steely determination in the pale eyes. "But this is no longer a simple matter of murder or even theft. Lord Doulton has entangled himself in war crimes for which he might very well be hung for treason. I suggest we turn the matter over to the War Office."

Hawksley gave a growl of frustration. He had dreamed too many nights of having his hands around Doulton's throat to abandon his blood-thirsty desire with ease.

"You believe they can see him hang?"

"If nothing else, they can certainly ensure that he is driven from England and never allowed to return," Biddles temporized.

Turning, Hawksley slammed his fist onto the mantle. "This is not the revenge I sought."

Biddles laid a hand upon his tense shoulder. "I understand, Hawk, truly I do. But now you have more to think of besides tasting Lord Doulton's blood."

Hawksley abruptly whirled about, his eyes narrowed. "If you say my damnable position—"

"I was thinking more of your fiancée," Biddles interrupted. "As much as it might rub at a gentleman's pride, you must now halt and consider what would happen to her if you were somehow harmed seeking out Lord Doulton, or worse, charged with his murder. Your first loyalty must be to her."

Clara.

The seething fury slowly eased as Hawksley allowed the image of sweetly feminine features to rise in his mind. It was astonishing. For months, nothing had been allowed to interfere in his fierce campaign to punish the man responsible for Fredrick's death. He had been ruthless and without mercy to any who stood in his way.

Now a tiny slip of a girl had reminded him that his life could be more than guilt and regret and anger.

She had reminded him that he had a future.

One he never thought to look forward to with such eager anticipation.

"I suppose you are right, damn you," he muttered in resignation.

Biddles offered a smile of approval. "Justice will be served, that I promise you, Hawk. In fact, if you will give me a few hours, I will assemble the appropriate gentlemen and we will bring our evidence to them this evening."

Hawksley heaved a wry sigh. "I never thought the day would come when you would advise caution, you sly ferret."

"Like you, I now have a great deal to lose by rash pride," he said simply.

Hawksley gave a slow nod. *Something to lose.* Yes. Biddles was right.

"Very well. We will do this your way."

"You will not be sorry."

Giving Hawksley a firm slap on his back, the slender nobleman turned to head back toward the window. In amazement, Hawksley watched as he slung his foot over the ledge and prepared to disappear.

"Biddles," he called in amusement.

"Yes?"

"There is a perfectly good door just across the room."

Biddles flashed a sly grin. "Anna would fear I was cheating upon her if I did not return home with a rip in my breeches and my boots marred by mud. Besides which, she enjoys lecturing me upon my disreputable habits. I cannot possibly disappoint her." He gave a wave of his slender hand. "Until later."

Clara studied the closed door to the library with an unfamiliar sense of indecision.

As a rule, she disliked the thought of intruding upon Hawksley. She knew intimately just how aggravating it could be to be in the midst of some deep thought or calculation and be interrupted. Which was precisely why she had always preferred to live on her own.

And she most certainly did not wish Hawksley to believe that he was about to tie himself to a woman who could not allow him so much as a few moments' peace without demanding his attention.

Still, she sensed that something was troubling Hawksley. It was unlike him to remain closeted alone for so long. Or to ignore the scents wafting from the kitchen.

And while she wished to respect his privacy, she could not bear the thought of him sitting alone and brooding when she might possess the means to comfort him.

Pacing the hall for several long moments, Clara at last sucked in a deep breath. She was being a nitwit.

Reaching out, she pushed the door open and crossed to the center of the library. Even in the shadows she had no difficulty spotting Hawksley, who stood beside the window staring into the darkness.

"Hawksley?"

"Yes?" he murmured without turning.

"What has occurred?"

There was a moment's pause before he shifted to regard her with a curious smile. "And why should you believe something has occurred?"

"You are never late to dinner when there is the scent of shepherd's pie in the air."

His expression abruptly lightened as a smile curved his lips. "Ah, you know me too well, kitten."

Carefully searching the features that had become as familiar as her own, Clara did not miss the edge of strain about the full lips.

"Did Biddles bring you bad news?" she asked softly.

His eyes widened. "Good God, how . . ." he began, only to give a pleased laugh as she bent down to pluck a lace handkerchief from the floor. "Ah, how thoughtless of Biddles."

Dropping it upon the desk, Clara offered him a teasing glance. "You are fortunate, sir, that it smells of brandy rather than perfume."

His beautiful eyes darkened as he took a sudden step forward and wrapped his arms firmly about her waist.

"Would you be jealous, sweet Clara?"

Clara was startled by the sharp, near-blinding fury that flared through her at the mere thought of Hawksley with another woman. What the devil was the matter with her? Such an intense emotion was hardly reasonable. Or even desirable.

It was, however, undeniable.

Hoping that her expression did not reveal the force of her reaction to his simple teasing, Clara managed a small smile.

"I assure you that you would never taste of my shepherd's pie again."

He gave a dramatic shiver. "A fate that does not bear contemplating. And one that neither of us need ever fear." He tugged her even closer, his gaze filled with tenderness. "I want no woman but you."

Her ridiculous fears were instantly banished as a comforting warmth filled her heart.

"And I want no man but you." She wrapped her arms about his waist as she smiled with open contentment. "A fortunate thing we are to be wed, is it not?"

"Not a fortunate thing," he murmured, "a miracle."

A miracle, indeed. She laid her head against his chest, delighting in the sound of his beating heart.

"Will you tell me what is wrong?"

He stiffened at her abrupt question, then just as she feared he might refuse to share what was troubling him, he heaved a deep sigh.

"Actually, everything is falling into place. Biddles has learned how Lord Doulton managed to get his hands upon the paintings."

She pulled back to watch his shadowed expression as he succinctly revealed the role of Lord Doulton's young cousin and the suspicion that two soldiers had been murdered in their sleep while he slipped away with the wagon of priceless treasure.

"Heavens . . . How could any man be so evil?" she breathed in disbelief.

"Greed is a powerful incentive," he assured her. "It has led more than one man to crime."

"But to kill with such ruthless disregard." Clara shuddered. "It is sickening."

"And at an end," he said in rough tones. "At least as far as Lord Doulton is concerned."

Clara stilled at his grim expression, a chill inching down her spine.

"What do you intend to do?"

"I intend to ensure that he pays for his sins."

Oh no. She knew that tone. It always preceded a gentleman behaving as an utter dolt.

She licked her lips. "Hawksley, you will not . . . do anything foolish?"

A raven brow arched. "Foolish?"

"You know precisely what I mean." She stepped back from his grasp with a frown. "Please tell me that you do not intend to confront Lord Doulton. I could not bear for you to take such a risk."

A wry smile curved his lips. "I have already been lectured by Biddles, kitten. He has convinced me to allow the War Office to seek justice."

"Thank goodness." She breathed a deep sigh of relief. "I was worried you would take matters into your own hands."

"It is what I desire." He held her gaze steadily for a long moment. "But not at the cost of losing you."

It took a moment for his words to sink in. Then without thought Clara threw herself forward to land heavily against his chest.

"Oh, Hawksley . . . I love you."

His arms instinctively wrapped about her, but she felt him stiffen in shock.

"What did you say?" he demanded.

As she realized just what she had confessed, an embarrassed heat flooded Clara's cheeks. Oh, Lord. That was not at all how she intended to reveal her feelings. In truth, she was not at all certain she intended to say the words at all. She did not know much of gentlemen, but she had overheard enough women bemoaning the fact that men tended to be oddly terrified by confessions of love.

"I . . ." She cleared her dry throat. "I believe you heard me quite well."

She gave a squeak as his hands encircled her waist and he lifted her until they were nose to nose.

"Actually, I fear I must be dreaming," he murmured. "Say the words again, my angel."

Well, he hadn't bolted, she assured herself. Nor had he swooned in horror.

In fact, his eyes held such an aching vulnerability that her fear was swiftly dissolving. Framing his face with her hands, she slowly smiled.

"I said that I love you, Hawksley."

With a groan he jerked her against his tense body, burying his head in the curve of her neck.

"Bloody hell, you cannot know how sweet those words are to my ear, Clara," he muttered in a rasping voice. "I have waited a lifetime for you."

Although deeply pleased by his fervent response, Clara gently cleared her throat.

"Um . . . Hawksley?"

"Yes, my love?" he murmured.

"I fear I cannot quite manage to breathe when you hold me so tightly."

He gave a choked laugh as he slowly lowered her

to the ground, although his arms remained loosely wrapped about her.

"Forgive me, there are times when I forget just how tiny and fragile you truly are."

She leaned against his chest, placing her ear over the rapid beat of his heart.

"Not so very fragile," she assured him.

"Fragile and beautiful and utterly mine," he whispered, kissing the top of her head. "Or you will be mine as soon as I can acquire a special license."

A surge of pleasure swept through Clara as she leaned back to meet his watchful gaze. "A special license?"

He tensed, as if bracing himself for an unwelcome blow. "Only if it meets with your approval. I did not think you would desire a large, traditional wedding. And to be honest, I am too selfish to wish to wait to make you my wife."

She gave a slow shake of her head. Surely this must all be a dream? Aging spinsters simply did not have gorgeous pirates tumbling over themselves to make them their bride.

"Are you certain, Hawksley?" she demanded.

His eyes blazed with a sudden fire. "More certain than I have been of anything in my life."

A whisper of warning that this was all too good to be true fluttered deep in her heart, but Clara sternly brushed it aside.

She wanted to marry Hawksley. She wanted to be his wife and to know that she would never be alone again.

Nothing else mattered.

"Then yes. I would very much like to be wed by special license."

Pressing a swift, possessive kiss to her lips, Hawksley stepped back with an oddly shuttered expression.

"I promise I will do everything in my power to ensure you do not regret your decision, Clara."

She gave a faint frown. "What could I possibly regret?"

"I . . ." He bit off his words with an absent shake of his head. "I must meet Biddles at the War Office. Will you wait up for my return?"

"Of course." She reached out to gently touch his cheek. "Is there something troubling you?"

He conjured a strained smile. "Nothing more than the fear that Lord Doulton will somehow manage to escape justice. The sooner I have this turned over to the authorities, the better."

Her vague sense of disquiet was not entirely banished, although she told herself she was being a fool.

Of course he was tense. He had waited months to revenge his brother's death. Now he was forced to depend upon others to ensure Lord Doulton paid for his sins.

It must be a bitter pill for a man with Hawksley's pride to swallow.

"I will be waiting here for your return," she promised softly.

"Thank you." He brushed his lips lightly over her forehead before turning and heading for the door.

On her own Clara sucked in a deep breath.

All would be well, she told herself sternly.

Hawksley would see to Lord Doulton and they would soon be husband and wife.

Life was astonishingly perfect.

There was no reason to worry.

No reason at all.

Chapter Seventeen

Clara remained in the library even after she heard Hawksley leave the house. She felt ridiculously on edge, and there was an odd comfort in being surrounded by the scent and feel of Hawksley that lingered in the room.

Allowing her hands to trail over the leather-bound books that lined the shelves, Clara smiled wryly. It was rather astonishing just how important Hawksley had become to her happiness. After all, she had known him for such a short time. And in truth there was a great deal of him that remained shrouded in mystery. But she could not deny that it seemed impossible to imagine her future without him in it.

She had reached the marble fireplace when she became aware of the sound of raised voices in the foyer. Coming to a halt, she frowned as she attempted to discern the low rumble of words that echoed through the air.

"Out of my way, you scurrilous cur."

"Sir, I really must insist that you await Hawksley's return."

She could detect Dillon's familiar growl, but she was quite certain that she had never before heard the first male voice.

As she debated whether it would be wiser to keep her presence a secret or to go to the assistance of the growingly agitated servant, the decision was taken out of Clara's hands when the door to the library was abruptly thrust open.

Startled by the unexpected intrusion, Clara took an instinctive step back as her gaze swept over the large form.

The first thing she noted was the obvious elegance of the stranger. From the precisely styled gray hair that framed a powerful countenance to the dark coat and black breeches, he spoke of pampered, arrogant wealth. It was an image that was only emphasized by the cold expression upon his bold, male features and hint of disdain in the blue eyes.

Clara instinctively found her muscles tightening. She was all too familiar with such noblemen and their unbearable conceit. They had certainly managed to insult and mock her often enough over the years.

And it did not make matters better to have him regarding her with a curl of his lips that indicated quite clearly he considered her as something that should have been tossed out with the morning rubbish.

"Gads, I might have known Hawksley would have some bit of muslin tucked away," he drawled in disdainful tones. "He has never possessed the slightest measure of decency."

"Bit of muslin?" Clara stiffened her spine as her

chin tilted to a fighting angle. She did not know who this gentleman might be, but she would be damned if she would meekly allow him to insult her in such a fashion. "Sir, you are offensive."

He offered a humorless laugh as he stepped further into the room. "You will find that I can be a good sight more offensive if you do not pack your bags and leave immediately."

She blinked at the abrupt command. Arrogance, indeed, she acknowledged in disbelief. How dare he enter Hawksley's home and begin tossing about orders?

"That is hardly your decision to make. I assure you that I am here at Hawksley's invitation."

"Oh, I am sure you are." The blue eyes held open scorn as the stranger deliberately made note of her threadbare gown and boots that were several years old. "Hawksley is never satisfied unless he has managed to surround himself with cutthroats, whores, and every other sort of ruffian he can collect from the gutter."

Clara clenched her hands at her side. It was that or toss a very large, very heavy book at the older man's skull. Goodness knew she could not possibly miss his inflated head.

"That is enough. I think it would be best if you left this house until Hawksley has returned."

The arrogant wretch appeared taken back by her cold retort. As if she were a beaten hound that refused to heel when he snapped his fingers.

Then a decidedly unpleasant smile twisted his lips.

"Ah, I begin to understand your reluctance."

"I beg your pardon?"

"No doubt Hawksley has promised you some sort of payment," he said as he reached beneath his coat to pull out a small purse. "Very well, I am a man of business. How much will it cost to have you pack yourself off? Five pounds? That is more than generous."

Clara caught her breath. Never in her six-and-twenty years had she ever been so insulted. Which was saying something considering the innumerable slights, snubs, and cut directs she had endured.

"I do not know who you are or what your connection to Hawksley might be, but I can assure you that you have made a most grievous error," she gritted in icy tones.

Opening his purse, the gentleman counted out a handful of notes and tossed them to the carpet.

"Ten pounds, and that is my final offer. I suggest you take it before I have you tossed out without so much as a shilling."

At the moment Clara thought if anyone was about to be tossed out, it was the smug brute standing before her. She might be half his weight and several inches shorter, but she was certainly angry enough to dump him through the nearest window.

"There is no amount of money you can offer me," she assured him with icy disdain. "I will have you know that I am Hawksley's fiancée."

"His . . . fiancée?" Just for a moment stark silence filled the room, and then he suddenly tilted back his head to laugh with insulting humor. "Oh, that is rich."

"I do not know what you find so amusing."

"Not even my son would dare to make a penniless tart with no breeding the next Countess of Chadwick."

It was Clara's turn to fall silent as she reeled in disbelief.

No.

It could not be.

It simply could not.

"Countess . . ."

His nose flared. "Please do not pretend innocence, it does not become a woman of your ilk. You are obviously a well-educated courtesan who would never be in the company of a common gamester. Your sort always holds out for a titled nobleman. In this instance you managed to snare a viscount. I must compliment you upon your obvious . . . skills."

Clara barely heard his insults.

Instead she grappled with the horrid, near-mind-numbing possibility.

Hawksley . . . the son of this hideous nobleman. A man who was already a viscount and destined to become the Earl of Chadwick.

"This is impossible."

"If you mean it is impossible that you would be engaged to my son, I must heartily agree. Even if he were foolish enough to make some rash pledge in the heat of passion, I can assure you that I will see you in hell before I allow him to humiliate his family with the likes of you."

Clara reached out to grasp the edge of the nearest shelf. Only pride and the refusal to reveal the least hint of weakness before the coldhearted bastard kept her from swooning.

"Dear Lord . . ."

Oblivious to her distress, the Earl of Chadwick pointed toward the discarded notes upon the floor.

"Take the money and consider yourself fortunate

you were not tossed out with nothing to show for your efforts."

Without warning, a fierce fury raced through her blood.

She did not know who was responsible for her raging anger, the evil beast standing before her or the fiancé who had lied to her from the beginning. Or herself for being such a naïve sap.

In truth it did not matter.

She only knew that she was hurting and in need of striking out at someone.

"I would sell myself in the streets before I touched a grout of your wealth," she assured him with biting contempt. "Do you know, I wondered how Hawksley could bear to turn his back on his own family, no matter what the difficulties that may be between you. Now I comprehend utterly."

An ugly stain marred the once-handsome countenance. "How dare you?"

"Quite easily." She moved until she was standing directly before him, determined to reveal that for all his power and social stature, she would not be intimidated. "You are a cold, horrid man who has lost one son and driven away another. You are destined to die alone and unloved. I would pity you if you did not so fully deserve your pathetic fate."

For a moment the cold fury in his eyes made Clara wonder if he might actually strike her. Then with an obvious effort he took a step back and gathered his well-honed disdain.

"You will never wed my son."

A bitter smile curved her lips. "At last we come to an agreement. Now, if you will excuse me."

She swept past him toward the door.

"What are you doing?" he demanded.

Clara did not even bother to turn about. "I am about to correct a near-tragic mistake."

A blessed numbness shrouded Clara's mind as she calmly returned to her narrow chambers and packed her bags. Logic warned her that soon enough the shock would fade and she would be forced to confront the pain of betrayal and disappointment.

For now, however, she intended to use her momentary reprieve to flee as far as possible from Hawksley. She would not allow him to know just how deeply he had managed to hurt her.

Taking only a small satchel of her most necessary items, Clara put on her bonnet and wrapped her cape about her shivering form. She could only hope that Hawksley would possess the decency to send the rest of her belongings. She certainly could not afford to replace them.

Once ready, she forced herself to walk down the stairs without looking back. What was the point? The memory of every nook and cranny of the house would be forever branded upon her mind.

No matter how much she might wish to pretend she had never entered the Hawk's Nest.

She breathed a sigh of relief as she reached the foyer without encountering the dreadful Earl of Chadwick. As furious as she might be with Hawksley and his father, she was certain she would later regret blackening the eye of a peer of the realm.

Opening the door, she had nearly reached freedom when there was the sound of hurried footsteps behind her.

"Miss Dawson . . ."

Clara heaved a heavy sigh as she forced herself to turn and regard Dillon's anxious expression.

"Please, not now, Dillon," she pleaded.

Something that might very well have been remorse rippled over his battered countenance. As damn well it should, she told herself, refusing to feel the least amount of guilt at his obvious distress.

He had pretended to be her friend when all along he was allowing her to be played a fool by Hawksley.

"Where are you going?"

Her chin jutted to a stubborn angle. "I am going home, where I belong."

"But it is far too dangerous for you to return," he insisted.

"No longer. Hawksley will ensure that Lord Doulton is dealt with this evening. I no longer have a reason to remain."

Dillon chewed his lip at her stiff words, easily sensing the strain beneath her calm façade.

"It is far too late to be catching the stage, miss. At least wait until morning."

She stiffened at the mere thought. Remain here? Where she would be forced to confront Hawksley and listen to his empty assurances he had never intended to rip her heart out?

Oh no. That would never do.

"I do not care if I am forced to walk, Dillon," she said fiercely. "I will not stay another moment beneath this roof."

A hint of desperation settled about Dillon as he twisted his hands together.

"If you will just wait a moment, I will call for the carriage . . ."

"No." Stepping forward, Clara gave the man a brief hug. She could not be angry with him. This entire fiasco could be laid entirely at the feet of Hawksley. "I will always remember your kindness to me, Dillon. Good-bye."

Feeling tears beginning to prick in the back of her eyes, Clara hastily turned and hurried for the door before she managed to become a babbling idiot.

At least she could leave with a bit of dignity.

Dignity that lasted until she reached the darkened corner of the street.

Coming to a halt, she glanced about the shadowed buildings that lined the street.

Well . . . now what, she brooded.

She did not doubt that Dillon had been correct when he insisted there would be no stages to be had at such a late hour. And she had no friends or acquaintances to call upon.

Obviously she would have to seek out the nearest hotel.

It was what she had intended to do before ever arriving in London.

Now, if she just knew where the devil one might be found.

Squaring her shoulders, she set off at a brisk pace, keeping her eyes upon the narrow street for a passing hackney.

She would survive this, she told herself grimly. She always survived.

With her head turned, Clara had no warning of the large form that suddenly stepped from behind a large hedge. Nothing but an unexpected whiff of peppermint and cloves.

On the point of turning, she did not even manage a scream when a blinding pain flared through the back of her head. Instead she slid silently to the damp ground, a wave of darkness smothering the panic that stabbed at her heart.

Hawksley was seated within the sacred inner offices of the War Office when a servant discreetly pressed a note into his hand.

Just for a moment he debated slipping it into his pocket unread. After all, what could be more important than the grim-faced gentlemen seated around the oval table?

Biddles had made good on his promise to assemble the sort of powerful aristocrats, military commanders, and even royal officials they would need to have Lord Doulton facing the noose. More importantly, they had listened to the rather far-fetched accusations without yet having them tossed into Bedlam.

Now was not the time to be distracted.

But even as his fingers closed about the folded paper, an odd premonition seemed to inch down his spine.

It was nothing more than a vague sense that all was not right. But it was enough to have him smoothing out the folds of the paper to read the hastily scrawled message.

Clara is in great danger. You must return at once.

His blood ran cold as he easily recognized Dillon's hand, and without thought he reached out to grasp Biddles's arm in a biting grip.

With a startled blink, the thin-faced gentleman turned to regard him with concern.

"What is it?"

It took a moment to force his stiff lips to work. For all his daring deeds and habit of flaunting death, he had never known true terror before this moment.

"Clara," he managed to rasp.

There was no hesitation as Biddles slipped a small pistol from his pocket and placed it in Hawksley's hand. "I will finish this business and collect Santos."

The crisp authority in his friend's tone was as effective as a slap to the face. With a sense of relief, Hawksley battled down the smothering panic so that he could once again think clearly. He would be no good to Clara if he was a raving lunatic.

"Thank you."

With a silent grace Hawksley slipped from the room; then picking up his pace to a full-out run, he burst out of the building, leaping into Biddles's waiting carriage with a curt command to return him to the Hawk's Nest.

It was a testament to Biddles's unconventional training that the driver did not hesitate for a moment as he set the horses into a brisk pace that did not waver until they reached the cramped townhouse.

Hawksley did not wait for the carriage to pull to a halt before he was leaping onto the pavement and charging up the path. Throwing open the door, he discovered Dillon awaiting his arrival with a pale countenance and his hair standing on end.

A piercing pain shot through him as he reached out to grasp the man by his shoulders.

Hellfire, it had to be bad. He had seen the stoic man face bullets without batting an eye.

"Dillon . . . what is it? Where is Clara?"

Anguish darkened the older man's eyes. "She is gone."

"Gone?" Hawksley gave a shake of his head. The man was babbling. Clara could not possibly be gone. She had promised. "What do you mean gone?"

The grizzled countenance abruptly hardened as the servant stabbed him with a glare that could have killed at a hundred paces.

"She packed her bags and left near an hour ago. I tried to stop her but she was too angry to listen to me." Dillon lifted a fist to shake it in his direction. "I warned you, Hawk. I told you to tell her the truth."

Very well, there could no longer be any doubt. His faithful servant had most certainly tumbled into lunacy.

"What the bloody hell are you babbling about? Why would Clara leave?"

"No doubt because she at last had the pleasure of meeting your offensive toad of a father."

Of all the dangers Clara might face, this was one he had not envisioned. How could he? The Earl of Chadwick had never bothered to call upon him before.

Now a sense of sick dread clutched at his stomach.

"Father . . . here?"

"Yes."

Hawksley muttered a string of vile curses beneath his breath. He did not doubt for a moment that his father had managed to be gloriously rude to poor

Clara. He had always possessed a remarkable talent to offend and insult others.

And worse, he obviously must have revealed Hawksley's identity.

Why else would she have packed her bags and left?

However ghastly his father might be, Clara would stand up to him without fear. That much he knew for certain.

Clenching his jaw until he thought that his teeth might shatter, Hawksley reached out to grasp the front of Dillon's coat.

"Do not give me that look, Dillon. Just tell me what has happened to Clara."

Clearly sensing this was no time to test Hawksley's temper the servant grimaced.

"I was concerned when she left so I sent Billy and John to follow her."

"And?"

"And a bloke snuck up behind her on the street and forced her into a carriage."

"What do you mean forced?" he rasped.

"He knocked her over the head and bundled her into the carriage before Billy or John could reach her."

Hawksley stood for a moment in numb shock before he turned and rammed his hand into the wall.

"Lord Doulton," he growled in self-disgust. "He must have discovered our suspicions and is hoping to trade Clara for our silence. Dear God, what have I done?"

Fighting back the bile that rose to his throat, Hawksley struggled to consider what must come next. He would have ample time later to flog himself for his self-ish stupidity. For now nothing mattered but finding Clara.

Absolutely nothing.

"We must begin a search immediately," he commanded. "I will start with Lord Doulton—"

"Actually, I have hopes such a search will not be necessary," Dillon interrupted. "Billy returned to warn me of Clara's abduction, but he left John behind to follow the coach. He will return when he knows where she is being held."

A measure of the tightness eased in his chest as he cast a rueful glance toward his loyal servant.

"Thank God my staff possesses a few wits even if their employer is a fool."

Dillon's expression eased to one of sympathy; perhaps the former thief sensed the raw, aching pain that throbbed deep in Hawksley's heart.

"We will find her, Hawk."

"Yes, we will. And then I will deal with Lord Doulton once and for all." He clapped Dillon upon the shoulder. "You have done well. Fetch me the moment John returns."

With a swirl of his greatcoat Hawksley turned to head down the narrow hall. He needed to collect his dueling pistols. They would ensure a far more lethal wound than Biddles's small gun.

And a shot of whiskey would not come amiss.

And perhaps a heavy object to whack against his head for being such an unmitigated ass.

If anything happened to Clara . . .

His steps briefly faltered as that blinding pain once again wrenched through him.

If anything happened to Clara he could not bear to go on living.

Of that he was absolutely certain.

And he would have no one to blame but himself.

He turned to lean his shoulders against the paneled wall as his knees threatened to give way.

Stop this, Hawksley, he grimly commanded himself. *Nothing is going to happen to Clara. Not if you have to walk through the very fires of hell to rescue her.*

"So at last you return," a too-familiar male voice groused from the door to the library. "And cast to the wind as usual."

The prickle of antagonism that always signaled when his father was near raced over Hawksley's skin as he slowly straightened to confront the unwelcome intruder.

"Father." His own tone was cold. The very last person he wished to deal with at this moment was the Earl of Chadwick. "I would say this is a pleasant surprise, but we would both know that it was a lie, so why do we not just forgo the niceties and you can be on your way."

The heavy brows lowered in an expression that the earl held in reserve for his younger son.

"I most certainly will not be on my way. Not at least until I have had my say."

Curling his hands at his side, Hawksley forced himself to brush past his father and into the library. He could not afford to be distracted. Not now.

"Whatever you have to say will have to wait until a later date. I have no time for your tedious lectures this evening."

Huffing with indignation, the older man followed closely behind.

"I have not traveled all this way to be put off."

"No one requested you to travel here." Reaching the desk, Hawksley pulled out his matching pistols and began to load them with practiced ease. "Indeed, I have never once invited you to do so."

"Hawksley. What the devil are you doing?" the earl growled. "Do not tell me that you have embroiled yourself in some uncivilized duel?"

"I am going to retrieve my bride."

"Bride?" Large hands abruptly landed on the desk and his father leaned forward to slay him with a murderous glare. "You cannot mean that shabby tart who—"

Hawksley was around the desk in the blink of an eye, grasping his father's lapels to haul him forward.

"Never . . . never speak of Clara in such a manner again," he gritted between clenched teeth.

The earl's countenance reddened with fury, but there was the faintest hint of unease in his pale eyes. As if he were caught off guard at the realization that Hawksley would at last make a stand against him.

"Who is she?" he attempted to bluster. "Some penniless stray you picked out of the gutter?"

Hawksley narrowed his gaze as he gave his father a shake. "She is a lady in the finest sense of the word and far too good for me. But if by some miracle I can persuade her to have me as her husband, I will devote the rest of my life to ensuring she never has a moment of regret."

"I forbid it, do you hear me, Hawksley?"

"You can forbid all you like, Father."

"She will never be welcome at Stonecrest."

Hawksley smiled with icy satisfaction as he dropped his hands. For years he had allowed himself to carry the wounds his father had inflicted. Nothing he had ever done had been good enough. Nothing could convince the aloof earl that his son could be anything but a disappointment.

Now he realized that it no longer mattered.

He did not need his father's approval. He did not even need his love. Not when he had Clara.

She completed him in a manner he could never have dreamed possible.

"Nothing would please Clara more than to know she need never darken your door," he informed the older man, his expression softening as he thought of his logical, practical, utterly delightful angel. "She possesses a fine distaste for your sort of pompous superiority. Did I mention she is quite the most intelligent woman I have ever encountered?"

The earl frowned, but Hawksley did not miss the faint tremor in his hands as he tugged his immaculate coat back into place.

Perhaps you are not quite so certain of yourself as you wish others to believe, he abruptly acknowledged.

"You do not fool me, Hawksley," the earl at last managed to mutter. "This is nothing more than an attempt to punish me. You think that by embarrassing your family with such an obviously ill-bred chit, you will have had your revenge."

Shoving the pistols in the waistband of his breeches, Hawksley gave a growl of disgust.

"God, listen to you, you starched prig. This has nothing to do with you. Nothing." He stabbed a finger in his father's flushed countenance. "I love Clara. I love her so much that I ache when she is not at my side. And you can make any damnable threat you want, but nothing will change that. She will be my wife. You can accept it or not. I do not give a damn either way. Now out of my way."

Stalking toward the door Hawksley did not even pause as his father chased behind him.

"Where the blazes are you going?"

"I am going to fetch the only person in this world who has ever truly cared about me."

Chapter Eighteen

The darkness stirred as Clara battled her way to consciousness.

And promptly wished she hadn't.

Even before she was fully awake she could feel the heavy throb at the base of her neck. A dull ache that seemed to have settled in for a good long stay.

The temptation to slide back into the numbing blackness beckoned only to be sternly squashed. Even with her senses dulled, she could determine that she was laid upon an unfamiliar mattress and shrouded by the stench of stale air and mold.

It was imperative that she discover where she was and why she had been taken. And to do so as swiftly as possible.

Her very life might depend upon it.

Gritting her teeth, she forced her heavy lids to lift.

At first she could see very little. An oppressive darkness filled the room, broken only by the weak glow of a flickering candle.

Above her she could make out a wooden beam

ceiling that was held up by thick stone walls. Stone walls that were damp and coated with a thin layer of mold. It was enough to make her shudder in horror.

Her gaze darted about, but she could discover no windows and only a narrow door across the room.

Blast. She had been hauled off to a cellar, she concluded with a trickle of fear. That was surely a bad thing?

No one carried a woman to a cellar without a ghastly purpose.

Ignoring her pain, Clara struggled to sit up. She would not have her throat slit while she lay helplessly on the bed. A courageous notion; unfortunately, she had barely pressed herself upright when the room began to swirl and she clapped a hand to her mouth as she feared she might sick up.

"Argh . . ." she groaned.

"Easy, my love," an unexpected voice murmured from behind even as a wet cloth was pressed to her neck.

Terrified to realize she was not alone, Clara sharply pulled away and turned to regard the man hovering beside the bed.

He did not look like a dangerous ruffian, she had to admit.

Indeed, he reminded her of nothing more sinister than a timid shopkeeper, or even a vicar.

In puzzlement she allowed her gaze to travel over the narrow countenance framed by rapidly thinning brown hair and eyes that seemed pale and watery in the dim light. Even his body was small and stooped, as if he spent more time bent over a book than brawling in pubs.

Still, when he held out a hand, she was swift to shrink from the approaching fingers.

"No . . . Do not touch me."

He slowly straightened, blinking at her in mild surprise. "I assure you I have no intention of causing you harm."

"Forgive me if I find that difficult to believe after you accosted me upon the street," she charged.

"Oh no, you are mistaken." He gave a fervent shake of his head, settling himself on the edge of the mattress. "It was I who rescued you from a dangerous footpad. Indeed, you might say that I saved your life."

Clara frowned. He seemed quite sincere in his astonishment that she would believe for a moment he would wish her harm. But even as she wondered if she had perhaps made a mistake he leaned forward enough for her to catch a vague scent of peppermint and cloves that seemed to cling to him.

A chill shot down her spine.

This was the same man who had attacked her. There was no mistaking that scent. But for some reason he was determined to convince her that she had nothing to fear from him.

She could not imagine what he wanted from her or what he intended to do, but it seemed best for the moment to play along.

Had her father not always said that it was best to humor a madman?

"Then it seems that I owe you my gratitude," she said slowly.

"You owe me nothing." He offered a smile that revealed several teeth that were beginning to rot. Well, that at least explained his odd scent, she told

herself. He no doubt used the cloves and peppermint to mask his bad breath. "I am only relieved
that I happened to be keeping a watch upon you
when I spotted the ruffian attempting to bundle
you into a carriage."

Her heart skipped a horrified beat even as she
struggled to keep her expression calm.

"You were keeping a watch upon me?"

"But of course," he retorted, not seeming to consider that she would find his odd behavior anything
out of the ordinary. "I very much wished to speak
with you, but I dare not reveal my identity by approaching you while you were in the company of
others."

Reveal his identity? Her gaze slowly roamed over
the shabby coat and loose breeches before returning to the expectant expression. Comprehension
dawned with a jolt.

"You are . . . Mr. Chesterfield?"

"Just as brilliant as I suspected, and even more
lovely," he breathed in appreciation. "Astonishingly
lovely."

For a moment Clara grappled to accept what was
happening. This was Mr. Chesterfield. The gentleman she had corresponded with for over a year.
The gentleman who was the reason she had
charged willy-nilly to London. The gentleman who
at one time had seemed precisely the sort of man
who would make a nice, stable husband.

The gentleman who had attacked her on the
street and now had her hidden in a cellar.

The gentleman she was beginning to suspect was
a raving lunatic.

Damn and blast.

"How did you know I was in London?" she demanded in what she hoped was a causal manner.

"I received your letter, of course. Forgive me for not responding, but it was impossible. I could not risk putting you in even more danger."

Clara stiffened, recalling the deadly ambush that had been set for her. "You knew I was in danger?"

"Not until too late," he swiftly assured her. "Believe me, had I known I would have done whatever necessary to protect you."

She wisely hid her doubt. For now it seemed best to pretend to accept whatever he might say.

"That still does not explain how you knew where to find me after I arrived."

He heaved an audible sigh. "In truth, I just managed to reason where you might be hiding. Rather tediously dull of me to have taken so long, but in my defense I have not quite been myself the past few weeks. Even after my servant came to me with the story of a beautiful lady arriving upon my doorstep with the renowned Hawksley, I still did not put two and two together." The rotting smile returned. "Having at last come to my senses, I was anxious to meet you face-to-face. Not, however, in such a painful manner."

She shivered as her hand instinctively rose to touch the lump on the back of her head.

"Where are we?"

He grimaced. "Ah yes, not the sort of accommodations that I had hoped to provide for you, but for the moment I have little choice. The cellars are preferable to a bullet through the heart."

"We are beneath your home?"

"My home for now," he corrected, a rather odd

glittering entering his pale eyes. "Soon enough I will be in the position to offer you much more than this."

Clara licked her lips. For once she did not blurt out the first thing that came to her mind. Not when that warning voice was whispering in the back of her head that one careless word might very well bring about another painful blow.

Or worse.

"Because of the money you hope to gain from Lord Doulton?" she asked cautiously.

"Lord Doulton?" he demanded in puzzlement.

"I know that he has stolen artifacts from the Vatican. Artifacts that he gained from his cousin, who murdered two soldiers in their sleep."

"Ah yes, a most heinous crime." He shrugged his narrow shoulders, seemingly unconcerned at her knowledge of the ghastly murders. "Although few men can resist the lure of untold fortune."

"I also know that Hawksley's brother came to you with a rare parchment that he desired you to translate."

"Rare?" The glitter in the pale eyes became hectic as he abruptly rose to his feet to pace across the narrow cellar. "'Tis priceless. The sort of document that a collector can only dream of possessing. Only a dolt such as Lord Doulton could have failed to realize its value."

"But you recognized it, of course."

"Of course." He glanced back at her with a hint of annoyance that she would doubt his brilliance. "I am a scholar."

Clara took careful note of his reaction. It seemed

that like every man, his pride was his weakness. Perhaps she could use it to her advantage.

"It is a petition of some sort, is it not?" she asked softly.

"The most famous petition in all of history." With a dramatic motion he pressed his hands to his heart. "A demand from King Henry VIII to Pope Clement to grant him a divorce."

"Good heavens," Clara breathed in shock.

"There, I knew you would appreciate such a wondrous treasure," he exclaimed, moving back to kneel before her.

"Most certainly." She cleared her throat, refusing to ponder for even a moment what such a document would be worth. Or what a man might do to get his hands upon it. "I even understand why you would try and blackmail Lord Doulton once you realized what the petition was."

"Blackmail?" Genuine astonishment rippled over the narrow countenance. "Do you believe me capable of such childish games? Besides, Lord Doulton is even deeper in debt than myself. What could he possibly offer?"

She gave a sharp shake of her head. "You are mistaken. I know that Lord Doulton was in possession of the finest works of art."

He offered a sharp, humorless laugh. "Oh yes. He came to me the moment they arrived with the notion that I might find buyers for him."

She blinked at the unexpected confession. "He came to you? Why?"

"I have connections throughout England with those gentlemen who enjoy possessing rare objects, and who are wise enough not to ask unpleasant questions."

She battled back her revulsion. God, this man was nothing that she had believed him to be. How had she not sensed such weakness?

"I . . . see."

He shrugged, not the least troubled by his illegal activities. "It is harmless enough. I receive a small commission to make such transactions. Certainly I could not survive on the small sum I receive translating manuscripts."

"Of course." She forced a stiff smile to her lips. "And Lord Doulton came to you to assist in these transactions?"

"Such a fool." He rose to his feet with a scowl of disgust. "I easily sold off the lesser works and the artifacts that could not be readily recognized. But I warned him from the beginning he could not possibly sell off such famous works of art. No collector would risk possessing a painting that had so obviously been stolen, especially not a collector who might not wish to have attention called to where he had received other works. That is not even to mention having the entire wrath of the Vatican brought upon his head. Still, he continued to toss away his newfound fortune as if it were endless."

Clara slowly absorbed his words, even as she edged herself toward the end of the bed and tugged her skirts to ensure they would not tangle in her legs if she needed to move swiftly.

"If you did not intend to blackmail Lord Doulton, then why did you write to me of money from heaven?"

The pale eyes widened in surprise. "You read my letter? How?"

She hesitated, uncertain how much to reveal. "It was hidden in Lord Doulton's safe," she at last confessed.

"And you managed to enter his home?"

"Yes."

There was only admiration in his expression as he gave a nod of his head. "Such a clever girl. I knew you were perfect for me," he murmured before his features hardened. "Unfortunately, after Fredrick's death, Lord Doulton began to lose his nerve. He had come to the conclusion that I was plotting behind his back, and he forced his way into my home while I was composing my letter to you. The fool pulled a pistol upon me and I was forced to flee for my very life. Once he left the house, I circled back and attempted to give the illusion that I had fled the city." A muscle in his cheek began to twitch. "I fear it did not occur to me that he would suspect that you were my accomplice and attempt to halt you from arriving in London."

"So that explains your watch and glasses," she muttered, recalling her confusion when she had searched his chambers. A pity she had not considered the possibility that he had never left.

"What did you say?"

"Nothing." She managed to get one foot onto the floor even as she sought to keep him distracted. "I am still uncertain where you intended to get your money."

"The petition, of course. It was hidden among the artwork, but Lord Doulton is too much a buffoon to ever take notice of a scrap of paper." A disdainful smile curved his lips. "He was so dazzled by the pretty colors that he missed the greatest treasure in his possession. And I had no intention of drawing it to his attention."

"You intended to take it from him?"

"When the moment was right." He abruptly smacked a fist into his open palm, making Clara jump in surprise. "It did not occur to me that he could possibly be so stupid as to use it as rubbish."

Slowly the puzzle pieces were beginning to fall into place, and Clara cursed herself for being an idiot.

She had committed the worst sin in logical thinking. She had allowed herself to be swayed by Hawksley and his intense suspicion of Lord Doulton. It had kept her from keeping her mind open to other possibilities.

Not that she would have readily turned her suspicions to Mr. Chesterfield, she reluctantly acknowledged. At least not beyond a spot of blackmail. He had been far too clever to leave a trail of evidence leading to his door.

She turned until her other foot was firmly upon the dirt floor.

"And then Fredrick arrived upon your doorstep with his vowels."

The thin features twisted into a frightening expression of fury. "I could not believe it. To see my fortune torn into bits . . ."

"You must have been devastated."

"You cannot know." A stain of red marred his cheeks. "A collector can work an entire lifetime and never have his hands upon such a historical relic."

Clara swallowed heavily, sensing the building tension

in the air. There was no doubt that Mr. Chesterfield was unstable. And that he might be capable of lashing out without warning.

"You hoped to sell the petition?"

"In time." He jerkily paced from one wall of the cellar to the other, barely even noticing her presence. "Unlike art collectors, those of us who deal in rare manuscripts have no need to display our collections like puffed-up peacocks and risk unpleasant speculation. The pleasure comes from simply holding a piece of history in our hands." He came to an abrupt halt, his breathing heavy. "Unfortunately, I have only half of the petition at the moment. That prig Fredrick refused to leave the remaining pieces."

"Most inconsiderate of him."

He rounded on her with a growl of anger. "It was . . . unthinkable. The petition was mine. It would have made me renowned among all collectors." He stilled as Clara instinctively shrank away from his pulsing fury, and then with an obvious effort he sought to send her a reassuring smile. "And finally I would be in the position to ask you to be my wife. You see, I was to have it all."

Hiding her rising terror, Clara swallowed heavily. There was something troubling her. Something beyond being held in a cellar by an obvious madman.

What was it?

Willing her reluctant brain to work, she bit her bottom lip and considered what she had learned thus far.

Mr. Chesterfield had been involved from the beginning. That much was certain. Still, he had gained little from the theft of the artwork. Nothing more than a small commission.

Except . . .

Except for the petition.

A petition that he coveted with a frenzied lust.

Clara felt an icy fist clutch at her heart.

"Did you tell this to Lord Doulton?" she whispered even though she knew the answer.

"That idiot. Certainly not."

"Then . . ." She hastily swallowed her words.

Careful, Clara, she silently warned herself.

Now was not the time to reveal that she had just figured out that Lord Doulton would have no reason to kill Fredrick.

Not when it was painfully clear that the person with the most pressing reason to wish the man dead was standing just a few feet away.

"What?" her captor demanded.

Determined not to panic, Clara stretched her lips into what she hoped was a reasonable imitation of a smile.

"I was just thinking how terribly clever you are."

He frowned, although it was obvious he was pleased with her seeming admiration.

"Not quite clever enough. I still do not have the remaining pieces of the petition, and without them what I do possess is nothing more than worthless rubbish."

"I do not doubt you will find them."

With a casualness he could not quite pull off, Mr. Chesterfield plucked at the sleeve of his worn coat.

"Actually, I had hoped you might be of service."

"Me?"

"It occurred to me that Fredrick might have given the vowels to his brother for safekeeping."

Her heart came to a full halt before jolting back to life with a painful leap.

Dear heavens, he suspected that Hawksley had the vowels in is possession. Which unfortunately explained his sudden interest in her.

An interest that was not at all reassuring.

"Hawksley?"

"Well, he does possess the reputation of being a dangerous enemy who has killed more than one man upon the field of honor. Who better to keep watch over such a valuable prize?"

She lowered her lashes, covertly glancing about the barren room. Her heart sank at the realization that there was nothing at all to use as a weapon. And worse, the only means of escape was the narrow door across the room.

However swift she might be, she could not reach the door before Mr. Chesterfield could halt her.

"A reasonable conclusion," she at last forced herself to rasp, knowing her only hope was to keep him talking and await an opportunity to flee. "But I fear you are mistaken. Hawksley knows nothing of the petition."

The pale eyes narrowed as he stepped toward her. "Now, now, my dear. You must not lie to me. I know that Hawksley has been asking awkward questions about historical manuscripts. Why else would he do so if he did not possess the vowels?"

The chill within her deepened. If Mr. Chesterfield believed Hawksley to have the vowels, then he was in grave danger.

No matter what had occurred between them, she could not bear the thought of him being hurt.

Quite prepared to sacrifice everything to ensure his safety, Clara slowly rose to her feet.

"That is why you brought me here? To discover if Hawksley possesses your petition?"

"Of course not." He appeared shocked by her accusation. "I have every intention of making you my bride. But you must see that I cannot ask you to live as a pauper with a man who is laughed at and mocked by his peers. You deserve a fine house with servants and a husband who can command the respect of all those about him. Everything I have done was for you. To please you."

The fierce edge in his voice assured Clara that he was perfectly serious. In his twisted mind he had managed to convince himself that everything he had done was for her. No doubt even the murder of poor Fredrick.

A tidy means of avoiding any unpleasant pangs of guilt.

She gave a slow shake of her head. "I am sorry if you truly did this for me. It certainly is not what I would have wished. Obviously neither of us truly knew the other."

His brows snapped together in an ominous manner. "What do you mean?"

She shrugged. "I have no taste for fancy homes or servants, and I assure you that the only respect you ever need have earned was my own."

"No." Whirling about, Mr. Chesterfield shoved trembling fingers through his hair. "There was no other way. I had to have the petition. I still have to have it. It is the only way."

Clara silently edged toward the door. She could almost feel what little sanity the man possessed slipping away.

She had to get out. And swiftly.

"Why?" she demanded in soothing tones. "I have told you I do not care for riches. Why can we not simply be happy with being together?"

"It is too late." Without warning he spun about, backing her toward the wall as his chest heaved with his tumultuous emotions. "I will not be denied what is rightfully mine. Now tell me where those vowels are or I will hunt down Hawksley and kill him as I did his brother."

Her hands clenched at her side until her nails drew blood, but her mind remained thankfully clear.

If she could not escape, she would at least make certain that nothing happened to Hawksley. That she could not bear.

"You are right, there is no purpose in lying when you are clearly far too clever for me," she retorted, surprised that her voice did not so much as waver. The Lord knew she had never been so terrified in her entire life. "He did have the vowels, but he had no notion of their worth. He gave them to me to study."

"I knew it." Stepping so close his foul breath threatened to overcome her, Mr. Chesterfield clenched her shoulders in a painful grip. "Tell me where they are."

Swiftly searching her mind for a suitable lie, Clara was distracted as she glanced over Mr. Chesterfield's shoulder to discover the wooden door silently sliding open.

Expecting Mr. Chesterfield's servant, she nearly

swooned in relief as a familiar male form stepped into the darkness.

Hawksley.

He had found her.

Unaware of his danger, her captor gave her a violent shake. "Tell me."

Her eyes never strayed from the fierce blue gaze as Hawksley moved forward and raised his arm. With one smooth motion he struck Mr. Chesterfield on the back of his head with the butt of his pistol.

There was a strangled groan before the villain slid to the ground.

Then silence filled the cellar.

Chapter Nineteen

For a moment Hawksley could do nothing but gaze at Clara.

She was rumpled, with dirt upon her face that he did not doubt she would soon be nagging to have washed off. And even in the flickering light he could detect there was an unnatural pallor to her countenance.

But she was alive.

Alive.

A violent wave of relief swept through him, and without thought he reached out to pluck her over the unconscious man on the floor and haul her against his chest.

"Bloody hell, you frightened me, kitten," he rasped, burying his head in her hair as he battled the tears prickling his eyes.

She was shivering as she laid her head upon his chest.

"It was Mr. Chesterfield," she muttered into his shirt. "He was the one who killed your brother, not Lord Doulton."

Having already concluded that the damnable

Chesterfield was far more involved than either of them had suspected when he realized where the carriage had taken Clara, Hawksley gave little attention to the revelation.

Later he would have time to take revenge upon the villain. For now his only concern was for the woman in his arms.

With tender care he ran his hands down her back in a soothing manner. "Shh . . . It does not matter at the moment. We can speak later."

"He said he did it for me." She shuddered in horror. "He said that he had to have the petition so that he could ask me to become his wife."

A fierce anger flared through him. God above, it was bad enough that the man had committed murder. But to try and shift his guilt to Clara?

He was surely the lowest sort of . . .

His furious thoughts were brought to a slow end as a small voice in the back of his head whispered that he had not been so terribly different. Oh, certainly his crimes were not nearly so heinous, but had he not assured himself that lying to Clara was for her own good? That he was protecting her by hiding the truth?

When all along he was simply ensuring his own happiness. Grasping his treasure by any means possible.

He had been selfish and utterly indifferent to the pain he was bound to cause this woman.

"No, Clara, what he did, he did for himself," he told her in low tones. "He was blinded by greed. Not an uncommon tragedy, unfortunately."

"It is so horrible."

He pressed his lips to the top of her tumbled curls. "It is over."

"Over." She leaned back to meet his searching gaze. "I can go home?"

Just as he was about to reassure her that he intended to take her home with all possible speed, a faint noise behind him had Hawksley smoothly spinning about, his pistol already lifted.

His arm lowered at the sight of Biddles and Santos as they strolled into the cellar.

With a smile toward Clara, the rat-faced gentleman moved to where Mr. Chesterfield still lay upon the dirt floor.

"It seems that we are too late, Santos."

"A pity." The smuggler moved to join them, using his boot to turn over the limp form. With a moan Mr. Chesterfield slowly opened his eyes and instantly cringed at the sight of the forms looming above him. Santos's lips twisted into an evil grin as he pulled a dueling pistol from beneath his coat. "I had hoped to discover if these pistols are worth the enormous sum I was forced to pay."

Biddles reached beneath his own coat, only to produce a lacy handkerchief that he used to dab at his pointed nose.

"We could tie him to the wall and have a bit of target practice, if you wish?"

Santos gave a small snort. "And what is the skill in that? Far better to loose him in the street and shoot him as he attempts to flee."

Mr. Chesterfield's groans raised an octave, his eyes wild. "No . . . I beg you." Reaching out, he grasped the hem of Clara's gown. "Beloved Clara . . . You cannot allow them to harm me."

Without thought, Hawksley kicked the offending hand away. "Do not dare to touch her, you worthless sod."

"Clara . . ." the villain pleaded.

Clutching Hawksley's arm, Clara pressed her face into his chest. "Please, Hawksley, I just wish to be away from here."

Swiftly he placed his arms about her, cursing himself for not having swept her from the horrid cellar the moment he arrived.

"Of course, my love." He cast a swift glance toward his companions as he led her to the door. "Santos, would you be so good as to haul this rubbish to the nearest magistrate?"

"With pleasure." His smile widened. "And if he should not wish to go?"

"We will discover if those pistols are worth their price," he said in clipped tones.

Santos deliberately pointed the pistol toward his captive's heart. "Indeed we will."

Realizing all his scheming and skulking and bloody efforts were to come to naught, Mr. Chesterfield abruptly let out a wail of despair.

"Clara . . . I love you. I did this for you. All for you."

Hawksley refused to allow Clara to even pause as he hustled her from the cellar and through the shadowed house. Not until they were upon the street did he at last slow their steps and turn his head to regard the gentleman following in their wake.

"Biddles, did you bring a carriage?"

"Yes, it is just down the street." Without waiting he was slipping through the darkness. "This way."

In silence Hawksley pulled Clara after the retreating form, his arm clutched tightly about her trembling shoulders.

Thankfully the carriage was not far, and bundling her inside, he unfolded a blanket to wrap about her before he slid onto the seat beside her. Once again pulled her into his arms.

With a quick word to his groom, Biddles joined them, and shutting the door they were on their way.

Only as they moved down the narrow street did Hawksley allow himself to relax his knotted muscles.

It was over.

Both Mr. Chesterfield and Lord Doulton would be forced to pay for their crimes, and Fredrick would at last be allowed to rest in peace.

More important, Clara was no longer in danger.

They could now look to the future with nothing at all to stand in their path.

Well, nothing beyond the fact that she had just discovered he had been lying to her since the moment they met, he ruefully acknowledged.

His teeth gritted in determination. He would not allow his stupidity to ruin what lay between them. Not when they so obviously belonged together.

"All will be well, kitten," he murmured as he laid his cheek against the top of her head.

For a moment she willingly leaned against his strength, but as the carriage picked up speed she slowly pulled away to regard him with a faint frown.

"Where are we going?"

"I am taking you home." His hand lifted to brush her still-pale cheek. "Where you belong."

"No." They were all startled by the sharp vehemence in her tone, and Clara paused to suck in a steadying breath. "I mean . . . I wish to go home to Kent."

Hawksley flinched as if he had just been struck. God, he wished that he had been. No blow could be as painful as the thought that she would ever leave him.

"You are tired and upset, kitten," he forced himself to say in placid tones, not wishing to battle with her when she was in such a fragile state. "We will discuss this in the morning when you are feeling more yourself."

The emerald eyes flashed with a dangerous fire. "Do not talk to me as if I am a child, Hawksley." She deliberately paused. "Or should I say, my lord?"

Damn.

He had hoped . . . what?

That being kidnapped by a raving lunatic would make his own sins seem trivial? Or that her potential brush with death would convince her that she must seize whatever happiness might be within her grasp?

It did not matter what he had hoped, he accepted with a faint sigh.

Clearly Clara remained furious at his seeming treachery.

"My dear, it is far too late to consider traveling such a distance," he pointed out in what he hoped was a reasonable tone.

Her expression settled in those stubborn lines that were all too familiar.

"Then take me to the nearest hotel. That was where I was going anyway. I will catch the stage out in the morning."

He battled back his flare of impatience. Clara

had every right to feel betrayed. Who could blame her for wishing to put as much distance between them as possible?

Still, he could not allow her to flee. Not until he had an opportunity to plead for her forgiveness.

"I cannot allow you to go to a hotel without even a maid. 'Tis not safe."

Her chin jutted upward. Never good.

"It is not your decision to make, my lord."

"We must speak." Reaching out, he grasped her cold hands in his own. "I will not allow you to leave without . . ."

She wrenched her hands free and turned to the silent gentleman in the opposite seat.

"Lord Bidwell, will you be so kind as to tell your driver that I wish to be taken to a hotel?"

The pointed nose twitched as Biddles gave a helpless lift of his hands.

"Regretfully, I must agree with Hawksley. A young lady on her own would not be entirely safe at a hotel," he murmured in a sympathetic voice. "They are often frequented by the sort of loutish dandies and rakes who consider a lone female as mere sport."

Hawksley was swift to pounce upon his advantage. "There, you see. Far better that you return—"

"However, you would be quite welcome as my guest," Biddles overrode his words with a smooth determination. "Anna would be overjoyed to have another female about, and in truth, she has nearly nagged me to death for the opportunity to meet you."

"Biddles." Hawksley regarded his friend as if he were suddenly transformed into a coiled viper.

And with good reason, he told himself.

The dirty, rotten traitor.

At his side, however, Clara was not nearly so offended.

"Oh, I could not impose," she murmured softly.

Biddles gave an airy wave of his hand. "Trust me, it is no imposition. You would be doing the both of us a great favor if you would come to stay. Anna has not felt quite up to her usual dizzying round of activities due to her delicate condition and is nearly mad with boredom. She would give a fortune to have someone for company besides my poor self."

Hawksley furiously attempted to think of some means to counter Biddles's defection. Unfortunately, he was too angry to come up with more than a few incomprehensible grunts.

Clara ignored him without effort. "If you are certain?"

"Consider it settled."

"Thank you."

Obviously outgunned, Hawksley was left with nothing to do but toss himself back into the leather squabs and glare at the man he had once called friend.

"Damn you, Biddles," he muttered.

The slender gentleman smiled with dry humor. "You can rake me over the coals later, Hawk. For now I believe it best we have Miss Dawson settled in a hot tub with a nice brandy to warm her."

Clara sucked in a deep breath. "Oh yes, a hot bath is precisely what I desire."

The rest of the trip to the Hawk's Nest was completed in thick silence. All the apologies and explanations that pounded through Hawksley's mind were stuck in his throat at the sight of Clara's drooping shoulders and air of weariness.

Now was not the time to press her. No matter how painful it might be to allow her to leave his side.

Waiting for the carriage to come to a halt before his darkened townhouse, Hawksley opened the door with more force than necessary.

Before stepping down, however, he paused to slay his companion with a hard frown.

"We will speak of this later."

Biddles merely smiled. "I did not doubt that for a moment."

Grinding his teeth in frustration, Hawksley was forced to leap lightly onto the street and make his way to his door. It was that or toss Clara over his shoulder and haul her off to his chambers.

Not the wisest notion, considering she had already been kidnapped once that evening.

He had barely reached the porch when the door was abruptly flung open to reveal a decidedly rumpled Dillon. His gaze traveled beyond Hawksley to the carriage already pulling away.

"Miss Dawson?" he demanded.

Sweeping past his servant, Hawksley headed straight for the library and waiting whiskey.

"She is well and in the hands of Biddles."

"But—"

"Not now, Dillon," Hawksley pleaded, sensing Dillon plaguing his heels as he moved down the hall. "Did you rid me of my father?"

The servant gave a loud snort. "'Twasn't a simple matter, but I at last managed to convince him that his presence at the Hawk's Nest was unwelcome."

Entering the library, Hawksley smiled ruefully as he poured two glasses of the aged whiskey and handed one to Dillon.

God knew the loyal servant deserved a drink after having to endure the old earl.

"No doubt he made an unpleasant scene?"

"He attempted to do so until I assured him that I would as soon toss him out the window as to listen to his cackling."

A weary smile touched Hawksley's lips. "I knew there was some reason that I liked you, old friend."

There was a moment of silence as they both sipped the whiskey, and then Dillon roughly cleared his throat.

"Miss Dawson . . . Will she be returning?"

Setting aside his empty glass, Hawksley shoved his fingers roughly through his hair. The image of Clara seated in Biddles's carriage, so small and alone, tortured his mind.

"I cannot say," he muttered. "I have made such a damnable muck of this."

"Yes, you have," Dillon retorted without mercy.

Hawksley glared at his companion. First Biddles and now Dillon.

What did a man have to do for a bit of sympathy?

"Perhaps I do not like you so much after all."

Dillon shrugged. "Calling a weed a rose does not make it a rose."

Not at all in the mood for a lecture, no matter how well deserved, Hawksley gave an impatient shrug.

"I must find Santos. I wish to ensure he had no difficulties hauling Mr. Chesterfield to the authorities and that Lord Doulton was detained before he could flee."

"Mr. Chesterfield." The name sounded more a curse on Dillon's tongue. "He was the man who kidnapped Miss Dawson?"

"And also the one responsible for Fredrick's death."

The servant frowned. "Not Lord Doulton?"

"Yet another mistake I have made." Hawksley heaved a sigh as he gave a shake of his head. "Do not wait up for me. I will be late in returning."

Before he could make his escape, the servant reached out to lay a hand on his shoulder.

"You ain't intending to pester Miss Dawson tonight, are you?"

"No. She is tired and need of rest. I will go to her in the morning." His lips twisted. "If she will even agree to see me."

Dillon gave his shoulder a reassuring pat. "She will see you, and perhaps this time you will be wise enough to tell her the truth."

A raven brow arched. "She already knows the truth. My father saw to that."

"I do not mean the truth of your name. I mean the truth of your heart," Dillon corrected. "Tell her you love her before you lose her completely."

Hawksley struggled a moment, still not at all comfortable with revealing such an intimate emotion. But as it became obvious that Dillon was not about to release him until he had his assurance, he gave a reluctant nod of his head.

"I will tell her all that is in my heart."

"Then all will be well."

Hawksley wished he could be so certain.

In truth, he felt as if he were standing upon the edge of a cliff awaiting someone to rescue him or push him over the edge.

A sensation that was certain to keep him pacing most of the night.

A long night that he might as well put to good use, he told himself sternly, pausing only long enough to collect his greatcoat before heading back out of the house.

Although he did not doubt for a moment that Santos could be fully trusted to deal with the villains, he wished the satisfaction of witnessing their downfall. God only knew that he had waited long enough for this moment.

With impeccable timing, John was returning with the mount Hawksley had left behind at Mr. Chesterfield's as he stepped from the house. Tossing the young man a coin, he hauled himself into the saddle and set off into the darkness.

Three hours later found Hawksley standing in the shadowed garden behind Biddles's townhouse.

He had easily managed to locate Santos and assured himself that both Mr. Chesterfield and Lord Doulton had been properly handed over to the authorities. He had even had the pleasure of hearing both gentlemen confess their sins before they had fallen to their knees to sob for mercy.

Giving Santos thanks for his assistance, Hawksley had turned his mount for home. It had been a long day, with enough turmoil to make the most unflappable gentleman feel as if he had been run over by a team of oxen.

But even as he fully intended to seek the welcome warmth of his bed, he found his path straying far from the shabby neighborhood he called home and instead trailing through the elegant streets of Mayfair.

Oh, he could not pretend that he did not know precisely where he was going. Not when he had entered the darkened mews and climbed over the high wall to land lightly in the private gardens.

Once there he stepped beneath the cover of an ancient oak tree and simply gazed at the lighted windows.

Somewhere within the house Clara was preparing for bed.

His entire body ached with the need to go to her.

He just wished to see her face. To know that she was well and not suffering from her ghastly experience.

But while it would be a simple enough matter to slip his way into the house, he knew it would be a futile gesture.

The walls that kept him from Clara were not made of stone and glass.

It was the faintest rustle of leaves that warned Hawksley that he was no longer alone. With smooth ease he had pulled out his pistol and pointed it toward the darkness at his side. At the same moment Biddles gave a soft laugh and stepped into a slanting ray of moonlight.

"I thought you would make an appearance before the night was through," he murmured softly.

Caught off guard at being so easily discovered, Hawksley returned the pistol to his pocket. "I am not here to bother Clara."

Oddly, Biddles did not so much as smile at his ridiculous behavior. A rather astonishing miracle. Instead he gave a slow nod of his head, his expression somber.

"You just needed to be near her?"

Hawksley was thankful for the shadows that hid his sudden flush. "Pathetic, is it not?"

"Not at all," Biddles retorted. "'Tis the usual behavior of a man in love."

Love.

Gads, but the damnable emotion had a great deal to answer for.

Turning his head, he glanced toward the townhouse. "Is she . . . well?"

"Remarkably well considering all that she has endured. Anna was tucking her in when I came here to await your arrival."

"Will she ever forgive me?"

"That, I fear, is beyond even my abilities to foresee," Biddles murmured. "However, I will assure you that Miss Dawson is far too logical to allow her wounded emotions to overcome her better sense."

With a frown Hawksley turned his attention back to the gentleman at his side.

"And what is that supposed to mean?"

"Just that while some women might be willing to sulk and indulge in their desire to play the wronged woman, Miss Dawson has no talent for such theatrics. She would never hold a grudge simply for the sake of holding a grudge."

Hawksley gave a slow nod. He was well aware that Clara did not delight in those tedious games that some women played so well. It was indeed one of the reasons he found her so delightful. He was never in doubt as to what was precisely upon her mind.

Both a blessing and a curse, he wryly acknowledged.

"True enough, but not quite the reassurance that I had hoped for."

"It is more than what most women would offer you."

He briefly closed his eyes against the tide of painful longing.

"Yes. Let us hope it is enough."

It was a rather bemused Clara who sat upon the window seat of the bedchamber as she pulled a brush through her damp hair.

Anna had proved to be every bit as welcoming as Biddles had promised. More so, in fact. A short, curvaceous woman with a smile that could warm an artic winter, she had swiftly taken Clara under her wing.

Before Clara was quite aware of what was occurring, she had been whisked into a hot bath and changed into a clean robe. Even then Anna did not stop hovering until she had ensured that Clara had eaten every bite of the delicious stew that had arrived in her chambers upon a tray.

Thankfully, her motherly clucking had not included any attempts to force Clara into unwelcome confessions, or even to discover why she had been landed with an unknown woman at such an hour.

Although Clara was never one to hide from her troubles or attempt to pretend that they did not exist, for the moment she was content to allow herself to be cosseted and fussed over. It was a novel and not unpleasant experience.

With a faint sigh Clara set aside her brush and reached to crack open the window. Anna had demanded that the servants light a large fire before her bath, and the heat pouring into the room was nearly overwhelming.

Leaning forward, she sucked in a deep breath of the fresh air, only to freeze at the familiar scent of male cologne.

Hawksley.

There could be no mistake.

Brooding upon his most peculiar behavior, Clara paid scant heed to the sound of her door softly being pushed open. Only when a hand gently touched her shoulder did she turn to meet Anna's quizzical smile.

"Clara, I thought you would be fast asleep by now. Is anything troubling you?"

Troubling her? Clara resisted the urge to roll her eyes heavenward. She wished it were so simple.

"Hawksley is down there," she said in clipped tones.

Anna shot a startled glance toward the darkened window. "You can see him?"

"No, I can smell him."

"Smell . . . ?" Anna gave a sudden chuckle. "Ah . . . cologne. French, is it not?"

"Yes." *And utterly fatal to women,* she silently added. *It should be outlawed.*

Twitching her skirts out of the way, Anna seated herself next to Clara at the window seat, her expression one of sympathy.

"Horatio did not reveal all, but I suspect that Hawksley has managed to break your heart."

It took a moment for Clara to realize that Horatio must refer to Lord Bidwell, then she gave a deep sigh.

"To wound it, anyway," she reluctantly confessed.

"Men." Anna gave a disdainful sniff. "What has he done?"

Clara bit her lip at the burning pain that clutched at her heart.

"He pretended to be something he is not."

Anna's brows drew together. "And what did he pretend to be?"

Clara clutched her hands into fists upon her lap. "A simple gentleman of strained means."

There was a moment of startled silence.

"And you are angered to discover he is instead a man of wealth and position?" Anna demanded in confusion.

"Of course."

"No doubt you have your reasons."

"I should think it obvious."

Anna carefully cleared her throat. "Perhaps you will humor me?"

Clara abruptly rose to her feet, twisting her hands together as she aimlessly paced the floor.

"For goodness' sakes, what do I have to offer such a man? I have no fortune, no proper breeding, and worse, I do not have the talent to play the role of a viscountess, let alone some day a countess," she burst out in annoyance.

"Obviously Hawksley believes you possess such a talent."

Clara choked back a sob. "No, he is absolutely certain I do not, and that is precisely the point."

Anna pressed a hand to her temple. "I think there must be something wrong with my brain, it does not seem to be functioning properly."

"Do you not see?" Clara turned back to her new friend, her expression fierce. "I am the very worst possible maiden to become Countess of Chadwick. I cannot even move among village society without having everyone laughing behind my back or, worse, seeking to avoid me altogether. Hawksley could not conceive of a better means of punishing his family than by having me as his wife." She gave a slow shake of her head. "The insult could not be more obvious."

Despite her evident logic, Anna frowned in bewilderment. "My dear, you cannot truly believe Hawksley's only desire to wed you is with the intent to embarrass his family."

Clara did not understand why Anna would appear so shocked. It was all perfectly plain as far as she was concerned. Hawksley had never made any secret of his bitterness toward his father. Or the fact that he wished nothing more than to forget his family even existed.

But the death of Fredrick had brought an end to his desires. He was now no longer the younger son who was allowed to go his own way. Instead he was the heir, and as such bound tightly to duty.

He could not escape his destiny.

But he could have his final revenge upon his father.

"What other reason could there be?" she demanded.

Anna gave a lift of her brows. "It could be that he truly cares for you."

Clara flinched. If this woman knew how much she longed for Hawksley's heart, she would not tease about such a thing.

"A gentleman who cared for me would not have lied."

Without warning Anna gave a tinkling laugh. "Clearly you know very little of gentlemen."

"What do you mean?"

"Gentlemen rarely behave as rational creatures, and only a woman who desires to end up in Bedlam would ever attempt to understand their feeble attempts at logic," she retorted dryly. "And a gentleman in love is the very worst of all. The more ridiculously they behave, the more certain you can be that they are floundering in the throes of their own emotions."

"Love?" Clara gave a sad shake of her head. "Ridiculous."

"Why?"

Clara spread her hands in frustration. Anna seemed such an intelligent woman. Why did she pretend that it was even thinkable that a handsome, wealthy, and titled gentleman would find her genuinely desirable?

"Gentlemen do not fall in love with women such as me," she gritted.

Anna slowly rose to her feet, her arms crossing over her waist.

"Oh no, what would any man want with a beautiful, intelligent lady who has managed to bring justice to the villain who killed his brother? Most unsuitable."

Clara gave a shake of her head. "You could not possibly understand."

"Actually, I understand perfectly. There was a time when I thought I should never find someone to appreciate me for who I am. My first season in London was nothing short of torture, and I assure you that I was most firmly condemned to the shadows as a wallflower."

Clara frowned in bewilderment. This pretty, vivacious woman a wallflower? It seemed unthinkable.

"You?"

"Yes, me," she assured the disbelieving Clara. "So you see, I know what it is to be considered an outsider. Still, as much as it made me wretched to be considered an outcast, it still would have been far easier to remain safely hidden in the shadows than to take the risk that someone could truly love me." A whimsical smile touched her lips. "I have never regretted a moment putting my faith in Horatio. There are times when you must simply follow your heart."

Clara could not prevent the small pang of envy as she gave a wry smile.

"Hardly the most sensible advice."

Anna moved to place her hands on her shoulders. "You desire sensible? Very well. Do not make any decision while you are weary and still smarting from your feelings of betrayal. You have plenty of time to decide what you wish to do with your future."

Clara hesitated. She could not deny that Anna's words held merit. How often had she been astounded by those people who would rashly make decisions when in the throes of some strong emotion?

Logic demanded that she wait until she could clear her thoughts before leaping to a decision that might very well be irrevocable.

"You are right, of course," she reluctantly agreed.

A mischievous twinkle entered Anna's eyes. "My suggestion is not entirely without ulterior motives.

I intend to fully enjoy the rare treat of having another lady in the house."

"You are very kind."

"Nonsense." Leaning forward, Anna gave her a swift hug. "Get some rest, my dear. The world might seem a very different place in the morning."

Chapter Twenty

As it turned out, the world did seem a far different place for the next several mornings. Never having had a sister or even a close female friend, Clara had no notion just how enjoyable it could be to devote her mornings to sipping her hot chocolate and discussing anything from the genius of Plato to fussing over which ribbons she was to tie in her hair.

Not that Hawksley was ever far from her thoughts, she had to ruefully acknowledge.

Too often she found herself turning to share something amusing with the man whom she had become accustomed to being at her side. Or awakening during the night to reach for warm arms that were not there.

And too often she found herself brooding upon whether or not she had been overly hasty in presuming his intentions had been dishonorable.

Certainly he had hidden the truth of his past, but did she have any genuine proof that he was only hoping to use her as an affront to his father?

Anything beyond her own fear that no gentleman of sense could ever love her?

At last convinced that she was prepared to confront Hawksley and discover the truth for herself, Clara deliberately arranged herself in the back parlor after luncheon.

She knew that Hawksley would call. He had called every day, although she had always refused to meet with him.

Today, however, she made no move to hide herself in her chambers when she heard him announced. Instead she kept herself firmly seated upon the delicate rose sofa, even when a large, heartbreakingly familiar form filled the doorway.

"Clara?"

Slowly lifting her gaze, Clara was shocked by the unmistakable pallor of the handsome countenance and the shadows beneath his beautiful eyes.

Her heart clenched in swift concern. He did not look at all well.

"Hawksley."

He paused awkwardly before clearing his throat. "May I join you?"

"I . . ." She gave a nod of her head. "If you wish."

Still with that same odd hesitation, he crossed over the threshold and moved to stand before the fireplace.

"You appear to have recovered from your ordeal," he at last broke the silence.

An unwitting smile touched her lips. "Yes, Anna has been very kind."

"She is a very good sort." His own smile was wry. "Far too good for the likes of Biddles."

"They are very devoted to one another."

"Indeed they are." An aching loneliness that struck Clara like a blow darkened his eyes. "I envy Biddles for that."

Abruptly rising to her feet, Clara barely kept herself from launching across the floor to hold him in her arms. Blast, but he seemed so . . . vulnerable. Almost as if he had been suffering as much as she had by being apart.

Instead she wrapped her arms about her waist and fought for a measure of sanity.

"Have Lord Doulton and Mr. Chesterfield been properly dealt with?"

His features abruptly hardened. "Both have decided they are quite anxious to seek the adventures offered by the distant colonies."

Clara was startled that Hawksley had agreed to such a punishment. She had presumed he would not be satisfied until the two were facing the gallows.

"Are you disappointed?"

He lifted a shoulder. "There is still a part of me that thirsts for blood, and should I discover they have ever dared return to England, I will not hesitate to put a bullet through their hearts, but there is another part of me that only wishes Fredrick to rest in peace." His expression abruptly softened. "He would not wish for scandal to touch our family."

"Unlike you?"

He briefly stiffened before he visibly forced himself to loosen his muscles.

"I deserve that, I suppose," he murmured. "I have certainly devoted a great deal of my life to playing the role of the wicked son."

"To punish your father?"

"In part." He took a moment, as if carefully considering his words. "But more than that, I think that I had simply accepted my father's assurances that I would never be of any worth. Why even make an effort when I was doomed to fail?"

She stilled at the stark words, her eyes darkening with pain. "Hawksley, you should not say such a horrid thing."

"Why? It is the truth," he retorted, his gaze easily capturing and holding hers. "Or it was until I plucked you from that carriage. Since then I have begun to hope that I could be more. That I could become the sort of gentleman who was worthy of earning your love."

Clara abruptly turned away. Oh . . . damn. He was always so bloody good at this.

"I would believe you more easily if you had not lied to me."

She heard him move to stand behind her, although he was wise enough not to try to touch her.

"I know I made a mistake, Clara," he admitted in a voice raw with emotion. "I was a fool, but I swear if you will give me the opportunity I will never disappoint you again."

She bit her lip as a sharp ache flared through her heart.

She had thought it would be difficult to forgive him for deceiving her. And even more difficult for him to restore her trust.

In truth, the only difficult thing seemed to be keeping herself from tossing herself into his arms and never letting go.

"I need to know why," she forced herself to

demand. "Why did you hide the truth of who you are?"

He heaved a ragged sigh. "It is . . . complicated."

Slowly turning, she met his gaze squarely. "Most of life is complicated."

"Yes." Lifting his hands, he scrubbed them over his pale countenance before at last continuing. "At first I did not tell you simply because I had refused to take on the title. I told myself that I would not do so until my brother's murderer was hanging from the gibbet." His lips twisted into a humorless smile. "I now realize that I did not want the title because then I would have to accept that Fredrick was truly gone. And of course, there was the horror of knowing that I had no choice but return to my family and the duties awaiting me. Even in my own mind it seemed far preferable to remain Hawksley."

She blinked, caught off guard by his stark realization of his own motives. In her experience, men rarely bothered to try and comprehend what led them to behave as they did.

Just being a man was enough to excuse any stupidity.

It was something.

"And when you asked me to be your wife?" she ruthlessly prodded. "Surely you did not believe you could keep such a thing hidden?"

"I . . ." He heaved a deep sigh.

"What?"

"It is all rather a muddle now," he confessed with a grimace. "But I suppose it all comes down to fear."

Her brows lifted in surprise. "You afraid? I do not believe it."

"You should. I have never been so frightened in my life."

"Of what?"

"You."

She gave a short laugh of disbelief. "You are not making any sense."

"No?" He stepped closer, his gaze smoldering with suppressed emotion. "For God's sake, Clara, I could barely convince you to marry me when you thought I was a penniless gamester living in the stews. I knew you would balk when you discovered I was a viscount."

A faint hint of color touched her cheeks at the truth of his accusation. Had she known who he was from the beginning, she never would have allowed him to worm his way into her heart. No matter how tempting.

"You could not have kept it hidden forever," she at last pointed out in stiff tones.

He smiled wryly. "As I said, it was all a muddle. I cannot claim to possess your powerful logic or ability to think in a rational manner."

He was very convincing, of course. Or perhaps she just desperately wished to believe him. But still he had not yet banished her greatest fear.

Gathering her courage, she at last decided to confront him directly. That was always the most logical approach, was it not?

Unfortunately, it was not always the easiest.

She unconsciously squared her shoulders. "Hawksley?"

"Yes, my love?"

"Did . . . did it occur to you that by wedding me, you would have a lasting revenge upon your father?"

He briefly closed his eyes as his lips twisted. "Of course I considered the notion my father would not approve, and I would not be human not to take some small pleasure in aggravating the pompous fool." He held up his hand as her lips parted in anger. "But if you think I would tie myself to a woman for eternity for the simple pleasure of annoying my father, you must be daft. Besides which, if I truly wished to punish my father, I would simply refuse to wed at all." He held her wary gaze with the sheer force of his will. "There could be nothing more cruel to such a proud gentleman than to realize that his ancient title was destined to be handed over to a distant cousin he considers the worst sort of mushroom. That would be a true revenge."

Oh . . . rats, rats, rats.

He was not supposed to undermine her with such ease. Not when it left her with no excuses left to deny her feelings for him.

Not when it left her vulnerable to the possibility of becoming his wife.

"No," she whispered in a husky voice. "I cannot."

Not surprisingly, his brows snapped together with a gathering impatience.

"Why?"

"Because I shall only make a fool of myself and you as well," she burst out. "I am not at all suitable to be a viscountess or a let alone a countess."

"According to my father, there is no one less suitable to be a viscount, let alone an earl, than myself, so we shall be perfect for one another," he dryly retorted.

Her lips trembled as she battled the threatening tears. "Please do not jest, Hawksley."

Without warning, he was moving forward to grasp her hands in a tight grip.

"Clara, my love, I do not understand what absurdity has made you believe that you are unsuitable, but I can assure you that my desire to wed you has nothing to do with making you my viscountess and everything to do with the fact that without you my life is empty." His eyes darkened to indigo. "I love you. And in truth, I do not believe that I can bear a future without you."

Her heart jolted painfully against her chest at his fierce words. He loved her. Loved her, Miss Clara Dawson. If only . . .

No, she sternly warned herself.

There was never any point in wishing for what could not be.

"Hawksley, you know that society will never accept me, nor will your family," she said in tones that defied argument.

He blinked, as if caught off guard by her words. "Miss Dawson, for being so terribly clever you can be remarkably dense."

Dense? Her?

That was certainly not an insult that had ever been hurled at her head before.

Strange, eccentric, and outright daft. But never dense.

"What is that supposed to mean?"

"Only that the moment Anna took you into this house, you were accepted by society. Indeed, they will now be flocking to gain your approval."

Her gaze narrowed in confusion. Good heavens,

Egyptian hieroglyphs were less baffling than the inner workings of polite society.

"I do not understand."

"Lady Bidwell, along with her good friend, Mrs. Caulfield, is the undoubted leader of the *ton*. Their friendship will ensure that no one, no matter how petty or vindictive, will dare to utter a word against you," he said firmly. "In truth, we will be besieged from dawn to dusk with invitations and pesky visitors the moment we announce our betrothal."

Betrothal.

Her heart skipped a vital beat.

"And your family?"

He grimaced as he gave a shake of his head. "Do you truly believe that my father would ever consider any female good enough to become Countess of Chadwick? Good lord, I could bring home Princess Charlotte and he would stick his nose in the air and condemn her for possessing a whore for a mother."

"But—"

His grip upon her fingers abruptly tightened. "Listen to me, Clara. I do not care if we live in my decrepit house or your cottage or flee to the Continent, which now that I think about it is not a bad notion, and I certainly do not care if we never spend a damn minute in society." His voice lowered to a husky plea. "All that matters is that we can be together."

"I . . ." As she met his pleading gaze, her voice trailed away. What the devil was she doing? She had been lost the moment this man had halted her carriage. Oh, she could return to her cottage and spend the next fifty years attempting to convince herself that she had done the only logical thing. It would certainly be more prudent. There would be no opportunity for disappointment. No uncertainty. No risk of having her heart crushed. Just an aching loneliness that would haunt her until the end of her days.

She was familiar enough with loneliness to know that it was not something she wished to endure for an eternity.

Perhaps it was time to take a chance.

Perhaps this dangerous, handsome pirate was just what a logical spinster needed to be happy.

"Yes," she at last breathed.

There was a shocked silence as Hawksley frantically searched her countenance, as if seeking to discover if she was vindictive enough to tease him at such a time.

"Did you say . . . yes?"

A tremulous smile touched her lips. "Yes."

Still he hesitated, his expression wary. "Precisely what did you say yes to?"

Reaching up her hand, she lightly stroked his cheek. "All that matters is that we can be together."

"Clara?"

She gave a soft chuckle. Gads, it seemed that she would have to be far more direct. She framed his face with her hands.

"I love you, Hawksley."

She felt him stiffen as his eyes flared with hope.

"Say it again."

"I love you, Hawksley."

His arms wrapped about her as he hauled her roughly against his chest.

"Again."

"I love—"

Her words were abruptly cut off as his mouth impatiently swooped down to claim her lips in a kiss she felt all the way to her toes.

In response she wrapped her arms about his neck and returned his kiss with a burst of joy.

She had no notion when she left her quiet home in Kent that she had set out on a dangerous, sinfully delicious adventure that would alter her future.

An adventure that included kidnapping, stolen artwork, smugglers, and madmen.

And that was not even to mention falling in love, which was perhaps the most sinfully delicious adventure of all.

Thank God for blue-eyed pirates . . .

Please turn the page for an exciting sneak peek of

Deborah Raleigh's

next historical romance

SOME LIKE IT BRAZEN

coming in 2007!

"For God's sake, Edward, halt your fidgeting before I have you tied to the bedpost," Lord Bidwell groused.

Edward Sinclair, Fifth Earl of Harrington, smiled with rueful amusement. He was a large gentleman with the thick muscles of a person accustomed to hard labor and chestnut curls that were brushed toward a countenance too bronzed for fashion and features too forceful for beauty. He was, however, blessed with warm hazel eyes and an unexpected pair of charming dimples.

Thankfully, he was also blessed with a rare good humor and patient nature. A stroke of fortune, considering most would have bolted after a fortnight of enduring Biddles's wretched notions of how to mold a proper gentleman.

"I defy any gentleman not to do a measure of fidgeting after three tedious hours of being brutally bathed, brushed, and bedeviled. I can assure you that I have been more kindly handled during taproom brawls."

"Halt your complaining. You are fortunate that your form is such that I had no need to order a corset. They are damnably uncomfortable, according to most," Biddles retorted with a supreme lack of sympathy. "Of course, they are all the rage since the prince has taken to wearing them. Perhaps we may yet consider one."

Edward lifted one warning brow. "You would not dare."

The slender, flamboyantly attired dandy with a narrow countenance and piercing eyes smiled with a bland superiority.

"Not only would I dare, my dear Edward, but I would twist, tuck, and squeeze you into it myself if I thought it necessary." With a flourish the gentleman produced a lacy fan to wave before his pointed nose. "I have warned you that all of society will be anxious to cast their judgment upon the new Earl of Harrington. Especially since they are already titillated by your elevation from farmer to earl in one fell stroke. Do not doubt that every eye will be searching for some exposure of your rustic manners and lack of worldly experience."

"Meaning that they will expect me to arrive at their soirées complete with mud on my boots and a cow in tow?"

"That is precisely what they will expect."

Edward smiled wryly. "It is not that I doubt your judgment, Biddles, which is always quite beyond question," he murmured. "But I must admit that I have yet to comprehend how being scrubbed until I am raw and then strangled by my valet, who by the way is taking inordinate pleasure in my torture, is to assure the *ton* that I do not reek of the country."

The ebony fan was abruptly snapped shut as Biddies advanced across the hideous paisley carpet. During his rigorous training in manners, deportment, and dancing since arriving in London, Edward had not yet had the opportunity to do more than make a cursory inspection of the enormous townhouse. Certainly there had been no time to renovate the opulent grandeur to a more simple style suitable to a bachelor of modest taste.

"Egads, Edward, how often must I remind you? A gentleman can always be distinguished by his attire, and most importantly by the tie of his cravat. It is what sets apart a true nobleman from those of lesser Quality."

Edward could not help but chuckle at the absurdity of his friend's words. It was precisely the sort of logic he would never comprehend, regardless of the number of titles that were dumped upon his unwilling shoulders.

"Do you mean to tell me, my dear Biddles, that among a nation with the greatest minds, the most progressive scientists, highly respected philosophers, poets, and warriors, all we have to set us above the savages is the perfection of a knot in a length of linen?"

There was a cough from one of the numerous uniformed servants who were crowded into the room until Lord Bidwell's unnerving gaze fell upon the hapless man.

"Leave us," he commanded. "I will speak with his lordship alone."

As one the servants anxiously filed out of the room, all too pleased to be away from the dandy's sharp tongue and habit of flaying those who dared to interfere in his torturous lessons. Only the well-trained valet was daring enough to linger a rebellious moment to pluck a tiny thread from the shoulder of Edward's mulberry jacket before he too joined the mass retreat.

Once alone with his friend, Edward strolled to glance at his form in the floor-length mirror. He grimaced at the satin white pantaloons and silver waistcoat. Such elegance might be *de rigueur* for an evening in London, but he felt a dashed fool.

Gads, he had seen trained monkeys who looked more comfortable in satin and diamonds than he did.

What did he know of society? He had not been raised to take his place among the upper ten thousand. Indeed, during most of his eight-and-twenty years he had been only vaguely aware of any connection to the aristocracy. The knowledge that he had become heir upon the death of the old earl, followed swiftly by the deaths of his son and two nephews, came as much as a shock to him as to the horrified Harrington family that viewed him as little better than a puffed-up encroacher.

The sudden slap of the fan upon his shoulder had Edward reluctantly turning to meet the glittering gaze of the elegant gentleman.

"Edward, there are few who are as well versed in traversing society as I," Biddles warned in stern tones. "Which, I flatter myself, is precisely the reason that you requested that I be the one to introduce you to society. I am quite as cognizant of the ridiculousness of the *ton* as you. Perhaps more so. But while I might secretly find the shallowness and too-common lack of intelligence a source of amusement, I have never made the mistake of underestimating the power that society wields. Never."

Edward heaved an inward sigh. His friend was right, of course. Even if he did not care a fig for the opinion of society for himself, he could not forget that he now possessed a far-flung family that depended upon him to maintain a certain dignity. One of the many burdens that had come with the title.

More important, however, was the knowledge that if he hoped to use his newfound position to help those he had left behind, he would have to win the confidence of his fellow noblemen. His seat in the House of Lords would be meaningless if he was seen as a bumbling simpleton without the necessary skills to move through society.

Or to demand entrance to the various gentlemen's clubs, which of course, was where the true power was hoarded.

"Forgive me, Biddles." He offered a faint bow of his head. "I do not mean to make light of my entrance to society. It is only that I feel awkward and not at all confident that I shall not make an utter ass of myself."

The thin features abruptly settled back into the familiar sardonic amusement.

"Do not fear, Edward. You may not be the most dashing or elegant of gentlemen, but you are intelligent and you do possess a measure of charm when you choose to exert yourself."

"Thank you . . . I think."

The pale blue eyes glittered. "And with a bit of luck you will not be a complete ass."

He tilted back his head to laugh at the tart compliment. Biddles would never be considered a comfortable companion. He could play the buffoon to perfection or suddenly reveal the razor-edged brilliance that had once made him the most successful spy the crown had ever possessed. But Edward did not regret his choice in seeking his help.

Despite the fact that Biddles was currently the proprietor of Hellion's Den, an elegant gambling establishment, he was undoubtedly a leader of society and the perfect companion to introduce Edward to the more fastidious *ton.*

"Well, I may wound several maidens unfortunate enough to be my partner upon the dance floor, and forget which fork to use, but at least my cravat is glorious perfection and my coat cut so tightly I can barely breathe. I trust no one shall mistake me for the gardener."

Biddles offered a condemning sniff. "As if any gardener could afford a coat cut by Weston."

"Or would be ridiculous enough to want one." Edward sucked in a deep breath. As much as he might long to remain in the dubious comfort of the drafty house, he knew that it was impossible. It was time to take his place as Earl of Harrington. Whether he desired the position or not. "Shall we be on our way?"

Lady Bianca, daughter of the Duke and Duchess of Lockharte, was in a towering fury.

Not an uncommon event.

Despite the endless parade of governesses who had tried to coax, coerce, and downright bully her into becoming a properly modest lady, she possessed a fiery temper and habit of speaking first and thinking later. Often much later.

In her defense, however, she was always swift to admit when she was in the wrong, and never took her ill humor out upon servants or staff who were in no position to defend themselves.

Not that any servants willingly lingered when Lady Bianca pitted her will against her father. 'Twas said below stairs that it was preferable to stick a hand into a hornet's nest as to stumble into a blue-blooded battle.

Even the butler, who was well known to consider himself just a step below royalty, was swift to scamper toward the servants' quarters when he heard the first of the delicate Wedgwood plates launched against the door.

Unaware of the household exodus to safer grounds, Bianca stomped angrily from one end of the vast library to the other. She briefly considered hefting a few of the rare leather-bound books at the door. They would make a much nicer thud than the china she had tossed. But while she was furious enough to throttle something, or better yet some-one, she had not plunged into utter stupidity.

The large, silver-haired duke with the powerful, handsome countenance could be astonishingly in-dulgent toward his only daughter. Most would say too indulgent. But he would have her head on a platter if she so much as touched one of his beloved books.

As if sensing her smoldering need for destruc-tion, her father settled more comfortably upon the elegant damask sofa and waved his hand toward the shelves of painted china.

"I do believe that you missed one of your mother's Wedgwood plates, Bianca, in case you are still in the mood to act like a petulant child," he drawled.

Bianca came to an abrupt halt to glare at her father. She could actually feel the hair on the nape of her neck stand upright. Like a bristling cat.

"This is unacceptable. You had no right to refuse Lord Aldron's offer of marriage," she gritted between her clenched teeth.

A silver brow arched at her scathing words. "As a matter of fact, I had every right. Despite your oft-time belief that you are in charge of the world and everyone in it, I am still your father and I will not have you toss away your future upon a practiced rogue. Certainly not one who would make you miserable within a week."

Bianca sucked in a sharp breath. She had known that the duke possessed no great fondness for Lord Aldron. How could she not? The two men had only to be in the same room for the ice to begin to form. But she had not thought he would sink to tossing about such slanderous insults.

"Lord Aldron is not a rogue."

"Bah. Only an innocent such as you would not know of his infamous reputation." Her father's expression hardened with an unfamiliar disgust. "For God's sake, he is a hardened rake, a gambler, and an adventurer who has been mired in scandal from the day he stepped foot into London."

Bianca resisted the urge to roll her eyes. Innocent or not, she was perfectly aware of Stephen's reputation. It was that hint of danger that had attracted her to him in the first place.

Well, that and his delicious blond hair and deep blue eyes, she acknowledged with a faint shiver.

For a young maiden who had been kept ruthlessly protected her entire life, what could be more fascinating than a gentleman who dared to ignore the tedious rules of society?

He was fiery, unpredictable, and most of all perfectly willing to teach her of the world outside her pampered existence.

Quite simply irresistible.

"You are hardly one to throw stones, Father," she retorted, her dark eyes flashing fire. "From all I have heard, you indulged in your own share of scandals when you were young."

"My scandals did not include fighting duels, hosting Cyprian Balls in my home, or leading innocent young females into danger."

Her brows snapped together. "Danger? That is absurd."

One of the very few who did not fear her temper, the duke rose to his feet and regarded her with a somber expression.

"I am not a fool, Bianca. I am well aware that the scoundrel has lured you from the house so you could attend boxing matches, horse races, as well as a bawdy pantomime that was not fit for the eyes of a harlot, let alone an unwed lady," he said in stark tones.

Her breath caught in shock.

Oh . . . cripes. So much for her carefully elaborate schemes to hide her exhilarating outings.

Obviously being a duke included knowing every damnable thing that happened in London.

It was with an effort that she met his accusing

gaze. "Do not hold Stephen to blame. It was upon my urging that he escorted me to such places."

"Which is the only reason I did not take a horse-whip to him, I assure you."

"And I only urged him to do so because I am sick to death of being treated as if I am a witless idiot without the ability to think for myself or to make even the simplest of decisions."

His eyes narrowed at her sharp words. "You are my daughter. It is my duty to protect you."

Bianca nearly screamed in frustration. On how many occasions had she heard the familiar lecture?

A hundred? A thousand?

Certainly it was trotted out whenever she happened to be in danger of having a bit of fun.

"I am not your daughter, I am a pretty doll you put on display and then tuck away when I am not of use. At least Stephen realizes that I am a woman perfectly capable of knowing something of the world."

"Oh, no doubt Lord Aldron has played his role well. He is, after all, a highly successful seducer and quite accustomed to doing whatever necessary to please a lady." He lifted a deliberate brow. "I wonder, however, if you have considered why the gentleman has shown such a marked interest in you after so assiduously avoiding debutantes?"

Bianca had a sudden vision of a cat toying with a mouse.

And she wasn't the cat.

"He finds me . . . fascinating."

"No, my child. What he finds fascinating is your rumored dowry."

She blinked in shock. Then blinked again.

"Father."

"The man is without a feather to fly with," the duke retorted in hard tones. "Despite having hocked every belonging he possesses, he is still mired in debt. There is not a gambling house in town that will allow him across the threshold, and his clubs have long since turned him away. His only hope to avoid fleeing to the Continent is to snatch a bride too naïve to see beyond a handsome countenance and shallow charm."

Bianca gritted her teeth. She would not listen to her father. She could not. To do so would mean that the gentleman who had stolen her heart, the one who had offered her the promise of a glorious future without tedious rules and expectations, was nothing more than a lie.

The servants had been wise to go into hiding.

"I will not listen to such slander. Stephen loves me."

The duke curled his lip in disgust. "Lord Aldron loves no one but himself."

"You do not know him as I do."

"I know him far better than you, Bianca." There was a brief pause before her father lifted his chin to a stubborn angle. "Which is precisely why he will never be your husband."

Her chin tilted to match his. Damn and blast, but she was weary of being dictated to as if she were mindless dolt.

At least Stephen made the pretense of listening to her desires.

"I am two-and-twenty, Father, and quite at liberty to do whatever I please. You cannot halt me from wedding Stephen." Her hands were planted on her hips in the unlikely event that the duke did not realize the extent of her resolution.

The duke calmly adjusted the cuffs of his elegant coat. Her teeth snapped together at his deliberate nonchalance.

"Perhaps not, but do you truly believe that either of you will be content living in some decrepit cottage or renting rooms in the stews?" He smiled without humor. "I assure you that it might seem charming enough in storybooks, but there is nothing pleasurable in scrubbing your own floors or freezing before an empty grate. Besides which, Lord Aldron would barter off his own mother before becoming a pauper."

"Pauper?" Her momentary bravado faltered with stunning speed. "You would disinherit me?"

Without warning, her father's eyes darkened with what seemed strangely close to regret.

"There would be no need for such drastic measures. I simply have nothing to offer as a dowry."

"But . . . that is absurd."

"It is the simple truth."

"I do not understand."

"Because I never intended you to understand," her father admitted with a harsh sigh. "With your beauty and position, I simply presumed that when you chose your husband, you would have the good sense to select one with a large fortune. It is, after all, what most maidens do."

Her brows snapped together. Most maidens were not the daughter of a duke, she thought with a tingle of panic. For God's sake, she had never devoted a moment to considering something so tedious as wealth.

"But what of my dowry?" she demanded.

"What do you think has funded your very expensive seasons for the past four years?"

For perhaps the first time in her young life, Bianca's swift wits deserted her. Her brain froze and she was forced to open and close her mouth several times before she at last managed to speak.

"Are you telling me that we have no money?"

There was a moment of silence before her father turned to stroll toward the large bay window. He kept his back turned as he at last cleared his throat.

"Being a duke is an expensive business, my dear. I have estates that need constant upkeep, a near battalion of servants to keep paid and pensioned, tenants to keep housed, your brothers schooled, and of course you and your mother properly clothed and bejeweled."

"But what of your rents and investments?"

His gaze remained trained upon the Mayfair street below him. "They would be adequate as a rule, but while London has devoted itself to pleasure, war has ravaged the world. Trade has all but disappeared, and not nearly enough able-bodied men remain to tend to the lands." He gave a frustrated shake of his head. "Put on top of that last year's unseasonable cold, and more fields than not lie fallow. Would you have me stand aside and watch my tenants starve?"

Well, for goodness' sakes. Of course she would not wish for anyone to starve.

Still, she found it difficult to accept that matters had come to such a desperate quagmire. Surely being a duke must count for something?

"But the war has ended," she lamely pointed out.

"That does not bring young men back from the grave to plant my fields, or fill empty pantries. Such devastation will take years to repair."

"Why have you not said something before?" she rasped.

Slowly he turned to regard her with a somber expression. "As I said, I simply presumed that when you chose to wed it would be to a gentleman of means."

The sickness in the pit of her stomach became outright nausea. The glorious future she had dreamed of for months was crumbling into dust.

"But . . . this is horrible."

"Not so horrible." Her father moved to gently pat her shoulder. "There are any number of suitable gentlemen who will be eager to wed the daughter of a duke. Especially one who happens to be as lovely as an angel."

She abruptly pulled away from his comforting touch, her eyes glittering with suppressed tears.

"Do you have no feelings at all? I love Stephen. I do not want any other gentleman." Her expression became one of deepest scorn. "Especially not one who only wishes to wed me because I happen to be your daughter."

With an insulting lack of sympathy for her wounded heart, her father gave a vague shrug. "Then approach Lord Aldron and tell him that you wish to wed without a dowry or a prospect for an allowance from me. Let us see precisely how quickly he leaps at the opportunity to have you for his wife."

Bianca did not even consider the notion of approaching Stephen. Not because she feared he would slither away the moment he discovered she was penniless, she hastily reassured herself. But simply because she would never wish for him to sacrifice himself in such a manner.

No matter how much it might hurt.

Knowing she could not hold back her tears for much longer, she glared at the gentleman who had managed to ruin her life in a few short minutes. Unwittingly, her hand lifted to clutch the silver locket that lay against her pounding heart. The necklace had been a gift from Stephen and held his precious portrait.

"I will never forget Stephen. Never," she announced in dramatic tones, then turning on her heel, she flounced from the room and headed for her private chambers to cry out her misery.

Discover the Romances of
Hannah Howell

BOOK YOUR PLACE ON OUR WEBSITE AND MAKE THE READING CONNECTION!

We've created a customized website just for our very special readers, where you can get the inside scoop on everything that's going on with Zebra, Pinnacle and Kensington books.

When you come online, you'll have the exciting opportunity to:

- View covers of upcoming books
- Read sample chapters
- Learn about our future publishing schedule (listed by publication month *and author*)
- Find out when your favorite authors will be visiting a city near you
- Search for and order backlist books from our online catalog
- Check out author bios and background information
- Send e-mail to your favorite authors
- Meet the Kensington staff online
- Join us in weekly chats with authors, readers and other guests
- Get writing guidelines
- AND MUCH MORE!

**Visit our website at
http://www.kensingtonbooks.com**